The Bethlehem Murders

Matt Rees

W F HOWES LTD

This large print edition published in 2008 by
W F Howes Ltd
Unit 4, Rearsby Business Park, Gaddesby Lane,
Rearsby, Leicester LE7 4YH

1 3 5 7 9 10 8 6 4 2

First published in the United Kingdom in 2007
by Atlantic Books

A CIP catalogue record for this book is available
from the British Library

ISBN 978 1 40741 382 2

Typeset by Palimpsest Book Production Limited,
Grangemouth, Stirlingshire
Printed and bound in Great Britain
by Antony Rowe Ltd, Chippenham, Wilts.

FSC
Mixed Sources
Product group from well-managed
forests and other controlled sources

Cert no. SGS-COC-2953
www.fsc.org
© 1996 Forest Stewardship Council

To Bo

All the crimes in this book are based on real events in Bethlehem. Though identities and some circumstances have been changed, the killers really killed this way, and those who died are dead just the same.

CHAPTER 1

Omar Yussef, a teacher of history to the unhappy children of Dehaisha refugee camp, shuffled stiffly up the meandering road, past the gray, stone homes built in the time of the Turks on the edge of Beit Jala. He paused in the strong evening wind, took a comb from the top pocket of his tweed jacket, and tried to tame the strands of white hair with which he covered his baldness. He glanced down at his maroon loafers in the orange flicker of the buzzing street lamp and tutted at the dust that clung to them as he tripped along the uneven roadside, away from Bethlehem.

In the darkness at the corner of the next alley, a gunman coughed and expectorated. The gob of sputum landed at the border of the light and the gloom, as though the man intended for Omar Yussef to see it. He resisted the urge to scold the sentry for his vulgarity, as he would have one of his pupils at the United Nations Relief and Works Agency Girls School. The young thug, though obscured by the night, formed an outline clear as the sun to Omar Yussef, who knew that obscenities were this

1

shadow's trade. Omar Yussef gave his windblown hair a last hopeless stroke with a slightly shaky hand. Another regretful look at his shoes, and he stepped into the dark.

Where the road reached a small square, Omar Yussef stopped to catch his breath. Across the street was the Greek Orthodox Club. Windows pierced the deep stone walls, tall and mullioned, capped with an arch and carved around with concentric rings receding into the thickness of the wall, just high enough to be impossible to look through, as though the building should double as a fortress. The arch above the door was filled with a tympanum stone. Inside, the restaurant was silent and dim. The scattered wall-lamps diffused their egg-yolk radiance into the high vaults of the ceiling and washed the red checkered tablecloths in a pale honey yellow. There was only one diner, at a corner table below an old portrait of the village's long-dead dignitaries wearing their fezes and staring with the empty eyes of early photography. Omar Yussef nodded to the listless waiter – who half rose from his seat – gesturing that he should stay where he was, and headed to the table occupied by George Saba.

'Did you have any trouble with the Martyrs Brigades sentries on the way up here, Abu Ramiz?' Saba asked. He used the unique mixture of respect and familiarity connoted by calling a man *Abu* – father of – and joining it to the name of his eldest son.

'Just one bastard who nearly spat on my shoe,' said Omar Yussef. He smiled, grimly. 'But no one played the big hero with me tonight. In fact, there didn't seem to be many of them around.'

'That's bad. It means they expect trouble.' George laughed. 'You know that those great fighters for the freedom of the Palestinian people are always the first to get out of here when the Israelis come.'

George Saba was in his mid-thirties. He was as big, unkempt and clumsy as Omar Yussef was small, neat and precise. His thick hair was striped white around the temples and it sprayed above his strong, broad brow like the crest of a stormy wave crashing against a rock. It was cold in the restaurant and he wore a thick plaid shirt and an old blue anorak with its zipper pulled down to his full belly. Omar Yussef took pride in this former pupil, one of the first he had ever taught. Not because George was particularly successful in life, but rather for his honesty and his choice of a career that utilized what he had learned in Omar Yussef's history class: George Saba dealt in antiques. He bought the detritus of a better time, as he saw it, and coaxed Arab and Persian wood back to its original warm gleam, replaced the missing tesserae in Syrian mother-of-pearl designs, and sold them mostly to Israelis passing his shop near the bypass road to the settlements.

'I was reading a little today in that lovely old Bible you gave me, Abu Ramiz,' George Saba said.

'Ah, it's a beautiful book,' Omar Yussef said.

They shared a smile. Before Omar Yussef moved to the UN school, he had taught at the academy run by the Frères of St John de la Salle in Bethlehem. It was there that George Saba had been one of his finest pupils. When he passed his *baccalaureate*, Omar Yussef had given him a Bible bound in dimpled black leather. It had been a gift to Omar Yussef's dear father from a priest in Jerusalem back in the time of the Ottoman Empire. The Bible, which was in an Arabic translation, was old even then. Omar Yussef's father had befriended the priest one day at the home of a Turkish *bey*. At that time, there was nothing strange or blameworthy in a close acquaintance between a Roman Catholic priest from the patriarchate near the Jaffa Gate in Jerusalem and the Muslim mukhtar of a village surrounded by olive groves south of the city. By the time Omar Yussef gave the Bible to George Saba, Muslims and Christians lived more separately, and a little hatefully.

Now, it was even worse.

'It's not the religious message, you see. God knows, if there were no Bible and no Koran, how much happier would our troubled little town be? If the famous star had shone for the wise men above, let's say, Baghdad instead of Bethlehem, life would be much brighter here,' Saba said. 'It's only that this Bible in particular makes me think of all that you did for me.'

Omar Yussef poured himself some mineral water from a tall plastic bottle. His dark brown eyes were glassy with sudden emotion. The past came upon him and touched him deeply: this aged Bible and the learned hands that left the grease and sweat and reverence of their fingertips on the thin paper of its dignified pages; the memory of his own dear father who was thirty years gone; and this boy whom he had helped shape into the man before him. He looked up fondly and, as George Saba ordered a *mezze* of salads and a mixed grill, he surreptitiously wiped his eyes with a fingertip.

They ate in quiet companionship until the meat was gone and a plate of baklava finished. The waiter brought tea for George and a small cup of coffee, bitter and thick, for Omar.

'When I emigrated to Chile, I kept the Bible you gave me close always,' George said.

The Christians of George's village, Beit Jala, had followed an early set of emigrants to Chile and built a large community. The comfort in which their relatives in Santiago lived, worshipping as part of the majority religion, was an ever-increasing draw to those left behind, sensing the growing detestation among Muslims for their faith.

In Santiago, George had sold furniture that he imported from a cousin who owned a workshop by the Bab Touma in Damascus: ingeniously compact games tables with boards for back-gammon and chess, and a green baize for cards;

great inlaid writing desks for the country's new wine moguls; and plaques decorated with the Arabic and Spanish words for peace. In Chile, he married Sofia, daughter of another Palestinian Christian. She was happy there, but George missed his old father, Habib, and gradually he persuaded Sofia that now there was peace in Beit Jala and they could return. He admitted that he was wrong about the peace, but was glad to be back anyway. He had seen Omar Yussef here and there since he had brought his family home, but this was their first chance to sit alone and talk.

'The old house is the same as ever, filled with racks of Dad's wedding dresses. The rentals in the living room and those for sale in his bedroom, all wrapped in plastic,' George Saba said. 'But now they're almost crowded out by my antique sideboards from Syria and elaborate old mirrors that don't seem to sell.'

'Mirrors? Are you surprised that no one should be able to look themselves in the eye these days?' Omar Yussef sat forward in his chair and gave his choking, cynical laugh. 'They lead us further into corruption and violence every day, and no one can do anything about it. The town is run by a shitty tribe of uneducated bastards who've got the police scared of them.'

George Saba spoke quietly. 'You know, I've been thinking about that. The Martyrs Brigades, they come up here and shoot across the valley at Gilo, and the Israelis fire back and then come in with their tanks. My house has been hit a few times, when the bastards did their shooting from my roof and drew the Israeli fire. I found a bullet in my kitchen wall that came in the salon window, went through a thick wooden door and traveled down a hallway, before it made a big hole in my refrigerator.' He looked down and Omar Yussef saw his jaw stiffen. 'I won't let them do it again.'

'Be careful, George.' Omar Yussef put his hand on the knuckles of George Saba's thick fingers. 'I can say what I feel about the Martyrs Brigades, because I have a big clan here. They wouldn't threaten me, unless they were prepared to face the anger of half of Dehaisha. But you, George, you're a Christian. You don't have the same protection.'

'Maybe I've lived too long away from here to accept things.' He glanced up at Omar Yussef. There was a raw intensity in his blue eyes. 'Perhaps I just can't forget what you taught me about living a principled life.'

Omar Yussef was silent. He finished his coffee.

'You know who else has returned to Bethlehem from our old crowd?' George Saba's voice sounded tight, straining to lighten the tone of the conversation. 'Elias Bishara.'

'Really?' Omar Yussef smiled.

'You haven't seen him yet? Well, he's only been back a week. I'm sure he'll stop by your house once he's settled in.'

Younger than George Saba, Elias Bishara was

another of Omar Yussef's favorite pupils at his old school. 'Wasn't he studying for a doctorate in the Vatican?' Omar Yussef asked.

'Yes, but since then he's been living in Rome as some kind of apostolic secretary to one of the cardinals. Now he's back at the Church of the Nativity. I know, Elias and I are only asking for trouble by coming home, Abu Ramiz. Perhaps you can't understand what it has been like for us. We grow up in this dismal place, wanting desperately to leave for another country where we can make money and live in peace. But the day always comes when you imagine the savor of real hummus and the intoxicating brightness of the sun on the hills and the sound of the church bells and the muezzins. You miss it so much you can taste the longing on your tongue. Then you come back, no matter what it is you are giving up. You just can't help it.'

'I'll go to the Church and say hello to Elias as soon as I get a chance.'

'Next month is Christmas, so I wanted to invite you to come with us to the Church to celebrate,' George said. 'And then you and Umm Ramiz will come for Christmas dinner at my house.'

'I would be delighted, and so will she, too.'

The two men argued over who should pay the check. Both threw money onto the table and picked up the other's cash to force it back into his hand. Then the shooting began. It was close enough that it sounded big and hollow, not like the whipcrack of faraway firing.

George looked up. 'Those sons of whores, they've started again.' He stood, leaving his cash on the table. 'Abu Ramiz, I have to go.'

They went to the door. Omar Yussef could see the tracer striping across the valley toward a house along the street. The big, bass bursts of gunfire from the village were directed toward the Israelis in the Jerusalem suburb over the wadi. The gunfire emanated from the roof of a square, two-story house only fifty yards away. There was a dark Mitsubishi jeep in the lee of the building. George Saba stepped into the street. 'Jesus, I think they might be on my roof again.'

'George . . .'

'Don't worry about me. Get out of here before the Israelis come. Not even your big clan will protect you from *them*. Good-bye, Abu Ramiz.' George Saba put an affectionate hand on Omar Yussef's arm, then went fast along the street, bending low behind the cover of the garden walls.

Omar Yussef put his hands over his ears as the Israelis switched to a heavier gun. It shot tracers that left a deceptively slow, dotted line in the darkness, like a murderous Morse Code. That code spelled death, and the warmth that he had felt during the dinner left Omar Yussef. He could no longer see George Saba. He wondered if he should follow him. The waiter stood nervously behind him in the doorway, eager to lock up. 'Are you coming inside, uncle?'

'I'm going home. Good night.'

'May God protect you.'

Omar Yussef thought he must have looked foolish, groping his way along the wall at the roadside, kicking his loafers in front of him with every step to be sure of his footing on the broken pavement. An awareness of fear and doubt came over him. He sensed movement in the alleys he passed, and shadows momentarily took on the shape of men and animals, as though he were a frightened child trying to find the bathroom in the darkness of a nighttime house. He was sweating and, where the perspiration gathered in his moustache and on the baldness of his head, the night wind chilled him. *What an old fool you are*, he told himself, *scrambling about in a battle zone in your nice shoes. Sometimes you can have a gun to your head and you still don't know where your brains are.*

The firing behind him grew more intense. He wondered what George Saba might do if he found the gunmen on his own roof again, and he decided that only when a gun points at your heart do you realize what it is that you truly love.

George Saba's family huddled against the thick, stone wall of his bedroom. It was the side of the house farthest from the guns. George came through the front door. The shooting was louder inside and he realized the bullets were punching through the windows into his apartment. He ducked into an alcove in the corridor and crouched against the wall. At the back of the house, his living room faced the deep wadi. It was taking heavy fire from the Israeli position over the canyon.

Sofia Saba stared frantically across the corridor at her husband. She was not quite forty, but there were lines that seemed suddenly to have appeared on her face that her husband had never noticed before, as though the bullets were cracking the surface of her skin like a pane of glass. Her hair, a rich deep auburn dye, was a wild frame for her panicked eyes. She held her son and daughter, one on either side of her, their heads grasped protectively beneath her arms. All three were shaking. Next to them, Habib Saba sat silent and angry, below the antique guns mounted decoratively on the wall by his son. His cheekbones were high and his nose long and straight, like an ancient cameo of some impassive noble. Despite the gunfire, he held his head steady as an image carved from stone. George called out to his father above the hammering of the bullets on the walls, but the old man didn't move.

Most of the Israeli rounds struck the outside wall of the living room with the deep impact of a straight hit. These were no ricochets. Every few moments, a bullet would rip through the shattered remains of the windows, cross the salon and embed itself in the wall behind which George Saba's family sheltered. Sofia shuddered with each new impact, as though the projectiles might take down the entire wall, picking it away chunk by chunk, until it left her children exposed to the gunfire. The hideous

11

racket of the bullets was punctuated by the sounds of mirrors and furniture falling in the living room and porcelain dropping to the stone floor from shattered shelves.

A bullet rang down the corridor and splintered the wood of the front door through which George Saba had entered. As he had dodged along the road in the darkness, he had been determined that tonight he would act. He had cursed the gunmen under his breath, and when a shot struck particularly close to him he had sworn at the top of his voice. Now he wanted only to crawl deeper into the alcove, to dig himself inside the wall until this nightmare stopped. If he stayed in the niche long enough, perhaps he would awake and find himself in his store in Santiago and this idiotic fantasy of returning to his childhood home would once more be merely a dream, not a reality of red-hot lead, blasting through his home, destructive and deadly. He looked over to the bedroom and caught his wife's pleading expression, as she struggled to keep the heads of their children hidden beneath her arms. He wasn't going to wake up in Chile. He couldn't hide. He had to end this. He got to his feet, sliding up the wall, pushing his back hard against it as though it might wrap his flesh in impenetrable stone. He took the tense, expectant breath of a man dropping into freezing water and dashed across the exposed corridor into the bedroom.

George Saba hugged his wife and children to

him. 'It's going to be all right, darlings,' he said. 'I'm going to take care of it.' He pulled them close so they wouldn't see that his jaw shook.

For the first time, his father moved his head. 'What are you going to do?'

George looked sadly at the old man. He wasn't fooled by the stillness with which Habib Saba held himself. It wasn't calm and resolve that kept the old man frozen in his self-contained posture against the wall. His father cowered in the bedroom because he was accustomed to the corruption and violence of their town. He lived as quietly and invisibly as he could, because Christians were a minority in Bethlehem, and so Habib Saba was careful not to upset the Muslims by standing up to them. George had learned a different way of life during his years away from Palestine. He put his hand on his father's shoulder and then touched the old man's rough cheek.

Quickly, George stood and reached for an antique revolver mounted on the wall. It was a British Webley VI from the Second World War that he had bought a few months before from the family of an old man who had once served in the Jordanian Arab Legion and kept the gun as a souvenir of his English officers. The gray metal was dull and there was rust on the hinge, so that the cylinder couldn't be opened. But in the darkness its six-inch barrel would look deadly enough, unlike the three inlaid Turkish flintlocks that decorated the bedroom wall beside it. George Saba tightened his hand around the square-cut grip and felt the gun's weight.

Habib reached out for his son's arm, but couldn't hold fast. Sofia screamed when she saw the revolver in her husband's hand. At the sound, her daughter peered from under her mother's arm. George knew he must act now or the sight of those frightened eyes would break him. He reached down and put his hand over the child's brow, as though to close her eyes. 'Don't worry, little Miral. Daddy's going to tell the men to stop playing and making noise.' It sounded stupid and, for the moment, he kept his fingers over the girl's face so that he wouldn't see the look of incredulity he felt sure would have registered on her features. Even a child could tell this was no game. Then he dashed through the front door.

CHAPTER 2

arkness smothered the valley swiftly,
sliding gray down the steep hillsides, blot-
ting out the scanty olive trees and shading
the romantic portraits of the martyrs in the cemetery, until it settled over the village of Irtas. In the
home of the Abdel Rahmans, no one turned on
the lights. To do so would have illuminated the
vegetable patch and the glade of pines outside,
through which the family expected their eldest son
to creep home soon for the *iftar*, the evening meal
to break the Ramadan fast. In the front room of
the house, Dima Abdel Rahman set down a tray
of *kamar al-din*. She placed the glasses of apricot
juice before the cushions where each member of
the family would sit to eat. The glass with the
most fruit floating in it, she put by the corner of
the low table, where Louai would want to sit so
that he could watch the windows for any threat.
Then she went to the open window for a moment
and, ignoring the excited, fluttery calls of her
mother-in-law from the kitchen, strained her eyes
into the shadows for a sight of her husband. She
adjusted her cream headscarf, which curved to a

pin below her chin and emphasized the strong oval of her face. Her eyes were a light, warm brown, like the foliage of Palestine's brief autumn, and her lashes were long. It was a kindly, confident face, though it was tainted by an undertone of recent loneliness and an anxious tightness about her lips. She shivered and hugged herself as the night's chill penetrated her bright holiday robe.

The building was well situated for these clandestine visits. Louai Abdel Rahman could move from his hideout in Irtas to this square two-story house a quarter of a mile along the valley without stepping into the open, where Israeli hit squads might see him. The cinderblock homes and winding streets of Irtas billowed across the lowest slopes and into the narrow bottom, looking from this end of the valley like rushing rapids washing through a crevasse, foaming against the precipices and cresting on fingers of easier gradients. At the edge of the village, the valley was a fertile place, the green plots of the *fellahins* spraying out around the famous gardens of the Roman Catholic convent tended by the Sisters of the Hortus Conclusus. Behind the Abdel Rahman house at the head of the valley were the ancient wells known as Solomon's Pools, which fed the main aqueduct of Herod's Jerusalem. With springs across the vale, the people of Irtas allowed themselves a luxury barred to other rural Palestinians, who strained to eke out the fetid contents of their cisterns through the eight dry months of summer: in Irtas there were tall, shady pine trees, as well as the squat, functional olives to which most villages were limited. Dima Abdel Rahman knew her husband could move about, hidden beneath the canopy of leaves, as though nature wished to be complicit in his struggle against the occupation. If the Israelis watched from above, Louai would surely see them, because the thick vegetation thinned and petered out as the hillsides cut up from the narrow floor of the wadi. The soldiers would be exposed on those bare slopes, even in the twilight.

Then Dima Abdel Rahman heard sounds among the trees. *It must be him,* she thought. She kept quiet, even though her mother-in-law called her to help with the serving once more. There was nothing moving that she could see, but the undergrowth crackled beneath careful footsteps. He was coming, for the first time in weeks. She straightened her headscarf excitedly once more and fiddled with the pin beneath her throat.

No matter how long Louai hid from the Israelis, she would never grow accustomed to the absences between his visits to the house where she lived with his parents, his brother and three sisters. They had been married only a year, but he had been underground most of that time. It was as her parents had feared. Before the wedding, they had consulted with their neighbor, *ustaz* Omar Yussef, a respected friend of her father and a schoolteacher who took a special interest in her. He had told Dima's father that, though there was a risk the girl soon would be widowed, there seemed to be love between the two young people and such feelings ought to be nurtured in these days of hate.

So Dima had given up her studies at the UNRWA Girls School in Dehaisha to marry Louai. She went to work in her father-in-law's autoshop, doing the accounts and answering the phones. At home she ended up doing the family's housework and dreaming of Louai's rare homecomings. It became a week or longer between his visits to the house, and each time he spent only an hour or two with her before he had to be gone once more. When he wasn't there, she was melancholy. Without her husband to enliven her nights, the days in the glass booth at the back of the garage were dull. Worse, Louai's father Muhammad and his brother Yunis grew cold toward her, as though they blamed her for the risks he took in coming through the darkness to the house. Or maybe it was something else.

Weeks before, a burly man in military fatigues had come into the autoshop when Muhammad and Yunis were out. He sat on Dima's desk, crumpling her paperwork with his broad backside, and tried to touch her cheek. 'I have something I need to buy from your family,' he said to her, 'but I'd pay double the price if they'd let *you* deliver it to me.' She moved away and the man laughed. Behind him, she noticed Yunis at the entrance to the garage. The man lifted his hand again, but then followed her eyes to her brother-in-law. He laughed again and left the autoshop. Yunis looked darkly at her and followed the man out, whispering insistently to him. He had barely spoken to her since that day.

When Louai last came home, Dima complained that his father and brother were distant with her. A quiet, calm man, he surprised her with his sudden anger. 'You have no right to judge my father and brother,' he shouted. 'These are not matters that concern you.'

Dima had no idea what 'matters' he meant – she had referred only to their icy manner about the house and office. But Louai quickly calmed himself and apologized. He said he was tense because of his confinement in a safehouse, but Dima knew he was lying. He was defensive, because he, too, was frustrated with his brother. Dima's suspicions about Yunis somehow were confirmed by Louai's outburst. Before he had left that last time, Dima had heard Louai and Yunis arguing. They had spoken in whispers. She couldn't tell what they were saying, but the tone had been heated. She had also noticed her husband stare sternly at his father after he embraced him in farewell.

As Dima Abdel Rahman stood at the window straining to see the source of the steps sounding in the undergrowth, she heard the steady footfalls stop. Then they began again, not so clearly defined, but rather a shuffle through the underbrush, as though the creeping man had suddenly relaxed.

'Oh, it's you, Abu Walid.'

It was her husband's voice. He spoke calmly, in a friendly tone. Dima looked toward the voice. For a moment she saw nothing, then at the edge of the pines a small red dot appeared, flitting unsteadily as though describing a circle of a small radius. It quivered to a halt, like a firefly settling onto a leaf. When the red dot was still, instantly there was a shot. Dima gasped, and it was as though the sudden extra oxygen fed her eyes, because she saw Louai. He stumbled from the edge of the trees. Dima couldn't make out his face, but she knew the denim jacket and the jeans she had bought for him before his last visit. His hand clutched his shoulder.

The red dot, again. Another shot cracked out of the darkness and Louai spun, his arms stretched wide, like a Sufi dancing in the divine trance of the *sema*, whirling, head back, one hand turned toward the earth, the other palm heavenward. He collapsed facedown in the cabbage patch.

Dima stared. Her mother-in-law came wailing into the room, crying out that the Israelis were invading. 'They will murder us all,' she called. 'Yunis, my son, come and bring your father to protect us. Muhammad, come to protect us, husband.' There were footsteps from the upper floor as the men awoke from their evening naps and hurried to the stairs. Dima felt as if she had been turned to stone. If she moved, she thought she might fall to pieces on the ground, her body dropping noisily in a cloud of dusty chips. With a fearful effort, she turned and ran to the door, knocking over a glass of *kamar al-din* on the way.

The killers could be out here still, Dima thought, *but I have to reach him and touch him. Don't let him be badly hurt.*

She stumbled through the cabbages and dropped to the ground at Louai's side. It was then that she realized she was sobbing and, as she turned her husband onto his back, her sobs became a scream. His wide eyes were blank and stared right through her. His tongue protruded palely between his lips. The denim jacket was wet, saturated with blood from the collarbone to the navel. Dima held his hand and touched his face. He was so beautiful. She looked at his hand. His fingers were long and slim, these fingers that touched her delicately when he came to the house. Why was the cause of Palestine worth more to him than their happiness and their love?

Louai's mother came through the cabbages. She knew the meaning of Dima's scream. She fell on her knees at her boy's side and laid her hands on the bloody torso. Dima heard the soft squelching of the wet denim as the old woman gripped it desperately. The mother lifted her hands, covered her cheeks in her son's blood and called out to God.

'Get away from him.'

Dima heard Yunis behind her. He grabbed her shoulder and shoved her away from her husband's corpse. He lifted his mother gently, but led her away from the body, too. She sobbed and cried, '*Allahu akbar*,' God is most great. As he passed Dima with his mother, Yunis caught her eye. His look was defensive and hostile. The glance confused her. Yunis looked away. 'Don't disturb anything. Leave the place for the police to investigate,' he said.

'The police?'

'Yes.'

'What is there for the police to investigate? The Israelis assassinated your brother. Are the police going to go and arrest the Israeli soldier who fired the shots?'

'Just do as I say.'

'The police will be useless unless a Palestinian did this. What Palestinian would kill a member of our family? What Palestinian would kill a leader of the resistance?'

Yunis averted his eyes. Dima stepped toward him, but he turned his gaze on her again and it was reproachful and violent.

Dima would have spoken more angrily, if it had not seemed like a desecration of her husband's body to use harsh words. When Yunis turned on the lights in the house, beams of fluorescent blue filtered outside. Their icy reflections shone in the pool of Louai's blood.

CHAPTER 3

Omar Yussef placed his purple leather briefcase carefully on his desk and opened the
shiny gold combination locks. He un-
clipped a Mont Blanc fountain pen from the
pocket on the inside of the lid. It was a present
from a graduating class of students, who knew
that he loved stylish things. He felt the pleasing
weight and balance of the Mont Blanc in his hand
and glanced at the pile of exercise books on his
desk to be graded. He wondered if the class whose
books lay before him would ever feel generous or
grateful toward their teacher. He began to read
through their short essays on the demise of the
Ottoman Empire. He spent a great deal of his
time, too much of it, angry with these children.
He tried not to be, but he couldn't stand to listen
to them when they rolled through the political
clichés of the poor, victimized Arab nation, subju-
gated by everyone from the Crusaders and the
Mongols to the Turks and the British, all the way
to the intifada. It wasn't wrong to see the Arabs
as victims of a harsh history, but it was a mistake
to assume that they bore no responsibility for their

own sufferings. In his classroom, Omar Yussef would step in and destroy their hateful, blind slogans. Yet he could see that it only made him angrier and left the students somehow mistrustful of him.

Omar wrote a 'C' grade in the margin of the first messy notebook, because he decided to be generous, and opened another. He was getting old. He thought of George Saba and the comforting feeling he experienced as they dined, that this pupil and others like him would be the proud legacy of Omar Yussef. He knew that his recent irritable outbursts in the classroom were caused by a combination of frustration at the ignorant, simple-minded, violent politics of his students and the sense that he was already too old, too distant from their world ever to change them. He knew it would be worse in a boys school, but there was such violence even in his girls that it shocked him. No matter how he tried to liberate the minds of Dehaisha's children, there were always many others working still more diligently to enslave them.

It was different when he taught at the Frères School. During those years, there were many fine young minds that had opened themselves to him. It wasn't just the pupils that had changed. Tension and hatred had engulfed Bethlehem, and on their heels came poverty and resentment and propaganda. Even a fine pupil like Dima Abdel Rahman was sucked into the violence. Her father, Omar

Yussef's neighbor, had called the previous night to tell him about the death of the girl's husband, Louai Abdel Rahman. The funeral would be in the early morning, when Omar Yussef was at work, but he planned to visit Dima Abdel Rahman in the afternoon. He had thought he might suggest that she return to her studies, but then he remembered that she truly loved her husband and he decided to wait before offering her any such proposals for her future.

It was at times like these, when the first light of the day was crisp in his empty classroom and the essays he graded were sub-par, that Omar Yussef wondered if he ought not to accede to the request of the school's American director and quit. Omar Yussef was only fifty-six years old, but Christopher Steadman wanted him to retire. He saw how the American looked at his shaking hands, reminders of the years of alcohol that were now behind him. They made him seem even more fragile than his slow, labored walk. Maybe Steadman only wanted a more vigorous man, but Omar Yussef hated him because he suspected the American really wanted a teacher who wouldn't talk back. Omar Yussef reflected that he had molded a sufficient number of fine young minds, like those of George Saba, Elias Bishara and Dima Abdel Rahman, enough to satisfy the most conscientious of teachers. Perhaps he shouldn't be driving himself crazy, putting his heart through the stress of confronting the entire machine of mad martyrdom propaganda and lies every day.

The first of his pupils entered. 'Morning of joy, *ustaz.*'

Omar Yussef returned the greeting, quietly. With the student's arrival, the comforting thoughts of his old pupils dissolved and he dropped back into the alien present, his senses heightened to the tawdriness of the school. The chairs scraped on the classroom floor as the girls seated themselves. The air filled with the background stink of unwashed armpits and bean farts. Omar Yussef looked down at the exercise book and pretended to be grading it. The pen shook in his fingers, as it always did these days. There was a tiny liver spot on the back of his hand, which presented itself to him as he turned the pages. It was new, appearing almost overnight, as though some genie had stolen into his bedroom while he slept and stamped him ineradicably as prematurely aged. When he thought of it that way, he wondered that the visiting spirit found him in his bed and asleep, for it seemed to Omar Yussef that he spent half the night urinating and the genie could just as easily have impressed its seal of superannuation on his dribbling penis. This was the real him and this was the reality of his life. Maybe he hadn't been such a prize even back when he was young. To the rosy, wistful picture of a youthful Omar Yussef, he ought to have added that his eyes would be bleary from drink and his mouth would be tight with the bitterness of one who feels he has much for which to apologize – to those he offended while drunk, but to himself most of all. Yes, perhaps he truly didn't need this in the morning. He would talk about retirement with his wife Maryam.

More students came into the room. Most were silent. They knew enough of Omar Yussef's strictness not to speak in class unless he appeared to be in a very good mood, which rarely applied to the opening of the morning session at 7:30 A.M. But one girl was too animated to hold herself back. Khadija Zubeida entered quickly and excitedly. She was tall and thin with black hair cut in a bob. There was an early bloom of acne high on both of her pale cheeks. Before she sat, she leaned over the desks of two friends: 'My dad called me before I came to school,' she told them. 'He arrested a collaborator. The one who helped the Israelis kill the martyr in Irtas. He said they're going to execute the traitor.' She spoke in a whisper, but in the quiet classroom it was audible to all, as was the snigger that punctuated it.

'Who was it?' one of her friends asked.

'The collaborator? He's a damned Christian from Beit Jala. Saba, I think. He led the Jews right to the man in Irtas, who was a great fighter, and he delivered the final blow with a big knife that the Jews gave him.'

Omar Yussef put down his pen before the shaking of his hand could propel it across the table. He

27

shoved the exercise book away from him and put his head in his hands to gather his thoughts. They had taken George, he was sure of it. He coughed to steady his voice. 'Khadija,' he called to the girl, hoarsely. 'Which Saba?'

'I think he's called George, *ustaz*. George Saba. My dad says he keeps dirty statues of women in his house and he offered to let the arresting officer take his daughter instead.'

The girls clicked their tongues and shook their heads.

'The Christian confessed, too. He said, 'I know why you came here. You came here because I sold myself to the Jews.' My dad gave him a good thump after he confessed.'

Omar Yussef stood and leaned against his desk. 'Come here,' he said, sharply. As the girl approached him, a little confused, he considered giving her the same blow her father claimed to have aimed at the collaborator. But he knew he must try harder than that: he was a schoolteacher, not a police thug. He wondered what the girl saw from the other side of the desk. He knew that his own eyes were tearing with rage and the slack fold beneath his chin trembled. He must have seemed pitiful, or deeply unnerving. 'What do I teach you to do in this classroom?'

The girl looked dumbly at Omar Yussef.

'How do I teach you to look at history?' Omar Yussef waited. He stared closely at the girl. There was no reply, so he went on. 'I teach you to look at the evidence and then to decide what you think about a particular sultan, or about the causes of a war.'

'Yes, that's right,' the girl said, relieved.

'So how do you know that this man was a collaborator?'

'My dad told me.'

'Who's your father?'

'Sergeant Mahmoud Zubeida, General Intelligence, Rapid Reaction Force.'

'Did he do the investigation, from start to finish?'

The girl looked perplexed.

'No, of course, he didn't,' Omar Yussef said. 'So you'd need to talk to all those who *did* investigate the case before you could come to the conclusion that this man was a collaborator. Wouldn't you?'

'He confessed.'

'Did he confess to you? In person? You'd need to talk to him. To understand him. To talk to his friends. Most of all, you'd need to find his motive for collaborating. Did he do it for money? Maybe he already has a lot of money and has no need of more. So then why would he do it? Was there anyone else who might have done it to set him up? Maybe a business rival?'

The girl shifted from foot to foot and scratched at the spots on her cheek. Omar Yussef saw that Khadija was about to cry. He knew that he was shouting now and leaning very close to the girl across the desk, but he didn't care. He was infuriated by the ignorance of an entire generation and saw it concentrated in this girl's thin shoulders and blank face.

'How could I know all that?' Khadija stammered.

'Because it's what you need to know before you condemn a human being to death.' Omar Yussef leaned as far forward as he could. 'Death. Death. It's not something light, something to giggle and boast about. This alleged collaborator is someone's father. Imagine having *your* father taken away and knowing that he will be killed.' As he spoke, it occurred to Omar Yussef that the girl probably had frequent cause to imagine her father's death at the hands of the Israelis in some stupid gunbattle. It was probably in Khadija's nightmares each night, coruscating and terrifying. It made Omar Yussef feel, for a moment, sympathetic. He stood up straight. 'Sit down, Khadija.'

Omar Yussef took out his comb and straightened the strands of hair that had fallen forward when he shouted at her. The class was silent. He returned his comb to his top pocket and sat. 'When you are gone from the world, what will you leave behind?' he said. 'Will you leave behind many children? So what? Is that a good thing in itself? No, it depends on what you will have taught them. Will you leave a great fortune? Then, what kind of person will inherit it? How will they spend it? Will people remember you with love? Or will they feel hate when they think of you? Start asking yourself these questions now, even though you are only eleven years old. If you do not ask these questions of yourself, someone else – maybe a bad person – will dictate the answers to you. They will show you their so-called evidence, and you will never see all the other choices available to you. If you do not take charge, someone else will gain control of your life.'

I might be talking about myself, Omar Yussef thought.

'This man, George Saba, was once my student. He was a very intelligent, good pupil. He was sensitive and funny. He was also moral. I don't believe he would become mixed up in anything criminal or bad.'

Khadija Zubeida didn't raise her head as she spoke sullenly. 'What evidence do *you* have?'

Omar Yussef was pleased with the question and he nodded at the girl. 'More than you, Khadija. Because you judge the case according to your feelings of hate for someone you've never met. I know George Saba and I love him.'

Well, that was a smart way to start the day, Omar Yussef thought. *I love the Israeli collaborator; I love the worst traitor. Next time anyone's looking for a dupe, stick me in jail and get my class to testify that I sympathized with a collaborator, which surely makes me a collaborator, too. Good job, Abu Ramiz. You need more sleep and an extra cup of coffee in the morning.*

When classes ended for the morning, Wafa, the school secretary was waiting outside the room.

31

She wore a thin, fixed smile and handed a small cup of coffee to Omar Yussef.

'God bless your hands,' Omar Yussef said. 'I assume this fine treatment means that you are preparing me for bad news.' The cup rattled against the saucer. His hand shook more than usual. *George*, he thought, *Allah help him*.

'Drink your coffee, *ustaz*,' Wafa said, and the smile became more affectionate.

Omar Yussef stared at her, waiting.

'The director wants to see you as soon as possible in his office,' she said.

'Thank you for the coffee.' Omar Yussef drank. 'It's delicious.' He returned the empty cup to Wafa. 'You see, I didn't even curse when you mentioned our esteemed director.'

'For a change. We must thank Allah.'

Omar Yussef entered Christopher Steadman's room and immediately the friendly warmth he had felt with Wafa changed to anger. At the side of the desk, next to the tall, fair figure of the UN director, was the government schools inspector who had forced the Frères School to terminate Omar Yussef's contract a decade earlier. Omar Yussef knew immediately what this would be about. The bastard from the government had stopped Omar Yussef tampering with the minds of the elite at the Frères School. Now he figured he could cut off his piffling influence over even the bottom of the pile here in the refugee camp, where, after all, the corrupt scum who ran the government recruited their expendable foot soldiers. Omar Yussef was angry, too, because he understood that he was being summoned into the presence of the inspector to give Steadman more leverage in his push for his retirement. 'Sit down, Abu Ramiz.' Steadman gestured to a chair in front of his desk. Omar Yussef noted that the American had picked up on the tradition of calling an acquaintance the 'father of his eldest son.

Only the day before, Steadman had asked Omar why Arabs called each other *Abu* or *Umm*? Omar Yussef explained that Palestinians each have a given name, 'so I am Omar,' he said. 'But we also are known as the father – *Abu* – of our first son. My first son is Ramiz, so people call me Abu Ramiz. The father of Ramiz. It is more respectful, more friendly.' Then he warned Steadman that if he made him retire, he wouldn't have anyone to pester with questions about Arab society. Steadman proceeded as though he hadn't noticed the aggression in what Omar Yussef said. 'If I had a son, which I don't, I always thought I'd call him Scott,' Steadman said. 'So I'd be Abu Scott.' Then he asked Omar what *Umm* means. Omar decided to confuse him: 'It means "Mother of." My wife is Umm Ramiz, just like I am Abu Ramiz. My son decided to name his first son after me, because he believes in following this tradition, so he is Abu Omar and his wife is Umm Omar, and their son Omar will one day name his son after his own father and be called Abu

Ramiz, too. And you,' Omar said, 'will always be just an American.'

Now, in Steadman's office, Omar Yussef could see that the American was trying hard to fit in. *All right, so you remembered*, he thought. *You called me the father of Ramiz, Abu Ramiz, but you won't make me like you so easily.*

The room smelled. That, too, was the result of Steadman's attempt to conform to local traditions. Before Ramadan, Omar Yussef joked with him that Muslims refrained from washing during the holy month and were offended by those who did. At first, he found it hilarious that Steadman took him seriously. The director evidently planned not to bath for the entire month. Omar Yussef regretted the joke now and sniffed the cologne on the back of his own hand to overcome the reek of body odor. 'Do you know Mr Haitham Abdel Hadi from the Ministry of Education?' Steadman asked.

You know perfectly well that I know him. I'm sure he's shown you his file on me, Omar Yussef thought. He remained silent.

'Well, I must tell you that Mr Abdel Hadi has received some complaints about your teaching. This is why I've called you in here today.' Steadman stroked his thin, blond hair back from a sunburned forehead. He brought his hand down with the palm open, giving the floor to the government inspector.

The government inspector read from a series of letters he claimed parents had written to his department. The letters quoted Omar Yussef criticizing the president and the government, lambasting the Aqsa Martyrs Brigades as gangsters, condemning suicide bombings and talking disrespectfully about the sheikhs in some of the local mosques. 'Last month,' the inspector said, 'some of the students were hurt in a demonstration against Occupation soldiers at Rachel's Tomb. The next day, teacher Omar Yussef told them that instead of throwing stones at soldiers, children should throw stones at their parents and their government for making a mess of their lives. This is a precise quote: for making a mess of their lives, throw stones at their parents and their government.'

'Is that what you said, Abu Ramiz?' Steadman asked.

Omar Yussef looked at the dark, sly eyes of the government inspector. He held his hand over his mouth, trying to make the gesture look casual. He hoped it would hide the angry twitching in his lip. He felt adrenaline filling him with rage. Steadman repeated his question. His innocent tone infuriated Omar Yussef.

'I don't expect you to be absolutely politically correct, Abu Ramiz. You're too old for that,' Steadman said. 'But I cannot accept this kind of thing. We work in cooperation with the local administration and we're not supposed to be breeding revolutionaries, or encouraging acts of violence.'

This stupid man really thought I wanted the children

to attack their parents. 'The children were already violent. They attacked the soldiers. I hope it's not revolutionary to point out that this is still an act of violence, whatever their reasons for doing so. I was suggesting to the children that the guiltiest target is not always the most obvious one,' he said.

'That is outrageous,' the government inspector said. 'To place parents and the government before the Occupation Forces as criminals against the Palestinian people.'

'It's politically correct these days to blow yourself up in a crowd of civilians. It's politically correct to praise those who detonate themselves and to laud them in the newspapers and in the mosques.' Omar Yussef banged the edge of his hand on the desk. 'But you say that it's outrageous for me to encourage intellectual inquiry?'

'You have a bad record, Abu Ramiz,' the government man said. 'Your file is a lengthy one. I will have to institute official proceedings against you, if you do not agree to Mr Steadman's proposals.'

Omar Yussef looked at Steadman. The square American jaw was firm. The lips were tight. Steadman adjusted his small round spectacles. He squinted and watched Omar Yussef calmly with his little, blue eyes.

So this bastard already told Abdel Hadi he wants me out of here. Who knows if they didn't cook this up between them? He decided he wouldn't make it easy for them. He would never retire. They could put him in a jail cell with George Saba before he'd accede to Steadman's weakness and pandering. 'This would never have happened when the school was run by Mister Fergus or Miss Pilar. They would never threaten me. Yes, I consider this a threat, not just from the government but from you, too, Christopher. I end this conversation.' He went to the door.

'Abu Ramiz, you may not leave yet,' Steadman said. 'We need to clear this up.'

'I am happy that you listened to my lecture about "Abu" meaning "father of,"' Omar Yussef said. 'Would you like me to refer to you as Abu Scott, as you suggested, after all?'

Steadman seemed taken aback by Omar Yussef's change in direction, and he answered warily. 'Yes. Like I told you, I always figured I'd call my son Scott, if I had one. So that makes me the father of Scott. Sure, you can call me Abu Scott.'

'It is a most appropriate name. In Arabic, Scott means *shut up*.' Omar Yussef stared at the confused American and the furious government inspector. 'Excuse me, but I have a condolence call to pay in Irtas. The husband of one of my former pupils has been killed by political correctness.'

CHAPTER 4

The path through the valley was marked by a languid stream of mourners for the martyr. They sauntered along the track to the Abdel Rahman house, chatting idly. Omar Yussef cursed himself for wearing only a jacket that morning, as the wind rushed down the valley of Irtas and through his tweed. He decided to put on a coat every day until April, no matter how bright the weather looked from his bedroom window when he awoke. He moved as fast as he could, but was passed by almost everyone, though they seemed to be in no hurry. He was thankful at least that he wore a beige flat cap of soft cashmere to warm his bald head and to keep his strands of hair under control in the stiff breeze.

Omar Yussef came to the end of the path. There were two oil drums with the palm fronds and black flags of mourning bending in the wind. The flags were mounted on bamboo poles and their ends clicked and scratched around inside the barrel as the wind whipped them, as though they thought they could escape. Omar Yussef wound through the rows of men sitting on white plastic garden chairs under the fluttery black tarpaulin of the condolence tent. He joined the queue of men who passed along the family receiving line, limply shaking hands and muttering that Allah would be merciful to Louai Abdel Rahman. At the end of the receiving line was a thin young man with a bony resentful face. Omar Yussef assumed this was the dead fighter's brother. The kid alternated his fierce glare between the edge of the woods beyond the vegetable patch and the entrance to the family's house. Omar Yussef held the youth's hand and asked him where to find Dima Abdel Rahman. He detected a flash of hostility before the young man told him she was inside with the women.

'Please go and get her. Tell her it's her old schoolteacher.'

The young man hesitated, while Omar Yussef kept his hand in his grip. Then he pulled his hand away and went into the house.

Omar Yussef would have liked to accept a small cup of *qahweh sa'ada*. Any other time of the year there would have been a teenager circulating with a plastic flask of the unsweetened coffee at a funeral. But it was Ramadan now, and there would be neither coffee nor anything else served until darkness fell. Omar Yussef didn't need Ramadan to remind him that there were things from which he ought to refrain. He remembered that when he was a student an old woman once slapped his face because he smoked a cigarette on a Damascus street during Ramadan. He ought to have kept her around to batter him every time he did something forbidden. How long, he wondered, would it have taken him to quit alcohol if he'd received a sharp jab to the head every time he sank a scotch on the rocks? Instead, he hadn't sobered up until his late forties. By that time, the spectacular relish of his early drinking days had vanished. Even he could see that he was pathetic. He had stopped because it embarrassed him to notice men twenty years younger look with pity at his bleary eyes and shaky hands.

From behind the mourning tent, there were three sharp, loud shots, but only Omar Yussef ducked. He turned quickly to follow the gaze of the other mourners. Along the path came a troop of Aqsa Martyrs Brigades gunmen. A big man who wore a bandoleer across his chest led them. Omar Yussef pushed his gold-rimmed glasses up along his nose and saw that it was Hussein Tamari, the leader of the Martyrs Brigades in Bethlehem. He carried the big gun everyone talked about. Tamari's head was widest at the bottom, bulky and jowly. He had a thick, black moustache and trim, black hair that seemed of necessity to be short, as there wasn't much real estate for it to cover. The top of Tamari's head narrowed to a third of the width of his neck. The tapering, in-bred head seemed to Omar Yussef to be a declaration that his brain wasn't the source of his swagger.

Next to Tamari walked a thin, dark man Omar Yussef had seen around town. His name was Jihad

40

Awdeh. There was a gray hat that looked like a furry fez on his head. Omar Yussef struggled to remember the name for this style of hat. No one wore such headgear in Bethlehem. Old men from the villages wore traditional *keffiyehs*, and kids wore American baseball caps. Most heads were bare. Jihad Awdeh's hat seemed extravagant and sinister. Omar Yussef thought immediately of Saddam Hussein, who used to wear just such a hat on winter occasions. *Astrakhan, that's what they call it*, Omar Yussef thought. He gave a short sardonic laugh and shook his head.

Hussein Tamari fired off a few rounds into the air with his massive machine gun as a mark of respect to the dead man, resting the butt against his hip and holding it in one hand with casually ostentatious power. It was a deep noise, wide and impressive, and Omar Yussef noticed that some in the crowd seemed about to applaud the show. The gun had a wooden stock and a dark metal barrel. It looked to be over four feet long.

The gunmen came under the tarpaulin canopy and, cutting in front of the line of mourners in the cold wind, shook the hands of the family members. Omar Yussef saw that Louai Abdel Rahman's father seemed particularly cowed and didn't look directly at the gunmen, though they lingered before him longer than was necessary.

Omar Yussef went to the door of the house. He glanced into the living room. There was a mural painted on the wall, a Swiss alpine landscape.

41

A fawn gamboled in the deep grass at the edge of a cool lake. A wooden house hugged the slopes of a snow-covered mountain, bright as a picture in a children's book and clumsily cartoonish. Many Palestinians decorated their walls with scenes of the Alps. It was, no doubt, a pleasure to gaze at such a prospect during the stifling summer, he thought. But perhaps it also was calming, as though by looking at the terrain of a peaceful country one could forget the violence all around, dream oneself onto a mountain elevation, breathing cleanly and easily. Omar Yussef noted that there were never any people in these murals.

In front of the alpine tableau there was a crowd of women. They improvised a song of blessings on the mother of the martyr for the bliss that her dead son would now be experiencing. A woman would chant a verse and the others would join in, clapping a rhythm, and another would take over for the next stanza. They did the same thing at weddings. At the back of the room, Omar Yussef noticed Dima Abdel Rahman. He waved for her to come outside. She half-smiled and walked to him. As she reached the steps, Omar Yussef saw the young man who was supposed to bring her to him watching balefully from the door of the kitchen.

'Allah will be merciful upon him, the deceased one,' Omar Yussef said.

'Thank you, uncle,' Dima Abdel Rahman replied. 'I'm glad you came.'

'Who's the kid I sent in to find you?' Omar Yussef gestured discreetly toward the youth.

'That's my husband's brother, Yunis.'

'He seems more angry than sad at his brother's death.'

'He seems more angry than anything,' Dima said.

They stepped away from the house and the mourning tent and came to the cabbage patch. Dima stared at the spot where her husband had died. She began to cry. Omar Yussef took a handkerchief from the pocket of his tweed jacket and gave it to her. She wiped her eyes and smiled, embarrassed. Then she pointed: 'This was where Louai died. I found him here.'

Dima cried again. Omar Yussef spoke quietly to her. 'It's appropriate that you should cry, my dear. Firing guns in the air is wrong. But crying is good.'

'Louai's mother said I should be crying out with joy now that he's a martyr,' Dima said.

'That's just a show for all these people. I'm sure she doesn't feel it deep in her heart,' Omar Yussef said.

'I just can't rejoice that he's dead, *ustaz*. I just can't.'

'When I was a young man, my dear father passed away. I remember crying, and all the people in the house told me I shouldn't, because my father lived to be an old man and I ought to behave like a man. But I had an uncle who understood me. He said, "Let the boy cry. Can't you see, he loved his father?" So don't worry. You can cry. And you can keep the handkerchief, too.'

Dima smiled through her tears. 'I was very happy when you were my teacher,' she said.

'You're a bright woman. I'd be very glad if all my pupils were like you.'

His pupils were Omar Yussef's legacy. After all his years of study and struggle, after his doubts that he was able to make a difference in their lives, the belief that he had truly left traces of knowledge and wisdom and goodness in other humans kept Omar Yussef from depression. Dima and George Saba and the few others like them must make the world the kind of place where Omar Yussef could live in happiness.

There were more shots from near the mourning tent. Dima gasped. 'Who is the man with the big gun?'

'That's Hussein Tamari.'

'The Martyrs Brigades leader?'

Omar Yussef nodded.

'I saw him at the autoshop once. He came when I was alone. I didn't know who he was,' she said, staring over the cabbages toward the gunman. Dima shook her head. 'Why did my husband allow himself to be killed, uncle? He never said he wanted to be a martyr, but everyone talks about the martyrs all the time. Maybe Louai started to think that way, too.'

'In the end, everyone dies. I'm getting old and I'm starting to feel death creeping through me, taking me over limb by limb, organ by organ. I hope my mind will be the last part living. But, in any case, some people might think it's better to go quickly, when you're younger, and to be remembered as a hero, rather than someone who clung on until everyone was sick of him.'

Dima seemed to want to talk, so Omar Yussef let her tell the story of the night her husband died. 'Before the shots, I heard Louai speak to someone, and then I saw something strange. I stood at that window there. I saw a red dot, like a light, that I now think was shining on Louai. It moved about, as though it was trying to settle on him. It was there, by that tree. Then he was shot. Two times.'

'You heard him speak? What did he say?'

'He said: "Oh, it's you, Abu Walid." He sounded relaxed.'

'There was someone else out here?'

'Yes, I suppose there must have been.'

Omar Yussef thought of George, arrested for collaborating in the death of this young man. But George was not called Abu Walid. 'You didn't see anybody when you came outside, except Louai?'

'I just ran to his body. I didn't think of anything else.'

'Who is Abu Walid? Which of Louai's friends is the father of Walid?'

'I don't know. There could be lots of people with that name, couldn't there?'

'Yes, but not so many who might have been on casual speaking terms with a man on the run

45

from the Israelis. A man who was in hiding for months.'

'I really don't know, *ustaz*.' Dima hesitated. 'There was something strange about the way Louai's brother reacted, too. He seemed angry with me.'

Omar Yussef paused, then he put his hand on Dima's shoulder. She looked down and smiled. He let his hand rest there. 'My sister, yours was a short marriage, but you were lucky enough to have that brief time with a man who loved you. You know enough about the way things are for women in our society to understand that this is a blessing.'

'Yes, uncle.' She blew her nose in his handkerchief. 'I have to go back to the kitchen now. I'll come and visit you soon. Please give my greetings to Umm Ramiz. A generous Ramadan.'

'Thank you. Allah lengthen your life.'

Omar Yussef was moved by the girl's emotion. He would have liked to stay with her longer. He didn't want to go back to the men in the mourning tent, so he shuffled through the grass to the trees. He leaned against the pine where Louai Abdel Rahman had been illuminated by a small, red light. Omar Yussef looked about him. A strip of grass had been wrenched from the ground in front of the tree. Maybe Louai had slipped and uprooted these blades when he was shot. Omar Yussef stepped a few paces to his right. A patch of grass and underbrush about the size of a man's prone body had been crushed and flattened behind a tree. This must be where Abu Walid – if he existed

46

– had waited. But why would he lie here? Had he shot Louai Abdel Rahman from this hiding place? There was only space in the flattened spot for one man, so there couldn't have been an Israeli hit squad there with him, whoever he was.

Omar Yussef looked closely at the spot. He ruffled the flattened grass stems with his foot. Something bright came to the surface. He bent stiffly and picked it up. In his palm he held a spent machine-gun cartridge. He kicked about in the flattened grass to see if there were more. Dima had said that Louai was shot twice. But there was only one cartridge case here. He couldn't see anything else on the ground.

Someone named Abu Walid had been here, lying in wait long enough to flatten the grass. Louai Abdel Rahman had known him. One spent cartridge case had been left behind. Did that mean Abu Walid had taken one shot at Louai, while someone in another location fired the other? What was the red light that Dima had seen?

Omar Yussef made his way back to the mourning tent. He put the bullet casing in the pocket of his jacket. Hussein Tamari was talking about Louai Abdel Rahman in a loud voice at the edge of the tent. 'The martyr,' he called him. It struck Omar Yussef that there was security in the thought that a man died as a martyr. There was no groaning and bleeding and wishing not to die in a case of martyrdom. For those who lived on, it was as though there had been no death.

There were different ways to defend oneself against the fear of death. Omar Yussef thought that only the dead could truly protect you from death. When you realize that someone is gone and always gone, there is no longing for their return. If death is simple and absolute, there is no doubt, no wondering whether the deceased received a good reward or was consigned to the flames – and doubt is a much more protracted torment than any kind of death. When you can look at a headstone and think simply to yourself, 'That lump of gray rock is what prevents the dust of my beloved blowing all over the cuffs of my pants, and that dust is all that there is left of him,' then you can truly live until you, too, die.

Omar Yussef ran his fingers over the cartridge casing. *That's what I believe about death*, he thought. *But murder is different.*

CHAPTER 5

Omar Yussef considered himself a long way from Paradise. No prayers preceded the *iftar* at his house. He broke each day's fast during Ramadan simply, with his family around the dining table in the drafty entrance hall of his old stone home. The lights already had been on in the house most of the dismal afternoon since Omar Yussef had returned, chilled through, from his condolence call to Dima Abdel Rahman. He was deeply disturbed by the thought of George alone in a jail cell, facing the possibility of a death sentence for collaboration. The heavy gloom of the overcast afternoon became cold, black evening. The streets, almost empty because of the threat of rain, were cleared utterly by the festive break fasts.

Omar Yussef's wife, Maryam, sent his grandson, little Omar, into the salon to call him to the table. Omar Yussef put down his tea cup and pressed his hand to the boy's cheek.

'What's for dinner?' he asked.

'Grandma's food,' little Omar said.

'What did she cook? Did she make something sweet for your sweet tooth?'

Little Omar nodded and wriggled away. Omar Yussef called him back and gave him a sugar cube from the china bowl on the coffee table. The boy smiled and ran to the door. Omar Yussef heard his wife bringing a pot to the table. Little Omar popped the sugar into his mouth. Evidently Maryam noticed him crunching it in his small jaw.

'Omar, you'll spoil the boy's appetite,' she called.

Omar Yussef came laughing into the hallway. 'You know the proverb, "The Lord sends almonds to those who have lost their teeth." Let the boy enjoy his sweets innocently, before he gets to the age where nothing is fun any more.' He took his seat at the head of the table, as the rest of the family filed in.

Ramiz, Omar's eldest son, came up the stairs from the basement, where he lived, carrying his youngest daughter. His wife, Sara, ferried a final pot from the kitchen to the table, and Maryam fussed the children into their chairs. When all were seated, Maryam spooned *ma'alouba* from the wide platter at the center of the table, serving her husband first. Omar scooped some of this rice and chicken into a clammy yellow Ramadan pancake. He loved Maryam's food and ate at home every night, unless he couldn't avoid an invitation to a restaurant. He spooned out a helping of *fattoush*, a Syrian salad of mint, parsley, romaine lettuce and chopped pita bread. He had only to place Maryam's *fattoush* in his mouth and the sharpness of her lemon vinaigrette would transport him to a café in the

Damascus *souk* where he had spent many wonderful times in his youth. Maryam hadn't been there with him, but somehow she seemed to have tasted what he had tasted. It was as though her cooking made a map for him of his life story. It was comforting, like a well-bound, old atlas that took your imagination across mountain ranges without the physical exertion, annoyance, and inconvenience of actual travel. He wondered if Louai Abdel Rahman felt the same way about Dima's cooking. Perhaps he hadn't been married to her long enough for the taste of her grape leaves to supplant that of his mother's in his memories of taste and happiness. Omar Yussef thought that, as the fugitive crept home through the dusk, he would have been struggling to concentrate on the dangers around him. A mother's cooking and its redolence of home was powerful for any Palestinian. He was comforted that at least the boy had died anticipating pleasure.

Omar Yussef watched his family take their first swallows of the meal. At the Ramadan break fast, he could sense the irritability of a day without food passing in the relief and comfort of the heavy, fatty goat's meat Maryam boiled in milk and the green chicken broth of her *mouloukhiyeh*, thick with cilantro and garlic and mallow leaves, poured over rice and beans.

Omar Yussef stopped eating after a few bites. There was something different tonight. It wasn't the quality of the meal itself, he was quite sure.

Rather it was the way his body responded to it. It was the herbs Maryam used that made her cooking so special to him, the black pepper and mint she mixed with garlic and kebab. But tonight he felt revulsion as he bit into the meat. It was as though, for the first time, he considered that the basis of the food and all its nourishment was dead flesh. Did something have to die so that he could live? Did the meat have to be flavored with spices to fool his tongue, to sneak a murder past it? How much killing can we swallow, so long as it goes down easy and doesn't tax our digestion? He glanced at his grandchildren and watched them push little lumps of animal flesh around their plates. Perhaps they instinctively understood what only now occurred to him. Everywhere there is hearty food, and it gives you a good feeling as it enters deep into your innermost organs. But if you are watching carefully, you will notice that death is gorging its way to the cemetery and you are its main course.

His eldest granddaughter, Nadia, filled his glass with water. She was twelve years old, with skin that was pale from passing the summer inside, under curfew, but her eyes were dark, with a light of intelligence gleaming in them. She was Omar Yussef's favorite grandchild. She loved to hear his stories. Nadia often asked him to tell her the story of how he came to this house.

It was fifty-six years since and Omar Yussef had been only a few months old, but, for the sake of the tale, he claimed to remember the arrival. His father told the servants to pack enough belongings to fill four carts. Others traveled lighter, expecting a short exile until the Arab armies expelled the Jews, but Omar Yussef's father later told him that he had known they would never return to their village. As the carts joined the refugees on the road to Bethlehem and Hebron, his father looked back at the village where he had expected his son one day to be headman like him and watched a tractor crossing the fields from the kibbutz with a handful of people walking behind it, heading for his village. 'It's gone, you know,' his father had told him, when his growing son first began to talk about politics. 'The village, the olive trees, the position of *mukhtar*. All gone. So forget about it. Don't listen to the people who think we can return.' Even as a young boy, Omar Yussef knew his father was right. The loss of land and privilege felt like less of a burden to him than it did to his friends, because he knew he always would have the protection and wisdom of his father.

The family came to Dehaisha on the edge of Bethlehem with the rest of their clan, which was called Sirhan. In Dehaisha, the peasants from their village set up in the canvas tents provided by the United Nations. Omar Yussef's father rented this stone house between Dehaisha and Bethlehem for twelve dinars. He paid the rent until he died, when his son took over the payments. The Sirhan clan

53

spread over the Bethlehem area, until it was a respectable group of about two thousand people, professionals and tradesmen. The clan was strong because its people never caused trouble with other families, and because some of them were influential in the political factions and had the protection of their militias. There were Sirhans who were powerful in the local branch of Hamas and others who climbed to prominence within the biggest faction, Fatah.

It made Omar Yussef happy that Nadia seemed to grasp his meaning when he told her this story, as though it were his dear, omniscient father who sat before her talking, rather than Omar Yussef. He felt he took on the nobility of his father as he spoke to her. Somehow, Nadia led him to the honorable essence of himself. He thanked her for the glass of water and squeezed her cheek.

The family finished their food in their accustomed quiet. The kids milled about the table absently as Sara went to prepare tea. Ramiz peeled an orange and dealt out segments to his children.

'I went to Dima Abdel Rahman today, for a condolence call,' Omar Yussef said as he sliced an apple.

'Ah, the poor one,' Maryam said. 'To be without a husband.'

'Is it so bad to be without a husband?' Omar Yussef laughed, brief and guttural. 'Sometimes you have been known to suggest that husbands are lazy and messy and a nuisance about the house.'

'Omar, you know what I mean.'

Maryam wagged her finger at him, jokingly. Lines stroked downward from her eyes and mouth, giving her face a sad cast, even as she smiled. She wore her hair in a soft wave, parted at the side and falling a few inches below her ears. She dyed it a stark raven color and always dressed in comfortable black clothing. As she aged, her skin had turned a deep gray, so that she sometimes stood out in a room like a single figure from an old movie inadvertently omitted from the colorization process.

The feelings of a man for his wife are very complex, Omar Yussef thought. *It's a shame our women can't acknowledge that their relationships to their men are not so simple, either. It would be a better thing.*

Omar Yussef needed the companionship he found with Maryam. She was born at the same time as he was, but in the north of Palestine, in Nazareth. Her family fled first to Jenin and then to Bethlehem. He had met her when they shared a taxi south from Jenin, where she still had relatives. He was beginning the final stage of his journey home from university in Damascus. They were bound together at first by their political views, their Arab nationalism. Defiantly, Maryam never covered her head as Muslim women do, though motherhood and the responsibility of the home eventually made her politics more simplistic, more average. She gave birth to three sons. Ramiz lived in the apartment downstairs, but the other two had emigrated, to the United States and to Britain. Instead of the politics of her people, Maryam fretted now about when she might see her faraway boys, a concern that could have applied to any mother anywhere in the world. *Perhaps it isn't Maryam who's become less smart. Maybe everyone was deeper back in my student days, when they didn't see the threat of a Zionist conspiracy everywhere*, Omar Yussef thought. It quietly infuriated him to hear Maryam talk about politics these days, but at least she never spoke of the dead as martyrs.

In any case, Omar Yussef wanted to talk to his son about George Saba and the thoughts about the case that had come to him after his visit to Dima Abdel Rahman. Ramiz ran a mobile phone business and his customers kept him informed about new developments in the town. Omar Yussef hoped his son might know something that would clear George's name.

'I can't help feeling that George is being set up somehow,' he said. 'I just don't believe that he would collaborate with the Israelis.'

'People will do very desperate things,' Ramiz said. 'George's business was selling antiques to Israelis on the bypass road. He can't do that any more, because there's a siege here, and his Israeli customers are afraid to come. So his business is suffering. Maybe he got desperate. Maybe the Shin

Bet got to him and told him they could solve all his problems if he did something for them.'

'It's because he's a Christian that he has been accused. That's all. It isn't because he *actually* collaborated.'

'Maybe it's because he's a Christian that he's willing to help the other side.'

Omar Yussef was shocked. 'I remind you that you were educated by the Frères. You studied at the very same Christian school as George Saba, the Christian school where I used to teach.'

'Dad, I'm just saying that people will do things under circumstances like these that we would never expect from them in normal times.'

'Like accusing all Christians of being traitors?' Omar Yussef leaned forward angrily.

'That isn't what I meant. But, look, Christians are already on the outside of our society, these days. Maybe they feel they owe less loyalty than a Muslim does.'

Omar Yussef put down the paring knife and ate some of the apple. 'I saw some of your loyal Muslims firing guns into the air at the mourning tent for Louai Abdel Rahman this afternoon.'

'I gave that a miss, because I went to the funeral earlier this morning,' Ramiz said. 'It was the usual show from the gunmen then. So they turned up at the mourning tent, too?'

'Yes. But something is strange about what happened at the Abdel Rahman's place,' Omar Yussef said. He looked around him to be sure the children were out of the room. 'You remember that Dima is a former pupil of mine. She told me that she heard Louai talking to someone outside the house just before he was shot. And she saw a red spot of light that seemed to be trying to settle on him.'

'He spoke to someone?'

'Yes. He said, "Oh, it's you, Abu Walid."'

Ramiz sucked on a segment of orange, slowly. 'Dad, let me say two things. First, when the Israelis use collaborators, they get the collaborators to go really close in, just to be completely sure that they've got the right man. When the collaborator gives a signal, they know the identification is made and they hit their target.'

'How do you know this?'

'Uncle Khamis told me when I visited him at the police station. He was reading an intelligence report on one of the Israeli assassinations in Gaza.'

'So Abu Walid is the name of the collaborator? The one the Israelis needed to lead them to Louai?'

'Yes, that sounds like it. Someone who knew Louai would have to make the identification, obviously. He would need to be close enough to recognize Louai, even in the dark.'

'Well, George Saba wouldn't recognize Louai. And George is Abu Dahoud, not Abu Walid. So there's the proof of his innocence.' Omar Yussef put down his food and threw his hands wide in excitement.

Ramiz hesitated. 'That brings me to my second point. Dad, please don't get involved in this. If you try to tell someone in the security forces about this, you might find they're working for the Israelis. They could silence you because you threaten to expose one of their agents. Also, the people who arrested George Saba wouldn't have just picked him up without reason. This was a good excuse to even a score with someone who must have crossed them. That's how it works these days.'

Omar Yussef thought of the night he had watched George Saba rush into the darkness toward the gunmen firing from his house. *Someone who must have crossed them.* He cursed himself for walking homeward down the hill, instead of helping George. Perhaps George ran into men that night whose ghastly revenge was now under way.

Maryam put her hand on Omar Yussef's arm. 'Don't do anything risky. You always criticize me for saying how bad these swine are. But the Israelis could come right in here and take you away, if they think you're trying to expose one of their collaborators.'

'I haven't done anything,' Omar Yussef said, irritated. 'The Israelis aren't coming for me.'

'Don't even *think* about doing anything. Please, Dad,' Ramiz said.

Omar Yussef was about to reply, but Ramiz raised his eyebrows and gestured with his head toward the kitchen door. Nadia was leaning against the doorframe, looking concerned. She held her index and middle fingers in her mouth, nervously. Sara came past the girl from the kitchen, carrying the tea. Omar Yussef wondered if Nadia had listened for long. He cursed the weakness he had shown. Because he thought he could save George Saba and protect the legacy of his teaching, he risked bringing his family into contact with the dirty side of the intifada. If he wanted a legacy, it was standing in the doorway, looking frightened, and it was he who scared it. He was a schoolteacher. He was not a detective. He could feel the bullet casing in his jacket pocket even now. It felt like a ton of molten metal. He wondered how soon he might get rid of it.

He held up a slice of apple. Nadia came forward with a half smile and reached for it. As she did so, her eyes caught something in the frosted glass of the front door. Omar Yussef turned to follow her gaze. There was someone there, silhouetted by the streetlamp and wearing a military beret. He felt a flash of fright and dropped the apple, before Nadia could take it.

The figure reached out and knocked on the door.

CHAPTER 6

Keeping his eyes on the door, Omar Yussef rose slowly from his seat. He felt a little nauseous. The silhouette outside rocked from left to right, as though it were trying to keep warm in the night chill. It knocked again. Maryam stood. She gave her husband a look of concern before she went to the door and opened it.

'Ah, Abu Adel,' Maryam said, warmly. 'Come in, come in.'

Omar Yussef felt his legs weaken with relief. He rested his hands on the table for support. He didn't have the constitution for a dangerous life.

The man at the door gave a bluff laugh. 'I just stopped in to say, *All the year, may you be well.*'

The family replied with other traditional Ramadan formulas. '*May Allah accept from us and from you,*' Omar Yussef said.

Nadia reached around her grandfather and took another slice of apple. She smiled at him as she bit into it, and the grin returned to him a little of his strength. He went down to the other end of the table to greet Khamis Zeydan.

'Consider yourself with your family and at home,' Omar Yussef said, in welcome.

Khamis Zeydan acknowledged the greeting and gave his friend five kisses on his cheeks. His face was scratchy with gray unshaven bristles. His eyes showed crafty amusement, relaxing from the accustomed state of high alert Omar Yussef noticed in them each time he ran into his friend about town. From the playful glint in those eyes, he figured Khamis Zeydan was already into the sauce pretty far tonight.

The Bethlehem police chief removed the blue beret that, in silhouette, had frightened Omar Yussef and smoothed his white hair, cut short and combed forward. He folded the hat and wedged it under his epaulette, which bore a white eagle, on the shoulder of his dark blue shirt.

Khamis Zeydan was the same age as Omar Yussef. They had known each other since their time as students in Damascus. In those days, they had been opponents in the bad-tempered politics of the university. Khamis Zeydan was an early devotee of Palestinian nationalism. He scorned Omar Yussef's faith that the Arabs would unite and liberate Palestine. Well, he was right about that. In Damascus, Omar Yussef and Khamis Zeydan had grown close, not over politics but over whisky. The two did their drinking and woman-izing together, though Khamis Zeydan, taller and blessed with blue eyes as rich as lapis, was more successful with girls. Khamis Zeydan followed the

PLO around the Mediterranean from Jordan to Syria, to Lebanon and Tunis. He lost touch with Omar Yussef because of the communication restrictions of the Israelis, and he lost his left hand to a grenade in Beirut. When he came to Bethlehem as chief of police their friendship was renewed.

Omar Yussef had been delighted by his friend's coming. Khamis Zeydan seemed to have changed so little, at first. But he soon saw that his friend the Police Brigadier Khamis Zeydan was dreadfully disillusioned and, as a result, often self-destructively drunk. Sometimes, when Omar Yussef stopped in at his office in the new police station on the corner of Manger Square, the reek of scotch in the warm room had turned the air stale and urinous.

When Khamis Zeydan came through the front door at the end of the *iftar*, the aura of alcohol about him was thick enough that Omar Yussef wondered if his friend would treat the children to one of his angry, foul-mouthed tirades about the government and his corrupt police colleagues. The amusement in the policeman's eyes suggested he wasn't far enough into his drunk to have un-covered his rage, but Omar Yussef didn't want to take the chance. With his hand on his friend's firm shoulder, he guided Khamis Zeydan into the salon.

The two settled into the heavy gold-embroidered armchairs. Maryam looked in through the door.

63

'Abu Adel, what would you like? Can I bring you some sweets?' she said, smiling at Khamis Zeydan.

'Maryam, our friend is diabetic,' Omar Yussef said. 'Bring him a *qahweh sa'ada*, and the same for me.' He turned to Khamis Zeydan and shook his finger. 'I won't let her corrupt you.'

'I am corrupt to the core,' Khamis Zeydan said, laughing. 'Umm Ramiz, I will eat whatever you set before me. I'm sure it will be the tastiest food with which a man may break his fast.'

'You haven't eaten since the fast?' Maryam was shocked. 'Come to the table. There's plenty of *ma'alubeh* left. You have to eat.' She turned to Omar Yussef and added, firmly: '*Particularly* if you are diabetic.'

'No, I had something with the guys up at the station just now, thank you.' There was embarrassment in Zeydan's voice. Omar Yussef understood that his friend needed no food so long as his hipflask was full.

The Brigadier looked undernourished, thin. His face was almost as white as his hair, so that one might not notice the neat moustache against the puffy paleness of his cheeks, if it weren't for the streak of nicotine that stained it below the nostrils. He lit a cigarette with his good hand. His left hand, a delicate prosthesis, rested on the arm of the chair, inside the tight shiny black leather glove that he kept over it at all times. Omar Yussef had once called on his friend at home in the morning and surprised him before he had dressed. He saw then that the false hand was made of a strangely washed-out green plastic, as though it were a bar of medicated soap or the flimsy limb of an alien creature. If he hadn't seen the ugly evidence of his friend's debilitation, Omar Yussef often thought, the glove would seem somehow sinister on a policeman, as though it were there to protect Khamis Zeydan's knuckles when he beat a suspect. Instead, it struck him that the glove undercut the toughness his friend needed to do his job, a reminder that he was less than a man of full power. Sometimes when Khamis Zeydan was very drunk, he would stare at the false hand, full of hate. When sober, he was self-conscious and would place the hand unobtrusively in his lap. So with the prosthesis now unregarded in its glove on the armrest, Omar Yussef figured Khamis Zeydan must be only half drunk.

Maryam brought the coffees and a plate of baklava for the guest.

'I didn't make it *sa'ada* for you, Abu Adel. I know you prefer it *mashuta*, so here it is, with a little sugar, just right.' She glanced at Omar Yussef, as though he had been rude to bring up Khamis Zeydan's diabetes.

'Maryam is very generous. She will also pay for your medical fees when the diabetes gets worse,' Omar Yussef said.

'Maryam's baklava is the best medicine,' Khamis Zeydan replied.

'I prescribe a long course of treatment,' Maryam said, with a gracious lowering of her head.

'Thank you. Doctor Maryam. Now please, I have to talk with our friend about something very important,' said Omar Yussef.

Maryam stared at him. *She knows I intend to discuss George's case*, Omar Yussef thought. Khamis Zeydan was a policeman as well as a friend. Omar Yussef was about to make his concerns somehow official and his wife stood, stumped, unsure how to stop him now that the Brigadier was in the room.

'Abu Adel,' she said, 'how are your wife and children in Amman?'

That's all she can come up with? Omar Yussef was not impressed.

'They're doing all right, thank you.'

'Maryam.' Omar Yussef glanced at the door.

'I'll leave you alone,' she said. 'But Abu Adel, don't let my husband do anything foolish.'

'These days, I believe it is Abu Ramiz who prevents me from foolishness,' Khamis Zeydan said.

Maryam closed the door.

Khamis Zeydan held out his good hand, palm upwards. 'What was that about?'

'She thinks I don't want to be a schoolteacher any more.'

'Did that bastard American persuade you to retire?'

'No, it's worse than that. She thinks I'd rather be a detective.'

'You'd make a very good detective. No one

would ever be scared of you. They'd trust you, because you're like the wise, honest uncle everyone wishes they had.'

'Then why don't you hire me?'

'There's no place for honesty in our police force.'

Khamis Zeydan nodded conspiratorially toward the sideboard. Omar Yussef stood and took out a bottle of Johhny Walker Black Label. He poured a big tumbler for Khamis Zeydan and put the bottle away. He handed the tumbler to his friend, who immediately took a stinging gulp and cleared his throat, clamorously. Omar Yussef sat and drank his coffee.

'I want to talk to you about George Saba,' he said.

Khamis Zeydan paused with the glass already on its way to his lips for a second slug. He looked hard at Omar Yussef. 'Are you going to tell me he's innocent?'

'Yes.'

'Well, you don't need to be a detective to know that.'

'You know?'

'Come on, he's a harmless guy.'

'But he's in your jail.'

'Preventive Security brought him in. He's in my jail, but he's not my prisoner.'

'How can you keep an innocent man in jail?'

'The jail is in Bethlehem, Palestine. It's not in Copenhagen or Amsterdam. I hope that answers your question.'

'There's something else. Look at this.' Omar Yussef took the bullet casing from his pocket and handed it to Khamis Zeydan. The policeman examined it for a moment. His pale face became stern.

'Where did you get this?' Khamis Zeydan asked.

'What type of gun does that come from?'

'Where did you get it?'

'Answer me first.'

'You don't want to know the answer. Neither do I, although unfortunately I already do.'

Omar Yussef sat quietly. They stared each other down.

Khamis Zeydan broke the silence first. 'It's the casing from a 7.62 millimeter bullet. Now where did you get it?'

'What kind of gun would fire a bullet like that?'

'A heavy machine gun.'

'A heavy machine gun like Hussein Tamari uses?'

'Yes, the kind Hussein Tamari uses,' Khamis Zeydan said, irritably. 'It's called a MAG.'

'How do you know?'

'Most of the guns in this town are Kalashnikovs. They fire 7.62 caliber bullets, too. But Kalashnikov bullets are only 39 millimeters long. This one was 51 millimeters long, before it was fired. That's the ammo for a MAG.' Khamis Zeydan glared at Omar Yussef. The playfulness was gone from his eyes. He looked very sober.

'Why are you staring at me so sternly?' Omar Yussef said. 'Look, tell me about Tamari. All I know is what circulates by gossip about town.'

68

'You've been in Bethlehem longer than I have, so you know his tribe,' Khamis Zeydan said.

'The Ta'amra.'

'Right. Until fifty years ago, these Ta'amra were desert nomads. They settled in villages east of town, but they still follow the old tribal codes. All the top Martyrs Brigades guys are Ta'amra. They're thugs and they run the place as a family racket.'

'All of the gunmen are relatives of Hussein Tamari?'

'All except one other guy, Jihad Awdeh,' said Khamis Zeydan. 'His family is from the Aida Camp, refugees of 1948 from a village on the plain toward Ramla, a small clan. Among the Ta'amra, he's an outsider, and they never let him forget it. So he's almost as much of a nasty piece of work as Hussein – he always feels the need to prove that he's more ruthless than the Ta'amra. It's the brutal zeal of the newly converted.'

'In the Bethlehem area, who has a gun that would use those cartridges?'

'A hundred or so Israeli soldiers.' Khamis Zeydan sounded angry. 'And Hussein Tamari. It's his symbol, as you know. He carries it on his hip everywhere, even when it'd be more convenient to use a pistol. He probably takes it to the bathroom with him. Now, Abu Ramiz, my old friend, tell me where you got this bullet.'

Omar Yussef recounted Dima's recollection of the murder and his discovery of the bullet casing

69

in the flattened grass. 'Who would want to kill Louai Abdel Rahman?' Omar Yussef said. 'Because the one who did that is the real collaborator, not George Saba. George doesn't own a MAG heavy machine gun. I don't think he could even lift one. Before the shots that killed Louai, his wife heard him speak to someone out in the darkness. He called him Abu Walid. Who could Abu Walid be?'

Khamis Zeydan lit another Rothman's. 'Abu Ramiz, a detective is a little like a psychiatrist. When you treat a mental illness, you had better know the workings of your own mind, or you risk becoming sicker than your patients. The disease can spread from one mind to another. That's how it is for a policeman. To catch a villain, you have to think like a villain, and when you think like a villain, perhaps you already are a villain. The problem is that if a psychiatrist makes the wrong diagnosis, it's the patient who pays. When a detective commits an error, the villain makes him pay for it.'

'Abu Adel, I want to find the real collaborator.'

'Are you listening to me? I'm trying to warn you that this is dangerous.'

'I don't need to be a detective to understand that.'

'I may be a police officer now, but I was, for many years, what the world chooses to call a terrorist. In Beirut, in Rome, Paris. Wherever the Old Man sent me. You know that. We were all terrorists, the people who now govern you. That gives me an advantage over you. I know what it is to face danger.'

Omar Yussef sat forward. 'You were all terrorists, you and your PLO buddies in exile. Now what? Now you are terrorized. By people like Hussein Tamari. I was never a terrorist, and I won't be terrorized, either.'

Khamis Zeydan grimaced, as though it was hard to swallow what he had to say. 'Get me another drink.'

Omar Yussef got the bottle of Black Label and put it on the table before his friend. The policeman poured a large shot as he spoke. 'Louai Abdel Rahman worked for me, supposedly. He was a sergeant at the Irtas police station. But you know how things are now. Everybody is a general. Everybody is a military genius. Everybody has to have a crack at the Israelis. No one gets to be a hero writing parking tickets and solving domestic disputes, but if you fire off a few shots at an Israeli car you're an instant resistance champion. Louai Abdel Rahman was not a bad guy. But he wasn't prepared to be a policeman. He was another fucking immature outlaw of the type that we're so good at breeding.'

'Why would anyone want him dead?'

'The Israelis would want to kill him because he shot a settler on the tunnel road last month.'

'He killed someone?'

'There's a lot of it about. Don't sound so surprised.'

'But who else would want him dead? A Palestinian, maybe?'

Khamis Zeydan was silent. His face was blank and cold. He drank the rest of the whisky in a single pull and crushed his cigarette in the crystal ashtray on the coffee table. 'I really must go, Abu Ramiz.'

'Wait, there's something you aren't telling me.'

'The only thing I have to tell you, Abu Ramiz, is this: whoever fired this bullet whose casing you found is sure to have many more bullets, and he probably doesn't care who he has to shoot to get what he wants. Do you understand?' Khamis Zeydan stood.

Omar Yussef rose, too. 'Give me that bullet. I want to keep it anyway.'

Khamis Zeydan pressed the cartridge casing into Omar Yussef's palm. 'You're a determined man, and I know you can be stubborn. But I'm your friend, and I really must tell you that this is not a matter for a schoolteacher to get involved in.'

'A schoolteacher? You said I'd be a good detective.'

Khamis Zeydan stopped in the doorway. 'In Palestine, there's no such thing as a good detective.'

CHAPTER 7

Hurrying along Dehaisha's main street, Omar Yussef headed for the UN school. The cold dawn wind lanced sharply through the valley, north toward Jerusalem, carrying the taint of diesel fumes. Omar Yussef had woken with a headache that grew worse now as he walked. He didn't doubt that it was the result of the stress brought on by Khamis Zeydan's warnings. He had barely slept that night after the policeman left his home.

Omar Yussef considered himself an independent thinker, a man who challenged the way most people in his community saw the world. But that night he had doubted himself. He lay awake thinking, *You're all talk, Omar. When it comes time for action, you're paralysed by worry, bullied by the thought that someone will hurt you.* When he did fall asleep, he jolted upright in fear. He thought Hussein Tamari was in the room. His heart was thundering, even as he told himself that there was no one there, no sound except Maryam's wheezy, light snoring. Did he really think Hussein Tamari had been present when Louai was killed, just because of the cartridges he had found? Why would the leader of the resistance in Bethlehem collaborate with the Israelis? Why would he want Louai dead? Khamis Zeydan had told him that Israeli soldiers used that big machine gun, too. Perhaps Louai Abdel Rahman was mistaken when he spoke to a man he believed was named Abu Walid. Maybe Louai only *thought* he recognized the person lying in wait for him. It had been dark already, according to Dima. It could just as easily have been a soldier from some Israeli hit squad, lying in wait between the pines.

When the first light came and Omar Yussef got out of bed, he returned to that thought. *If I get close to finding out who Abu Walid is, there's a danger he might try to stop me, even to hurt me, no matter how much protection I have from my clan and its connections with tough guys in Hamas and Fatah. But if there's no Abu Walid, if Louai Abdel Rahman simply made a mistake, then there's no one out there who'll feel threatened by me. I could be placing myself in danger, but only if I'm on the trail of the man who truly has framed George Saba, in which case I'm doing the right thing and this man deserves to be unmasked.*

That moment clarified for Omar Yussef what he must do. He tried to keep those thoughts foremost in his mind as he walked to the school.

A Blackhawk chopped southward above Omar Yussef's head. The Israeli helicopter flew in and out of the low, dark clouds on a reconnaissance mission over the camp. The resonant thudding spooked a mentally handicapped boy in his early twenties whom Omar Yussef often saw when he was on his way to the school. Usually the boy, whose name was Nayif, bounded along the street with exaggeratedly long strides, talking animatedly to himself and wagging an admonitory finger at approaching taxis. When he heard the baritone flutter of the helicopter, the boy panicked. He put his hands on his elongated, egg-shaped head and wailed incoherently. Omar Yussef approached him. He smiled at the boy and held out his hand with the palm upwards, as if testing for rain. The boy did the same, looking up at the clouds. After a moment he grinned and, in his slurred speech, said, 'It's only raining, uncle.'

Omar Yussef nodded and put his hand on Nayif's shoulder reassuringly before he walked on.

It was true that it would rain soon from the clouds that licked the Blackhawk. It would come hard. The streets would be mud where the tanks had cut them up. The dusty topsoil would tinge the rain the color of urine and, where it gushed down the slopes, it would ride over the top of Omar Yussef's wing tips and leave them sprinkled with grit that would take him careful hours to polish away. Omar Yussef was not a believer, he usually had trouble remembering Koranic quotations, but the words of that book on the subject of rain came to him as he left the handicapped boy: 'Know that Allah restores the earth to life after its death.' Allah, of course, claimed that he would perform the same restoration to the believers on the Day of Judgment. Omar Yussef looked about him as he approached the UN school. The dirty alleys of the camp seemed most desolate in the first, flat light of a winter's day. Allah didn't restore life to earth. He multiplied the number of lives on earth, but allowed their quality to diminish and their essence to drain away. Omar Yussef had never thought that life was a waste – what true educator could think that way? He wondered when it would be that Allah would restore life to him. Hell, he would have to do it for himself, and the case of George Saba would be his vehicle.

A tall black stone cut to the shape of the map of Palestine stood on a plinth outside the school. Its dimensions marked the complete area of Palestine, from the squiggle of the Lebanese border down to the long V of the Naqab Desert, the scope of the state to which the camp's leaders insisted its refugees would return. The statue was intended to make those aspirations firm and real and enduring, like stone. Every time Omar Yussef passed it, he felt as though the block might topple onto him, crushing him with the hopeless rigidity of his people's politics. His eye picked out the spot on the smooth stone map where his village once stood. His *father's* village, he corrected himself. Omar Yussef had no village.

Omar Yussef heard the light rap of rain on the

76

cashmere of his flat cap. He looked up and a drop landed on his lips. He remembered the hand he held out for rain before the handicapped boy. *I made it rain,* he thought, mocking himself.

Omar Yussef entered the UN school. He walked down the corridor, greeting the other teachers as he passed them. He went to Christopher Steadman's office, knocked and entered.

The UN director didn't stand and Omar Yussef didn't sit. The smell of body odor was gone. Someone must have found a way to tell Steadman that the history teacher had played a trick on him, or perhaps the American simply decided that he must wash, even if it violated Ramadan. Omar Yussef stood before the desk and said, 'I'm ready to consider retirement.'

Omar Yussef detected the barely disguised smile that nibbled at the edges of Steadman's lips before the American made a serious face. 'I think that's a wise decision, Abu Ramiz.'

'I will make a final decision at the end of the month. In the meantime, I want to take a leave of absence. Perhaps if I don't come to work for a couple of weeks, I'll realize that I enjoy not working and I will decide definitively to retire. You won't object to that, I'm sure,' Omar Yussef said.

'I guess it'll be hard for us to manage without you.' Steadman made a sucking noise between his teeth, as though he were wrestling with an awkward dilemma, but Omar Yussef thought it sounded like the hiss of a serpent. 'I'll have to teach some of your classes, and we'll also hire a part-timer. But we'll get by.'

Omar Yussef felt contempt for this man. He could see the relief on his face now that his problem with Omar Yussef appeared almost to be resolved. The American would be rid of a teacher who talked back. He would not have to explain to his own superiors why the government complained about his school, just because of the teaching methods of one ageing curmudgeon. Sometimes Omar Yussef wondered if he was too hard on his own people. *Look at this American*, he thought. *He grew up with all the advantages of freedom and democracy and money and education, yet he's exactly the same as our bureaucrats who bow to the government, even when the rules are scandalously violated.* Certainly, Steadman didn't care about the children at the school. His salary wasn't dependent on the quality of their education. In a couple of years, he would be drawing his UN stipend for handing out condoms to truckdrivers in Mozambique or running a carpet-weaving workshop in a women's prison in Kabul.

As Steadman spoke approvingly about retirement, Omar Yussef almost changed his mind. He couldn't leave the children to be taught the government's odious version of history by second-rate hacks or, worse, by Steadman. But he needed the time to find the truth, to save George Saba. He turned and left Steadman's office.

CHAPTER 8

Omar Yussef pulled his car out of the old, sandstone shed in the olive grove behind his home. As he drove around to the front of the house, Maryam looked out of the kitchen window. Her face registered the shock of finding him away from the school, but he pretended not to see her and curved out onto the wide main road toward Bethlehem and Beit Jala.

Omar Yussef was a poor driver and he took the slick roads slowly. It didn't worry him that other cars passed him in a frenzied stream, or that frustrated taxi drivers would ride their horns until they finally found an opportunity to overtake him. At the junction where he would make a left for the climb to Beit Jala, a slim-waisted policeman ran half-heartedly back and forth, vainly trying to direct the flow of vehicles. Omar Yussef turned slowly across the oncoming traffic, which slid to a halt with a chorus of beeps.

Omar Yussef felt grimly determined after his meeting with Steadman. He ran the facts of the Abdel Rahman case through his mind repeatedly. If he found the connection with George Saba, he would be able to identify the real collaborator. He would have to prove it, but to uncover the identity of the man who had, in fact, led the Israelis to Louai Abdel Rahman would at least be the first step. If the Israelis killed Louai without a collaborator to help them, though, it would make Omar Yussef's task much harder. Everyone wanted a scapegoat for the assassination, and it would be easier for him to persuade them to substitute another guilty party than to face the possibility that there was no one to blame except the untouchable soldiers. But there was certainly someone in the bushes when Louai Abdel Rahman died, and it was that person whom Omar Yussef needed to find.

It was hard for Omar Yussef to see as he drove. He leaned forward and rubbed the inside of the windshield with his handkerchief. His view remained obscured by a light rain. After driving even more slowly for a period, he remembered to turn on the windshield wipers. The summer dust still lay on the plastic blades and muddied his view with wet, brown smudges, until the rain cleared the window. He gripped the wheel tightly as he snaked up to Beit Jala. A truck came down the hill too fast and Omar Yussef, swerving, almost came to a halt. The cars behind him gave out a chorus of protest, as though their brakes were attached to their horns. He moved on again. The wipers made a moaning sound. The rain had stopped. Omar Yussef pulled over so that he could turn off the stammering wipers, then drove to the top of the hill. He passed the Greek Orthodox Club and recalled his dinner with George Saba. The damp gray stone of the Club looked desolate, like the asperous face of a lost, old man.

A single gunman guarded the final stretch of road before George Saba's house. He signaled dismissively for Omar Yussef to pull over and jumped out of the way as the car came to a halt with less control than he had evidently expected. Omar Yussef enjoyed making the gunman skip onto the sidewalk. He hated these types, barely more than boys, who stared down their elders with cold faces and contemptuous gestures. Respect for older people was one quality he always instilled in his pupils, and these gunmen certainly lacked it.

'What's the matter with you? Are you trying to kill me?' the gunman yelled.

Omar Yussef turned off his engine and took his time getting out of his car.

'You can't park here. This area is reserved for my roadblock.'

Omar Yussef turned a full circle demonstratively in the street. 'There's plenty of room,' he said. 'Even a tank could pass through here, and I expect that if the Israelis did drive a tank down here you wouldn't be around to stop them.'

'Where are you going?'

The gunman's rudeness made Omar Yussef angry and a little reckless. He returned to his car and turned the key in the door. 'I had better lock it. I know that you people are involved in car theft. My car might be a target for thieves, because, thanks to you,' he said, looking along the street, 'it's the only car in the village that doesn't have a bullet hole in it.'

The gunman looked at once furious and cowed. *After all*, thought Omar Yussef, *he can't deny that my accusations are true*. Perhaps, for a moment, the young man wrestled with the vestiges of respect for his elders that gradually was draining from him, as from everyone else. Maybe he hadn't been in the Martyrs Brigades long enough to override that tradition with their new arrogance.

'I said, where are you going?' the young gunman called. His voice was irritable but hesitant.

Omar Yussef sensed that the youth was already in retreat in the face of the older man's confidence. 'I'm a detective and I'm conducting an investigation of importance to national security. Now keep an eye on my car or Hussein Tamari will have your head.'

The gunman kicked a stone along the gutter and looked down. It was the gesture of a resentful, beaten, little boy. Omar Yussef smiled.

The street was empty. Even without the dull spread of the rain clouds, it would have been a sorry place. The windows of the houses on the left were shattered by bullet holes and filled with sandbags. The houses on the right must have been worse. Their backs faced across the valley to the

Israeli positions and took the full impact of the gunfire. From the shelter of the street, though, Omar Yussef could enjoy the lovely old Turkish arches and the pleasing squareness of the houses and the clear air left by the rain. Though the clouds had threatened for days, this was the first downpour. He breathed the rising scent of the wet dirt with pleasure as he approached George Saba's house. He climbed the stairs and saw that the disrespectful gunman still watched him from the curb by his car. He knocked on the door. There were black blast marks around the jamb and the wood was splintered.

George's wife Sofia leaned out of a window. 'Hello, Abu Ramiz, good morning. Can you go to the door at the side of the house? This one is broken and can't be used. I'm sorry. The police blew it open when they came for George.'

Omar Yussef waved and took the steps down to the basement. He noted that Sofia's head was bandaged, though she disguised it with the kind of headscarf women sometimes tie behind their ears to do housework.

Habib Saba embraced him in the doorway. His eyes were red from two days of tears, and they filled again when he saw Omar Yussef. He excused himself and guided the schoolteacher inside. 'Forgive my emotion, Abu Ramiz, but you are the first Muslim who has been to see us since this trouble.'

'That's a terrible shame, Abu George.'

Omar Yussef followed Habib Saba up the stairs to the salon. The room was lit by a single bulb. Sandbags covered the broken windows. It was drafty and cold, and the rain brought out a strangely rank smell of the sea from the damp-ened sacks of dirt. There were two racks of wedding dresses. Omar Yussef could barely see in the gloomy room. He could just make out that some of the dresses were partially burned. Their thin plastic packing was torn and the hems were smeared with the milky brown of extinguished flames.

Habib Saba noticed that Omar Yussef squinted in the darkness. 'George had some nice, old lamps in here, but the policemen took them.' He smiled. From a teak dresser, splintered by a half-dozen bullet holes, Habib Saba lifted a statuette of a nude woman reclining in a contorted position. 'I thought they had taken her, too. But I found her in the corner behind the sofa. I think someone must have thrown her at the wall. She was a little scratched, but she seems to have come through all right. I shined her up, because there was ash or some kind of burned material attached to her. Do you like her?'

Omar Yussef took the statuette in his hands. The model's hair swirled beneath her head, her neck stretched painfully, and her left hip jutted unnat-urally, as though it would pierce the skin. 'It's a Rodin?'

Habib Saba nodded. 'Well, a copy, of course.'

'That French fellow always made this young woman pose in positions of such extreme discomfort. I think she must have felt the pose reflected some terrible pain within herself, or she would never have been able to let herself be used like this,' Omar Yussef said. Though the metal of the statuette had already survived being cast onto the floor by one of the policemen, he was nervous holding it. It was the feeling he experienced when cradling a small child, fearful that he might expose its delicacy to damage.

'The model ended her life confined to an insane asylum, so I imagine you're right about the pain, Abu Ramiz,' Habib Saba said. 'The piece is called *The Martyr*.'

Omar Yussef gently replaced the statuette on the dresser. 'There really seems to be no way to escape that word, does there?' He laughed with the clipped sound of a man clearing his throat.

Sofia brought a plate of cookies and coffee. 'I made the coffee *sa'ada*, as you like it, Abu Ramiz,' she said.

'God bless your hands,' Omar Yussef said. 'May there always be coffee in your home.' He put his hand gently to her head, pushing the headscarf back so that he could see in detail the purple and green of a bruise that spread from beneath her bandage. He touched her arm lightly. Sofia gave a pained smile and left the room.

'Consider yourself with your family and in your home,' Habib Saba said. He tried to make the traditional formula sound contented, but Omar Yussef saw that the old man scratched the back of his hand nervously.

Omar Yussef drank some coffee. The sofa where they sat was tight against the wall. Omar Yussef gestured to the stone behind him. A half-mile beyond it were the Israeli guns. 'I hope this is thick stone, in case the shooting starts.'

Habib Saba laughed. 'We will protect you from all danger, so long as you remain on our couch, drinking our coffee and giving us the pleasure of your company.'

George's children came nervously to the doorway. Habib called them over and they greeted Omar Yussef. They were usually warm children, but today their greetings were perfunctory and shy, as though their marrow had been removed and their hearts deadened. Omar Yussef put his hand on the head of the boy, Dahoud, who was seven. George Saba was about as young when Omar Yussef first knew him. He could see George in the boy's face now. He had always perceived a great nobility in George's high forehead and his blue eyes, and he recognized the identical elements in the boy's makeup. 'Where do you go to school?' he asked.

'The Frères School,' the boy mumbled.

'Just like your father. I used to be his teacher there, you know. He was very clever. I expect you are clever, and so is your sister, just like your Daddy.'

Habib asked the boy to bring his cigarettes. The girl retreated toward the kitchen. 'She won't leave her mother's side for more than a moment,' Habib Saba said, quietly. The boy gave him his Dunhills and followed his sister out of the room. Habib watched the space where the boy had stood, as though he thought that by concentration he could fill it with the presence of his own son.

'When George wanted to leave for Chile all those years ago, I tried to change his mind. Do you remember, Abu Ramiz?' Habib Saba lit a cigarette and inhaled sharply. 'I was so selfish. I wanted my son to be here, with me. I didn't care even that his prospects were obviously quite limited here. I just wanted him close. But you convinced me to let him have his own life, his freedom. Abu Ramiz, you were right then. But I kept telling him that he should come back. I never let him rest in Chile. To my shame, I used to write to him about my loneliness after his dear mother died. I was quite aware that he would not be able to stand the guilt. So in the end he gave in to me, and now look at the result. He'll be punished for this thing, this crime that he could never truly have committed. He's a Christian, an outsider. Even the other Christians will be frightened to stand up for him. He is alone, as all Christians are when they come up against authority in our town. It's my fault for wanting what a traditional father would have wanted, to have his son near him. You are much more modern than I, Abu Ramiz.'

'It's not wrong to love your son and to want to enjoy his presence,' Omar Yussef said.

'Now I won't have his presence and perhaps I won't have a son, either.'

'One day of George is better than a lifetime with a more ordinary son.'

'But each day without him is a lifetime.'

Omar Yussef put down his coffee cup and broke an almond cookie in two. As he tasted it, he turned fully toward Habib Saba. 'What happened, Abu George?'

The older man sighed. 'I was in the back of the house. It was around dawn. I remember that the muezzins had just finished their call to dawn prayers. I was in bed, but I wasn't asleep. I haven't had a good night's sleep since the shooting began in this valley. Even when I'm asleep I dream about the gunfire. I heard an explosion. The police had blown the front door out of its frame. You can see the damage there, where I nailed what was left of the door back in place. The police came in and took George. Sofia screamed at them, so they knocked her out – you saw the bruises on her head. They held the rest of us at gunpoint.'

'But before that. Three nights ago, after George and I ate at the Orthodox Club. There was shooting. He left me to come and see what was happening. What took place then?'

Habib Saba looked very weary. He crushed his cigarette in the lip of a coral-pink conch shell. 'They were shooting at the Israelis from our roof, directly above where we are sitting now. George took an old pistol, an antique that was hanging on the wall. It wasn't even loaded, and if it were, I'm sure it wouldn't fire. But it looked dangerous enough. He went onto the roof and he chased them off.'

'Who were they?'

'You know, these Martyrs Brigades swine.'

'Which ones?'

'I don't know.'

'Did George know them?'

'He didn't say. Anyway, what do you mean "know them"? He doesn't mix with those people.'

'No, but most people in town would recognize the leaders. They don't try to hide, unless the Israelis come, of course.'

'George didn't say anything. He didn't mention any names. He seemed very anxious and excited.'

'Where is the gun he used against them?'

Habib Saba crossed the room stiffly. He opened the drawer of a French roll-top desk, pulled out the old Webley and gave it to Omar Yussef. The gun was heavier than it looked, almost three pounds. The metal was partially oxidized and the butt was worn, but at night it would have been impossible to detect the revolver's flaws. Omar Yussef pulled on the trigger. It was stuck by rust and dirt.

'You could soak it in oil for a week and I doubt that those parts would move,' Habib Saba said. 'It was a British officer's gun that was kept by

Ghassan Shubeki after he retired from the Jordanian Legion. You remember Shubeki, Abu Ramiz? That gun must be a half century old.'

George was braver and more desperate than Omar Yussef had thought to have confronted the gunmen with this old piece of junk.

'I would like to take this with me,' Omar Yussef said.

'You are welcome to it. It makes me sick to see it.'

Omar Yussef put the gun in his jacket pocket. It weighted the material so heavily that he felt almost as though he were wearing it on a strap over his shoulder. He wondered if it would damage his jacket or spoil the cut, but for the sake of his investigation he put aside his concerns about his clothing.

'Did you see nothing that night when George went to the roof to confront the gunmen?'

'I looked out of the bedroom window at the street after the shooting stopped,' Habib said. 'I saw two men getting into a big car. One of these jeeps they make these days, you know the type that looks like it's half car and half jeep. The expensive type, although I assume it was stolen. One of them was smoking, because all I could really see was the light at the tip of his cigarette. One of them carried a big gun.'

'What kind of big gun?'

'Abu Ramiz, I make wedding dresses. I don't know one gun from another. All I can tell you is that it was a big gun.'

Omar Yussef tried to picture the MAG that Hussein Tamari fired into the air at the wake for Louai Abdel Rahman. It was certainly a big gun. Could Hussein Tamari himself have been on the roof when George went up there with his defunct pistol? 'Did it have a big, long barrel, with a wooden butt, about a meter and a quarter long altogether, a bipod to support the end of the long barrel, and a chain of bullets so that they could be fed through and shot very fast?'

'Abu Ramiz, it was dark. I was very scared and concerned for my son. If the gunman had been wearing a wedding dress, I could describe to you the style of the pearl beading, even in such darkness. But not a gun. In any case, why do you ask about that gun? And why do you want George's Webley revolver? What are you up to?'

'I'm preparing for retirement, Abu George.'

Habib Saba shifted forward on his chair, nervously. 'Are you going to do something risky?'

I already have, Omar Yussef thought.

When he left Habib Saba, Omar Yussef climbed the steps at the side of the house to the roof. He paused at the top, breathing hard. He looked at the flat roof. Perhaps the Israelis kept it under observation in case the gunmen returned. They might shoot him with one of their sniper rifles from all the way across the valley. Ramiz had told him they had rifles that could shoot with shocking accuracy at distances greater than a kilometer. The soldiers might even be able to tell that there was

91

a gun in the pocket of his jacket from the way the material was pulling. He shrugged to shift the weight. He had to check the scene of the confrontation between George and the gunmen, so he took the last step onto the roof.

Rain gathered in a puddle near the shot-out water tank. Omar Yussef assumed the gunmen had positioned themselves at the edge of the building. Perhaps they lay down to take advantage of the cover provided by the small wall that ran around the roof. He made his way to the far side of the roof, glancing over the valley, wondering if some Israeli sniper had a nervous, slouching middle-aged man wearing a flat cap in his sights. His feet crunched on the slivers of the destroyed solar panels from the water tank.

Something glimmered in a puddle by the wall. Omar Yussef bent and picked out an empty cartridge. Shaking the water off it, he felt in his pocket and took out the cartridge he had found in the grass where Louai Abdel Rahman died. He compared the two. They were identical as far as he could tell, bigger and longer than rifle bullets. He had seen rifle bullets before, lying on the desk in Khamis Zeydan's office; they would be like pinkies next to a ring finger if you placed them side by side with one of the casings in Omar Yussef's hand. Khamis Zeydan had identified the first cartridge as belonging to a MAG and also said that there were no other such guns in Bethlehem, so Tamari's famous machine gun must have been on this roof. Unless Hussein Tamari lent it to someone that night, the head of the Martyrs Brigades must have been here when George Saba confronted them.

Omar Yussef could see nothing else on the roof. He slipped the two cartridges into his pocket. They tinkled against the Webley. *The Israelis have excellent surveillance equipment,* he thought. *Maybe they can see right through my jacket and pick out two spent cartridges and a uselessly antiquated gun in my pocket.* As he left the roof, he thought that the Israelis would care nothing about the Webley or the MAG casings. Only he understood just how dangerous those objects were.

CHAPTER 9

When Omar Yussef reached his car, the sullen, young gunman who had tried to intimidate him glared suspiciously. Omar Yussef wondered how long this kid would last. The youngster surely would run as soon as he heard the growl of a tank coming over the hill from the settlement, but the soldiers might get him anyway. Or he might become lazy and step out where a sniper could pick him off. It was no wonder he was aggressive and tense, but that didn't make Omar Yussef any more sympathetic toward him. He started his old Peugeot and spun the car around on the narrow road. The gunman jumped out of the way. Omar Yussef watched him step off the curb and glower after the car as it dropped down the hill.

Before he left Beit Jala, Omar Yussef pulled into a parking lot fronting a row of shops. A group of gunmen clustered before the grilled chicken restaurant on the corner. The restaurant was shuttered and wouldn't open until the end of the day's Ramadan fasting. Omar Yussef gave the gunmen a scornful glance and mounted the steps to the platform that ran along the shopfronts. As he passed through the clutch of gunmen, they stepped aside politely. 'Joyful morning, uncle,' one of them said.

Before Omar Yussef could think, he returned the greeting: 'Morning of light.'

The gunmen went on talking quietly. Omar Yussef wondered at himself. He was so angry with their general rudeness that his resentment was particularly acute at a rare moment such as this when they behaved well. *Do I need so much to blame them for all the things that are wrong in our society that I can't even see them as human beings any more? Perhaps they've been up all night on patrol,* he thought. *Some of them, at least, are willing to sacrifice their family lives for what they consider to be their duty. Some of them die for it, too.*

Omar Yussef came to a dingy storefront. The picture window was covered by a gray venetian blind. He opened the door. A middle-aged woman rose from behind her desk when she saw him. She was thick around the middle, but well dressed. She wore an Yves St Laurent scarf around her neck, and earrings by the same designer gleamed from her fleshy lobes.

'Welcome, Abu Ramiz,' she said. She reached out her hands to hold his shoulders and kissed Omar Yussef on each cheek.

'Nasra, you have a new haircut,' Omar Yussef said.

The woman's hair was short at the sides, blow-dried and combed back. It was a deep red, though

Omar Yussef knew that this was not her natural color.

'Do you like it, Abu Ramiz? I have to keep looking young or Abu Jeriez will fire me and hire a pretty little girl.'

'That will be the day his business fails. He always tells me you run everything.'

Nasra gave a deep, smoky laugh and guided Omar Yussef to the office at the back of the room. The door opened and Charles Halloun looked out.

'Abu Ramiz, I knew it must be you. No one makes Nasra laugh as you do,' he said. He grasped Omar Yussef's hand and pulled him into the office. He nodded at Nasra to prepare coffee.

Charles Halloun seated Omar Yussef on the couch and only then did he sit at its other end. His hair was black and trim. He had a long, shapeless nose and thick, agile eyebrows. He wore a check tweed sport coat, a brown cardigan, and a brown woolen tie. He looked like a bumbling old Oxford don.

Halloun's father had been accountant to Omar Yussef's father. The sons now kept the same relationship.

'You just missed your son, Abu Ramiz. He was here to deliver some papers. His account is fast becoming one of my biggest jobs.' Halloun rubbed the bulbous end of his nose. 'Ramiz inherited your brains, I must say. Mobile phones are an amazing business.'

'Ramiz is very smart. But I can't claim so much credit for that. I don't understand at all how these phones work.'

'As long as the cash isn't counterfeit, who cares where it comes from?' Charles Halloun laughed, twirling the pointed end of his eyebrow.

Nasra brought in two coffees and a glass of water. Like the Sabas, Nasra and Halloun were Christians who knew that Omar Yussef didn't observe Ramadan and would enjoy a drink.

'God bless your hands,' Omar Yussef said.

'Blessings. How is Umm Ramiz?' Nasra asked.

'Well.'

'And Zuheir and Ala?'

'Zuheir is visiting us later this month. He's coming in from Wales to celebrate the *Eid* with us. Ala just changed his job and is selling computers in New York.'

'Tell them I want to see them when they visit.' Nasra smoothed her skirt and closed the door behind her.

'Double-health and well-being in your heart,' Charles Halloun said as Omar Yussef began to drink his coffee.

Omar Yussef put the coffee on the table. 'Abu Jeriez, I will ask you a direct question. How is my family provided for?'

Charles Halloun sat forward. The dense eyebrows drew close to the bridge of his nose in concern. 'Is something wrong with your health, Abu Ramiz?'

'No, not really.' *Not yet.* 'I'm considering retirement. If I were to stop earning at the school, would I be able to continue to live as I do?'

'Well, you have the income from the investments your dear father made. There are some shares in the Arab Bank, some Egyptian bonds, and there is the rent from the land Abu Omar purchased in Beit Sahour shortly before he passed away. Most of this has been reinvested, because you live on your UN salary. But you could draw an income from it. I think retirement probably wouldn't alter your lifestyle too much.' Charles Halloun cocked his head. 'Are you sure it is only retirement that's on your mind, Abu Ramiz? You're a young man.'

'I'm fifty-six.'

'But you're in good health, thank God.'

'Yes and no. I no longer consume alcohol, but I drank enough for a lifetime before I quit ten years ago. It's only five years since I stopped smoking, and I sometimes feel a little short of breath even today. I don't exercise, except for walking to the school in the morning. And, well, there are some things that I won't go into except to say that they cause me a great deal of worry, which I'm sure is something of a stress on my heart.'

'No alcohol, no cigarettes? Your life is one long Ramadan.'

'But for almost fifty years, it was a continuous *Eid.*' Omar Yussef laughed. 'Rest assured that my retirement will preserve my health. I only want to

98

know all the facts about my financial situation before I make any final decisions.'

'I shall prepare a report for you with some projections of the income that you would be able to live on.'

'All I need is food and money to treat my grandchildren to presents. I don't travel very much, just once a year to Amman with Maryam to visit my brother, and once a year a vacation in Morocco by myself.'

'This should be no problem, Abu Ramiz. You will be able to afford to continue with those trips.'

The two men drank their coffee.

'I spoke to Ramiz this morning about something delicate,' Charles Halloun said. 'I thought perhaps you might discuss it with him, too. He wants to expand his business, to open several more mobile phone shops around the Bethlehem area. The problem is that expanding businesses tend to attract the attention of some disreputable types these days. There are a number of them that have been taken over rather suddenly by the Martyrs Brigades.'

'You mean protection money?'

'No, that's old hat. I mean, they take over. Just like that.' Charles Halloun snapped his fingers. 'These days they come to the house of the owner with a contract and say, "Sign it over to us or we'll kill you and take the business anyway."'

'You're worried this might happen to Ramiz?'

'All the gunmen use mobile phones. They can

see that it's a real business. That attracts them. Look how they just took over the Abdel Rahman auto shops.'

Omar Yussef felt his heart draw an extra pulse. 'What?'

'When the Israelis killed Louai Abdel Rahman, the family lost its protection within the resistance factions. So long as Louai was alive, no one could touch the Abdel Rahmans, unless they wanted to fight the part of the militia that was loyal to him. Their auto shops became very successful. They have one in Irtas, two in Bethlehem and one in al-Khader. But as soon as Louai was killed, the Martyrs Brigades went to his father and told him to hand over the keys to the business. Now it's all in the hands of Hussein Tamari's brother.'

'I'm shocked,' Omar Yussef said. 'Louai has only been dead two days.'

'Nothing Hussein Tamari does could shock me.'

Omar Yussef thought back to the mourning tent for Louai Abdel Rahman. When Hussein Tamari came along the path firing his MAG in the air, it wasn't just a noisy sign of tribute: it was a threat. He remembered how Louai's father had looked disturbed by something Hussein Tamari said to him, even as he was supposed to be offering his condolences.

'No,' said Charles Halloun. 'The resistance-hero pose doesn't fool me. I've known that bastard Hussein Tamari for exactly what he is ever since he jailed me for tax evasion.'

Omar Yussef looked perplexed.

'Oh, I didn't evade any taxes, Abu Ramiz,' Charles Halloun said. 'It was a racket. Tamari pulled the same trick on a dozen other businessmen here and in Hebron, too. Six years ago, he came here with a squad of Preventive Security officers. They were disrespectful to Nasra, and they took me away. They didn't confiscate any of our files or records. There was no investigation. They just took me to the jail in Jericho and locked me up. Tamari told me, "Look, you haven't paid your taxes. Give me thirty thousand dollars or I'll have you accused of collaboration with the occupation and you'll sit in this cell until you rot."'

'What did you do?'

'I told him to fuck himself and demanded to see a lawyer. Pardon my language, Abu Ramiz.'

'That's all right. And so?'

'He laughed in my face. Then he slapped it.' Charles Halloun gasped at the memory. 'He tortured me, Abu Ramiz. I don't like to tell you everything he did to me, but let me just say that every time I stand up I still get a shooting pain through my back and it reminds me of my time with Abu Walid.'

Omar Yussef looked up. *Abu Walid.*

'I was in the jail in Jericho for a week,' Halloun said. 'I didn't eat the whole time. They gave me a little water, but the bastards urinated in it and I was so desperate I drank it. They shaved one side of my head and made me wear a dress. In the end, they gave me a phone and I called Nasra. I told her to get the money from the bank and hand it over. Even then, Abu Walid gave me another beating before he sent me home.'

'Who is Abu Walid?'

'Hussein Tamari. The bastard father of a bastard son. Did you never meet Walid, his eldest boy? He's a bullying swine, too. Ask any teenager around town. They've all got their lumps from that nasty scum. Just like his father.'

Omar Yussef felt the weight of the Webley and the two spent cartridges in his pocket. Here was the information he needed. Abu Walid. Was Hussein Tamari the man in the bushes to whom Louai Abdel Rahman spoke before he died? How many men would there be among those gunmen who were known as 'the father of Walid'? With Louai dead, Abu Walid took over the Abdel Rahmans' business. He had a motive, something to gain from Louai's death. But was he also the killer?

Omar Yussef said farewell to Charles Halloun and Nasra. He drove down the hill to Dehaisha. He had always been sure that George Saba was innocent, but now he believed he knew the identity of the real collaborator. He felt his pulse rise and his knuckles whitened as he gripped the steering wheel tightly. How was he going to prove that George Saba had been set up by the head of the resistance in Bethlehem? He knew that he must carry on, for the sake of George and for the sake of his town, which was quickly becoming a place where these gangsters could do whatever they wanted. Khamis Zeydan had told him this was a dangerous path to take. It wasn't getting any less risky.

Omar Yussef parked his car in the sandstone garage behind his house. He came in through the basement door and went up to his bedroom. He opened the drawer beneath his closet. His socks filled the drawer, bulbed in matching pairs. He took the Webley from his pocket and shoved it into the back of the pile. He looked about guiltily and closed the drawer.

What did I bring this gun here for? I'm behaving like a detective, he thought. *I'm gathering evidence. This gun is evidence, so I have to keep it. But I'm scared. Things could become dangerous, if a man like Hussein Tamari is involved. How will I react if Tamari confronts me? Already I'm frightened by the presence of a useless, antique gun amongst my socks.* He rolled the two MAG cartridges in his palm, thick and stubby. He imagined them filled with gunpowder and tipped with a lead slug.

Omar Yussef went into the salon. He picked up the phone and dialed Khamis Zeydan.

'I need to talk to George Saba,' he said.

There was a pause. 'Come and see me in the morning. At eight A.M. At my office.' Khamis Zeydan hung up.

Omar Yussef sat in silence. He listened to the blood pumping hard through his temple. He thought of

103

what Charles Halloun had told him about his income. It wasn't retirement he was planning for. He wanted to be sure that Maryam would be comfortable if he came to some harm. He felt determined. Nothing would happen to him, so long as George Saba needed his help. If he didn't stick to his path, George wouldn't be the last victim of Hussein Tamari.

I'm not a victim, Omar Yussef thought. He held his hand out before him and laughed. For the first time in years, it wasn't shaking.

CHAPTER 10

The bells in the Church of the Nativity resounded about Manger Square as Omar Yussef crossed to the police station. The tourist shops on the south side would open later, though few pilgrims braved Bethlehem now. There were no buyers for the cherubic newborn Christs, which lay in silent rows along the shelves in the windows of the Giacomman family's store, gazing blandly at the equally numerous Virgin Mothers. The earthy scent of yesterday's *foule* drifted from the shuttered restaurant next door. Omar Yussef never ate breakfast, but the smell of the fava bean mash made him crave a plate. His hunger made him cold and he pulled his coat up at the collar.

Omar Yussef traversed the carefully laid-out expanse of stone paving and tree planters in the square. In the thin light, the dark buttresses of the Armenian monastery that fronted the church were as foreboding as the tolling bells. The liveliness that he remembered of the church in his youth was gone, swamped by the Muslims of the surrounding camps and villages, who came like him as refugees and with swelling numbers soon felt entitled to treat the once-Christian town as their own. The symbol of Bethlehem, the basilica of the birthplace of Christianity, was beleaguered, its massive stone walls a futile bastion against a hostile religion and a declining congregation. It seemed like a place for burial, not birth. George Saba's cell was in the police station at the corner of the square closest to the church. Omar Yussef imagined George assaulted by the ominous pealing of the bells that reckoned his slow minutes of imprisonment, just as they chimed a doleful countdown to the extinction of the Christians in his town.

At the corner of the square, a voice called. 'Greetings, *ustaz*.' Omar Yussef turned to see a thin priest crossing the empty road toward him with long, bouncy strides. The priest wore a black Catholic robe with a white dog collar. There were gray socks under his open sandals. His skin was olive and speckled with the kind of black whiskers that always need shaving. His black hair was thin and curly, standing above his scalp like the fuzz on a hairy man's chest. In no more than two years, he would be completely bald. His thick glasses made his eyes seem tiny.

'Elias,' Omar Yussef said. 'I'm so happy to see you. George reported that you were back from the Vatican. We spoke proudly of your achievements.'

'Yes, I'm back. Can you believe it? I just couldn't keep a safe distance,' the priest said. 'It's wonderful to see you, Abu Ramiz. You look so well.'

'I have never trusted the word of religious men, and now I understand why. I am not in such great health, to tell the truth.'

'Perhaps I am just so delighted to see you that I feel everything must be perfect.'

'I wish it were so, Elias.' Omar Yussef looked toward the police station. 'I am going to visit George in his jail cell now.'

Elias Bishara pushed his heavy glasses up his nose. 'Tell me if there is anything George needs,' he said. 'He could have no greater friend than you, Abu Ramiz, but perhaps he will ask for a priest. I would like to minister to him.'

Omar Yussef wondered if Elias Bishara already was thinking ahead to George's last rites. He wasn't ready to accept that, yet. 'I will let him know.' He shook Elias's hand.

Khamis Zeydan met Omar Yussef at the door of the police station and walked him down the rough steps to the cells. It was cold in the corridor, though Omar Yussef was sure that the chill he felt was as much because of the location as the winter morning. Khamis Zeydan glanced sideways at his friend as he unlocked a metal gate and ushered him through. They passed two cells that were empty except for old, cheap prayer mats laid out on the beds.

'This was where I kept the Hamas people, back when we actually used to arrest those types,' Khamis Zeydan said. 'Then we received orders to free them. Now there's no one here except your friend.'

At the end of the corridor, he unlocked another grille. It was George's cell. 'I'll wait at the end of the row here,' Khamis Zeydan said. 'Just call me. But don't be too long, for Heaven's sake.' Omar Yussef could tell the gruffness was a screen for his friend's nervousness. He wasn't sure if that was because the policeman didn't want to be discovered allowing a visitor to the collaborator or because he feared that Omar Yussef's investigation would lead to trouble and now he was implicated in it.

George Saba stood up from the sagging camp bed in the corner of the bare room. His face was puffy, unwashed. Omar Yussef saw that the stubble of George's beard was surprisingly thick with gray, though white only touched his head around the temples. His hair was tangled and stuck out from his head at strange angles. He looked like a man who had slept for years, but without resting soundly. George Saba embraced Omar Yussef, who could not help but wrinkle his nose at the stale smell of his friend's neglected body.

'Abu Ramiz, I'm so happy to see you.'

Omar Yussef found himself at a loss. It saddened him to the point of tears to feel George's shirt against his face. The cotton was cold and so were the hands that now held his fingers.

'George, it's freezing in here.'

George nodded toward the cell window, barred and glassless. He tried to smile, but it was a sad attempt.

'Take my coat,' Omar Yussef said, pulling off his short herringbone overcoat.

'I really can't, Abu Ramiz. You'll get cold.'

'I've got a jacket on underneath. See? Take it.'

'I don't think it'll fit.'

Omar Yussef made him try the coat. It was ridiculously tight around the bigger man's arms and barely closed across his belly, but it was clear that George felt the overcoat was a reprieve from a terrible torture.

'May God compensate you for this,' he said.

Omar Yussef immediately shivered in his tweed jacket. He gestured to George to sit with him on the bed.

'What happened on the roof, George, after you left me at the Orthodox Club?'

'I took an antique British pistol that I was intending to sell in my shop and went onto the roof. There were two gunmen up there firing a massive machine gun. I told them to get off the roof, but they only cursed me. So I held the gun on them. They weren't sure about it, but in the darkness it looked threatening enough, I guess. I only recognized them when they were leaving. One wore a fur hat. His name's Jihad Awdeh. The other one carried the big gun.'

'Hussein Tamari?'

'That's him.'

'The two men at the top of the Martyrs Brigades in Bethlehem. You picked a prize pair to face off with, George.'

George smiled, bitterly. 'Hussein Tamari did all the shooting. I thought I should watch Hussein Tamari more closely. He was the one with the gun after all. But there was something that drew my eyes to Jihad Awdeh. He seemed so menacing. I can't really describe it. There was a moment just before they went down from the roof: Jihad bent to pick something up and stuff it into his jacket. It was more than one thing, in fact, metal things, I think, that were spread on the roof. He gave me such an evil look. It would chill me even now, if I weren't already too cold to feel anything. Then the two of them went down the stairs and left.'

'Perhaps Jihad was picking up the empty cartridges from the bullets, for some reason. You see, I found only one on the roof when I went up there yesterday. He must have missed it.'

'Why were you on the roof of my house? What are you up to, Abu Ramiz?'

Omar Yussef didn't answer the question. 'Do you have any enemies who would set you up?' he said.

'Just those two, as far as I can tell. This is hardly the way some customer would avenge himself on me for overcharging on an antique chesterfield, is it? Tamari and Awdeh said they'd get me. But I figured they would just come and beat me, or even kill me on the street. I didn't think they'd shame me like this.'

'Did either one of them threaten to kill you?'

'I think they both did. No, I believe it was only Hussein who actually said he would make me pay.

But then as they left Jihad made a gesture like he was cutting a throat.'

Omar Yussef looked about at the bare walls of the cell. The mustard paint was covered in small graffiti, the scribblings of bored men venting their anger or doodling about their dreams of a good meal. The toilet bucket in the corner suffused the cell with a rank odor, despite the open window. The wall and floor beneath the window were damp where yesterday's rain had come in. Omar Yussef sighed, and his breath made a steamy path from his mouth into the freezing air.

'Why did you go to the roof, George?'

George Saba smiled. 'Abu Ramiz, I went up there because you told me to do so.'

Omar Yussef looked perplexed.

'In your class on the Arab Revolt of 1936, you said that the so-called Arab heroes were really just gangs. They went about robbing villagers of their food and killing those who resisted, and all the time no one could take them on, because these killers were portrayed as the brave men standing up against the Zionists and the army. They ended up killing more Palestinians than Jewish farmers or British soldiers. You said that if the people had stood up to them early on, the gangs would have backed down and there could have been peace.'

'But I didn't mean . . .'

'When you're a stimulating teacher, you had better be careful. You never know what you might inspire people to do.' George laughed and put his hand on Omar Yussef's. 'Don't worry, Abu Ramiz. It's not your fault. I thought about it for days, every time they came to the neighborhood to shoot across the valley. Finally I knew I had to act. You see, I thought I understood the gunmen better than you, better than my Dad. In South America, I saw thugs like them. They were cowards when they were confronted. Remember, I lived in Chile when the military dictatorship was forced to give up power. But unfortunately there is no one here to back people up, no law. The criminals have made themselves the law. They shoot at some soldiers, and it transforms them into the representatives of the national struggle. That makes them unassailable and they can abuse anyone they want, particularly Christians who are weak already. That was my mistake. I didn't see that clearly enough. But I don't regret it.'

'Our town has changed terribly since you first went to Chile, George.'

'I've lived a life of many changes. I learned that change is a good thing. But here in Palestine change is always for the worse. Christian villages are overrun by new Muslim residents, and instead of living together in tranquility, it becomes a bad place for Christians. Even to change a situation of hatred, they only make still more hatred. Love is not an option. It's the choice of an idiot who wants to end with nothing, robbed and abused and humiliated. The result is that, in the end, everyone's convinced that the only way to alter the bad relations between Christians and Muslims, or between Israelis and Palestinians for that matter, is to wipe out the other side. To kill them all. Like they'll kill me, now.'

Omar Yussef had seen that coming. 'No, they won't, George. They can't.'

George Saba inclined his head, almost as though he pitied Omar Yussef. 'When they bring a collaborator to this cell, it's all over for him. It will be a public execution, like the ones they held in Gaza.'

'I will stop it, George,' Omar Yussef said. 'I know that you've been set up by Hussein. I just need to prove it, and I will.'

'Abu Ramiz, don't get into trouble.'

'I already have some proof. I will get more, and I will save you.'

'I have no desire to join the ranks of the martyrs, and of course as a collaborator I won't get such a title. There will be no Paradise for me. But if there were, I wouldn't expect to see you there for a long time yet. I warn you not to place yourself in danger. It will only result in two deaths, where these bastards would be satisfied with one.' George laughed. 'Maybe I should rethink. If I'm going to die, it might be better to think of myself as a martyr, after all. I'm dying because of my religion, aren't I?'

'You're a Christian. You don't believe in martyrdom.'

'Abu Ramiz, that isn't true. All right, so we don't

believe like the Muslims do that anyone who's killed just now goes up to claim his bliss with seventy-two beautiful black-eyed virgins. But even if we don't believe in those lovely *houris*, we Christians have our martyrs, nonetheless. I traveled in Europe. The cathedrals there are full of paintings of Christian martyrs. My namesake, Saint George, you know, was a martyr, not just a dragonslayer. I suppose the difference is that we Christians accept martyrdom, but we don't seek it.' George Saba paused. He continued, slowly. 'I want you to go to my family. Tell them to leave. Even now, while I'm still in jail. I don't want them to live here as outcasts, and I'm worried that someone will try to harm them, too. Tell them to go to Sofia's family in Chile.' He put his hand on Omar Yussef's arm and turned away to hide his tears. 'Make sure that my father goes with them. He listens to your advice.'

'I don't think he'll go. Not without you.'

'Abu Ramiz, for Heaven's sake, they're all in danger, too. You don't know what those men will do.'

They heard quick footsteps along the corridor. Khamis Zeydan came to the door and unlocked it.

'I'm not finished,' Omar Yussef said.

Khamis Zeydan concentrated on the final key. 'I must leave the station now, so I'll have to lock him up. Unless you want to spend the next twenty-four hours shivering in here with George, I suggest you get out of the cell now. Come on. I have to hurry.'

George stood up. He kissed Omar Yussef's cheeks. 'Tell my family what I said, uncle.'

'Allah lengthen your life,' Omar Yussef said. He touched George Saba's face. The beard was prickly.

Khamis Zeydan called from the doorway and Omar Yussef went out. As the policeman locked the door, Omar Yussef looked through the bars at George. The coat he had left behind seemed pathetic, inadequate, stretching across the broad shoulders of his friend. He wished he had brought food or a book to leave with the prisoner. Then he followed Khamis Zeydan slowly along the corridor.

'Hurry up, Abu Ramiz, please. I have to go.'

'What's the rush?' Omar Yussef was irritated to have his time with George cut short. The emotion of his meeting burst out of him now. 'Can't you have any decency?' he yelled at Khamis Zeydan. 'Can't you let me be with that boy a little longer, that innocent fucking victim?' He lowered his voice in case George could still hear, but he spat out the words angrily. 'You bastards are going to kill the best student I ever had.'

Khamis Zeydan stepped close. He was about to speak. A police officer came to the head of the stairs. 'Abu Adel,' the policeman said, 'the squad is ready.'

Khamis Zeydan called back that he was on his

way and the junior officer rushed out of sight. 'It's an emergency, as you can see,' he said to Omar Yussef.

'What is it? The Israelis have invaded Bethlehem once more and you have to run away?' Omar Yussef's voice was bitter.

Khamis Zeydan looked grim. 'No, Abu Ramiz. Someone has killed Dima Abdel Rahman.'

Omar Yussef couldn't speak. He looked with disbelief at Khamis Zeydan.

'None of us will survive except Allah,' the policeman said. 'Let's go.'

CHAPTER 11

The wind drove cold through the open sides of the jeep. The policemen hunched their shoulders inside their parkas. One of them made his teeth chatter loudly to amuse the others. From the front seat, Khamis Zeydan turned and silenced his men with a disapproving click of his tongue. Omar Yussef shivered in his tweed jacket. He almost regretted the coat he had left with George, but he could stand a little chill for a short time if it made his friend more comfortable in that bare cell.

The freezing drive to Irtas seemed to go on forever. In the time it took the jeep to leave Bethlehem and cross the hill to the Abdel Rahman family's house, Omar Yussef felt that his mind raced a distance ten times further. Who could have killed Dima Abdel Rahman? He felt sure her end was connected to that of her husband. It occurred to him that Louai's killing might perhaps not even be linked to his status as a resistance figure. If Louai had died at the hands of the Israelis for his actions against them, Omar Yussef couldn't see how that would lead to Dima's murder. Even if they targeted him as a terrorist, they wouldn't care about his wife. Only if Louai were killed in some criminal conspiracy did it seem possible that his murder would also bring this girl into the compass of death.

Omar Yussef rubbed his hands and blew on them. He grabbed the side of the jeep as a sharp corner threatened to toss him from the bench. It was as though the sudden bend snapped his mind into a new channel. The road sloped down toward the valley of Irtas and Omar Yussef could see the Abdel Rahman house and the glade where he had stood with Dima, and then it hit him: it was because of him that Dima died. Someone had seen her talking to him. Someone noticed her gesturing toward the spot where Louai died and telling the story of how it happened. The cause of her death could be that she had talked to Omar Yussef.

Nauseating pain gripped him in his guts. Wedged between two policemen on the benchseat of the jeep, he wanted to sway side to side in grief. Had he killed her? His stupid ideas about investigating Louai's death and saving George Saba had only accomplished the death of an innocent girl. He closed his eyes and saw himself in his classroom making a joke, and Dima was laughing. She was such a pretty girl, with a serious face, which was only more beautiful when laughter crossed it. In that way, she reminded him of his granddaughter Nadia. What would he give now to be back in that classroom listening to Dima reading aloud her homework paper on Suleiman the Magnificent, rather than bouncing down the hillside in a police jeep to see where she died? He heard her voice, deep and gentle even when she had been a child, telling him about her husband's death, and he wondered what the last words had been that she spoke in her precise, intelligent diction.

Khamis Zeydan turned to his squad and issued orders to cordon off the Abdel Rahman house, as the jeep reached the floor of the valley and sped toward the murder scene. When he sat back, his eye caught Omar Yussef's for a second. It scared the schoolteacher, because it was such a severe, intent, dark glance.

Omar Yussef watched the police chief. Perhaps no one had seen him with Dima at the mourning tent after all or, if they did, no one thought it suspicious for an old teacher to console his former pupil. Who had Omar Yussef told about that conversation with Dima? Who knew that she had told him about 'Abu Walid'? He felt confused. He thought he had told his son and his wife, but he couldn't quite remember. The only person he was sure he had told was Khamis Zeydan.

The police chief looked back at him again, but Omar Yussef glanced away immediately. Could it be that his old friend had betrayed him? Had Khamis Zeydan informed Abu Walid that Dima was able to incriminate him? If so, that meant the policeman knew who Abu Walid was. But why would he tip him off? It wouldn't have been the first time Khamis Zeydan was involved in a double game. He had followed his people's leaders all over the Arab world and Europe, assassinating rivals, murdering innocent people who got in his way. *I was, for many years, what the world chooses to call a terrorist.* Yet this was worse. This was his old friend Omar Yussef whom he had betrayed.

The jeep pulled into the field outside the Abdel Rahman family's home. The officers piled out noisily, stamping their feet to get their bodies moving again after the cramped ride. Khamis Zeydan distributed them around the house with a clap on each shoulder and the point of a finger. He reached up to help Omar Yussef down from the jeep, holding out his prosthetic hand in its tight black leather glove.

'I can get down myself,' Omar Yussef said.

Khamis Zeydan turned and strode toward the family, which was gathered by the cabbage patch in front of the house. Omar Yussef stepped stiffly off the back of the jeep and landed awkwardly on a clump of grass that disguised a small rock. His ankle twisted. He shook his foot and grimaced. He followed Khamis Zeydan and noted that his friend seemed to move with greater power now that he was on an operation, in command. *Or perhaps he just seems stronger now that I believe he played some part in the death of an innocent girl. She may even have died while I was in his company this morning.*

One of the policemen went to the glade where Louai had died. He stood sentry over a lumpy object covered in a white sheet. Omar Yussef stopped. *That must be Dima's body.* He choked on a gulp of bile and coughed to get his breath. He turned his eyes to the ground, but he swayed, dizzily. He looked up at the gray sky and spread his legs to steady himself. He breathed deeply until he felt able to follow Khamis Zeydan.

The police chief was listening to Muhammad Abdel Rahman describe how his daughter-in-law's body was found. The old man went silent as Omar Yussef approached and stared suspiciously at him with his black eyes, but Khamis Zeydan told him to continue.

'I awoke for the dawn prayer and found my son Yunis downstairs. He told me that he saw something through the window. We came out to look, and over there, we found her, just where her body remains now. We put a white sheet over her. From the position in which we discovered her, I believe some sex pervert must have killed her.'

'Did you see anyone else?' Khamis Zeydan said.

'No one. It must have happened during the night. We all turned off the lights at the same time last night.'

'What time was that?'

'Just before twelve. We are all up late for Ramadan these days. We have a lot of family visitors, as well as people wishing us their condolences for the death of my son Louai.'

'Did anyone visit you last night? Was there anyone in the house who didn't usually stay here?'

'No, our guests left at least half an hour before we went to sleep. Dima went to her room at the same time as the rest of the family.'

There was something unemotional and organized about Muhammad Abdel Rahman's answers that disturbed Omar Yussef. He spoke up: 'Did Abu Walid come to see you last night?'

Muhammad Abdel Rahman looked angrily at Omar Yussef. 'You are not a detective and I'm not a schoolboy. Why should I answer a schoolteacher's questions? Fuck you. This is not your classroom. Go and order someone else around. I'm not one of your refugee children.'

Khamis Zeydan put his hand on Muhammad Abdel Rahman's chest and gave it a warning tap. 'Watch your mouth, Abu Louai. I brought *ustaz* Omar Yussef here as my friend. You had best be civil to him. But it is true that he's not authorized to investigate.' He looked sharply at Omar Yussef.

'Then you ask him that question,' Omar Yussef said to Khamis Zeydan. 'Ask him what I just asked.'

Khamis Zeydan took Omar Yussef aside. 'I think he's already answered it, quite clearly, don't you?' he whispered, firmly. He turned back to the family. 'Let's go and see the body. There's no need for you to go through this again Abu Louai. Please wait here.'

Under the pines, Khamis Zeydan looked at Omar Yussef, hard and questioningly. Omar Yussef nodded. The policeman lifted the white sheet.

The body lay on its side. Black hair spread around the head, as though the corpse were drifting in still water. A spray of that hair fell across the face. Khamis Zeydan lifted it and Omar Yussef recognized Dima Abdel Rahman. She was pale and her lips were the color of a bruise. Her eyes were open only slightly, as though she were rousing herself from a long sleep. Her tortuous posture reminded Omar Yussef of the Rodin statuette in George Saba's living room. He had held that bronze of a prone woman tenderly in his two hands, fearing to let a work of art drop to the ground. He wanted to lift the body of Dima Abdel Rahman, to cradle her as he had the statuette and to discover that she was merely posing for a sculptor. Omar Yussef cursed himself. He had held her just as securely as he did that naked *objet d'art*. She was his pupil and her father was his friend. He encouraged her to come to this house because he believed she would find love here. Instead, it was a place of death. He had dropped something much more fragile than a bronze cast. He punched a frustrated fist into the palm of his hand.

'Her throat has been cut,' Khamis Zeydan said. 'There's something shoved in her mouth.' He pulled at the end of a piece of cloth until a few damp inches of it dangled from between her teeth. 'She's been gagged.'

Only then did Omar Yussef notice the gash across the jugular and the coagulated blood on Dima's shoulder and outstretched arm. He experienced

123

the choking sensation once more. The coldness of the morning left him and he was very hot. He removed his flat cap and let the wind chill the sweat on his scalp. He shivered.

Khamis Zeydan lifted the sheet further. Dima's nightdress was ripped from the hem as far up as her shoulder blades. There were scratches on her naked buttocks.

'Has she been raped?' Omar Yussef asked.

Khamis Zeydan covered the girl with the sheet. 'It looks like it, but she'll have to be examined.'

Omar Yussef came close to Khamis Zeydan. '*They* are involved, aren't they? It's them.'

'The father and brother? Yes, I expect they are the ones who did it.'

Omar Yussef had meant the Martyrs Brigades. He frowned.

'No one could come out here and take a woman from inside the house without the family hearing,' Khamis Zeydan continued. 'It had to be the father and brother. It might be an honor killing, or maybe she knew something about them that made them want to silence her.'

'But the father more or less admitted that Abu Walid had been here. That's why he got so angry when I asked him about it. Maybe it was *him*. Maybe it was Abu Walid again.'

Khamis Zeydan looked hard at Omar Yussef. 'We don't know who Abu Walid is.'

'I think we do.'

'But we don't. Not for sure.' There was a warning

in Khamis Zeydan's eyes. 'Abu Walid could be any number of different people.'

'There's only one Abu Walid who could have left behind the bullet casing I showed you.'

'That bullet casing was from a massive machine gun. It's too bulky to bring on an ambush here.'

'You told me Abu Walid takes that machine gun with him everywhere. It's his symbol, you said, his emblem. You said he probably even took it to the bathroom with him. So maybe he would bring it to an ambush like this.'

'The Abu Walid to whom you're referring is a murderer, I agree. But he hasn't killed anyone without what he, at least, would think of as a good reason.'

'Then we have to find the reason he killed Dima.'

'Then you'd also have to find the reason Muhammad and Yunis would protect him after he killed her.' Khamis Zeydan clicked his tongue. 'I shouldn't have brought you. I thought it would cure you of this obsession. I thought that once you'd seen a dead body you'd realize that you aren't a policeman. You're a schoolteacher. Stick with that.'

'You're right. I'm a schoolteacher. I taught this girl, who now lies dead. I taught George Saba, who'll be dead soon unless I help him, because nobody else will. I'll tell you what I taught them, too. I taught them that the world is a good place and that they must use their intelligence and their hearts to contribute to its improvement. Do you see that if I let these things happen without taking any action, I've been lying to thousands of little children for decades? Most of all, I've been lying to myself.'

'Don't make it such a big thing. It's not all about you.'

'Listen to me, sometimes I feel like I'm not in the best of health. I feel that for a man in his mid-fifties I move slowly, my hands shake, I ache in every part of my body. I feel like death is taking me over.'

'You're not old. This is just your morbid reaction to seeing a corpse.'

'It's more than that.'

'Why are you so obsessed with death?'

'I'm waiting for my own murderer.'

Khamis Zeydan threw up his hands and stared at Omar Yussef. 'This is crazy,' he said, walking away. 'I've got an investigation to conduct. I have a lot of interviews with potential witnesses here. I'll have one of the men take you back to Dehaisha.'

Omar Yussef's head, which had felt so hot, was cold now. His shock at seeing Dima's dead body was replaced by a determination not to let go of Khamis Zeydan now that he had him rattled. He put on his cap and followed him across the grass.

'You're not really investigating, are you? You know something and you won't tell me what it is. It's a charade, asking these people questions. There's something they know, and you know it, too. What is it?'

Khamis Zeydan turned. 'I heard that you retired from teaching. I think you ought to reconsider. I think you ought to go back to work, so you don't have so much time on your hands. It's making you crazy to be a prematurely retired guy. I shouldn't have let you see George Saba, but it was a humanitarian gesture for an old friend who I sensed was in distress. Well, I'm sorry I let you into the jail. Now go back to the school and leave this to a professional.'

Omar Yussef grabbed Khamis Zeydan's shoulder. '*You* told them, didn't you? You told Hussein Tamari.'

'What are you talking about?'

'You're the only person I told about what Dima said to me. You're the only one who knows she told me about Abu Walid. You passed it on to Tamari and he came here and killed her. You're in with them.'

'Now you're making me angry, Abu Ramiz.'

'Why should I be surprised? Ever since we finished university, you've made your living by terrorism. You said so yourself.'

Khamis Zeydan pushed Omar Yussef's hand from his shoulder. His jaw was tight and he growled out his words. 'Believe me, I wish I was finished with all that. But maybe it's not possible. Life is terrorism, so spare me your indignation. Life is one big infiltration of our secure defenses. Some people put bombs on buses and blow them up: those are terrorists. Some people speak to you and their words blow you up: what would you call those people? Life is a condemned cell. If your friend George Saba finds himself locked up on death row today, it's only because he never had the brains to realize that he lived his whole life there. That's the only way to protect yourself, Abu Ramiz – to understand that you're always under sentence of death and to try to get a temporary remission.'

Omar Yussef was shocked. 'I can't believe you think this way,' he said, quietly.

'Well, I certainly hope you didn't believe I was operating on high moral principles. I assume you know me better than that.'

'This wasn't how you used to be.'

'Things have changed. I discovered that our people's struggle is run like a crappy casino, and after forty years gambling in it the only chip I have left is the one on my shoulder.' He swung his arm with its gloved prosthesis to take in Dima's dead body under the white sheet, the armed policemen, the hostile glare of Muhammad Abdel Rahman and his son Yunis. 'I lost the bet, as you can see. I fucking lost.'

Khamis Zeydan pushed his beret back and rubbed his forehead. His anger seemed to leave him and Omar Yussef thought he looked pained, sad, lonely.

'There's more to this business with the Abdel

Rahmans than you know, Abu Ramiz,' Khamis Zeydan said. 'Excuse me.' He walked quickly to the Abdel Rahman family. He beckoned Muhammad to follow him to the salon and told the women to go back into the house and await questioning.

After the family entered the house, no one remained by the cabbage patch except the police cordon and Yunis Abdel Rahman. Omar Yussef felt his ankle seizing up where he'd twisted it descending from the jeep. He limped over to Yunis.

'May Allah bless her,' Omar Yussef said.

Yunis barely nodded his head. *He's a handsome man*, Omar Yussef thought. *A handsome boy, really*. His face had a fine, almost feminine jaw and light hazel eyes. His neck was thin, a skinny teenager's neck. Omar Yussef read an arrogance in him of the kind that the young so often wore these days, full of the sense that their elders had failed to fight hard enough for the freedom of Palestine, convinced that they would be the ones to make the great sacrifices that would liberate their land. It was the pity for their humiliated elders and the anticipation of surpassing them in a hurry that made young men like Yunis Abdel Rahman insufferable to Omar Yussef. How many times had he faced the same aloof, defiant expression he now saw on this boy's face, in the UN schoolyard or on the streets of Dehaisha? But there was something else here, something more hostile, reckless, guilty. That was it, Omar Yussef thought, as he looked closely at the boy: *I don't think I've ever seen anyone who looked more ashamed of himself and more desperate to hide it.*

'May this sadness end all your sadnesses,' Omar Yussef said, offering another formula of condolence. 'Who would have imagined that I would be back here again so soon after your brother's death?'

Yunis looked over to the corpse and back to the cabbage patch. He seemed to be imagining that other body, his brother's, clad in denim and splayed across the green leaves on the ground.

Omar Yussef decided to test Yunis. 'Where will you work now?'

Yunis looked puzzled.

'Now that the Martyrs Brigades have taken over your family autoshops,' Omar Yussef explained. 'Where will you work?'

'It's not your business.'

'Your employment? No, perhaps it's just that as an old schoolteacher I always worry about young people.'

'That's not what I meant. The autoshops are not your business.'

'Neither are they yours anymore.'

'We'll manage.'

'Why did they take the business away from you?'

Yunis was silent again.

'I thought they were Louai's friends,' Omar Yussef said. 'He was in the same faction as the leaders of the Martyrs Brigades. They should be looking after his family, not stealing its livelihood. And why did they come and kill Dima?'

'Who told you that?'

Omar Yussef feigned surprise. 'That's the conclusion of the police.'

'The police just got here.'

'You know that the police operate on intelligence information, not on things that they find on the crime scene. You see, the crime scene can be tampered with, or even set up, faked. But intelligence, the things their informants tell them, that's something the police can rely upon.'

Omar Yussef watched the boy very closely. Yunis's left eye twitched nervously. Omar Yussef decided to press the boy. He spoke more loudly, with almost casual, confiding assuredness. 'Look, they came here to kill Dima because they feared that she knew something about Louai's death – something that they wanted to hide. It was they who killed Louai, not the Israelis. This Christian guy that they've arrested had nothing to do with it. You know that.'

'How would I know?'

'What if the Martyrs Brigades killed Louai and blamed the Israelis, so that they could take the family business from your father? You were helpless to prevent it. But the Martyrs Brigades found out that Dima knew something about them. Maybe that she saw something or heard something when she was waiting for Louai to come home that night. So they killed her. They made it look like some kind of sex crime, so that people would assume it's just a random nasty pervert who took her life.'

'The Martyrs Brigades are fighters, strugglers for our people.'

'Like your brother?'

'Yes. Like my brother.'

'How well did you know him, eh? Did you really know everything that he was into?' Omar Yussef looked over at the white sheet, lumpy with the body beneath. 'They have all kinds of tests these days. Genetic tests. You've seen where Dima's backside was scratched? They'll be able to look under the fingernails of any suspect and check that the fragments of skin they find there came from her buttocks, when the killer scratched her.' He turned and looked at Yunis's hands. The boy pulled his fingers tight into fists. 'They'll probably check you, too.'

'How could I have done this to my sister-in-law? You're crazy.'

'Haven't you heard of honor crime?'

'How had she offended the honor of our family?'

'You tell me.'

'I don't have to tell you anything. You aren't even a policeman. You're a schoolteacher.' He walked away from Omar Yussef quickly. Then he stopped. 'You should have taught Dima better. If you had, she wouldn't have ended like this. She came out here to meet a man for sex and he killed her.'

'That's a pretty desperate explanation and I know you don't believe it.'

132

'If you taught her better, she would be alive. It's you that killed her, you son of a whore. They ought to check under *your* fingernails.' The boy went fast around the house and into the garage with his hands shoved deep in his pockets. Omar Yussef heard the loud revving of an engine, as though Yunis were pumping the gas to make a racket as ringing as the scream he could not allow himself to emit.

Omar Yussef hobbled toward the white sheet. The policeman guarding the body nodded. Omar Yussef knelt stiffly on the damp grass. He lifted the corner of the sheet and looked at Dima's face. Her cheeks puffed where the cloth remained balled in her mouth. Her eyes stared blankly into the dirt.

Omar Yussef looked at his hands. What did he have under his fingernails? Who had he scratched during his years as a teacher? Had he taught these children to be discontented, unable to accept the reality of their society? Had he given them principles that would surely be violated by the world around them, dooming them to cynicism and disillusion? *If you looked beneath my nails*, Omar Yussef thought, *Yunis was right about what might be found there. There would be traces of the skin of Dima Abdel Rahman, of George Saba, of how many others?* Gently he put his fingers on Dima's lids and closed her eyes.

CHAPTER 12

O mar Yussef waited among the pines for Khamis Zeydan to complete his interviews with the Abdel Rahmans. A photographer came to document the details of Dima Abdel Rahman's death for the forensic record. He flipped the sheet off her, snapped her face in close-up and scuttled around to get a shot of the body in relation to the house twenty yards away. He joked crudely with the policeman guarding the corpse about Dima's marred backside. Omar Yussef turned away and leaned his face against the bark of a tree trunk.

Omar Yussef had spent his life teaching history, the facts and meanings of real occurrences. But he tried to keep himself free of the corroding effect of the historical events through which he had lived. He had never experienced life as a nomadic fighter, as Khamis Zeydan had. He didn't become a hateful thinker, a deceitful propagandist, like so many people around him. He wasn't untouched by his people's trouble, but he felt as close to pure as it seemed to him a man in control of his senses might be. He lived in the house his father had once rented, and he taught in a classroom that was, for reasonably intelligent pupils, a chamber that transported them to another time, safe from the destruction and prejudice around them. As he leaned against the pine, he wondered if he was sacrificing this purity and sanity to the investigation he had taken upon himself. Perhaps he remained an honorable, proud man entirely because he was insulated from the corrupting world in which his compatriots lived. Already, he could feel his grip on himself weakening, and it was only five days since he had dined with George Saba – days in which death and suspicion and fear were all around him as never before. He sensed that he wanted revenge for Dima's death. He didn't care who might suffer or die, so long as someone's body could pay and he could be reasonably sure that the new victim bore something related to guilt for the girl's killing. It was this thought that scared him most, that he might be just like everyone else after all, weak and vindictive and murderously righteous.

There seemed to be only one way out. He would stop his investigation. He was a schoolteacher. George Saba required help and Dima needed revenge, but Omar Yussef was not the man to provide either. He had to protect himself from the darkness deep in his soul. He thought of the night he had parted from George at the restaurant in Beit Jala, how he had stumbled home down the hill and how shapes in the dark alleys had taken on the forms of men and animals, nightmarish and insubstantial. This was how he thought of his own mind now, its shadows gathering until they became parasitic phantoms that breathed inside him just as surely as he lived. It occurred to him that the shadowy figures he imagined that night might have been impelling him to return to George. Who knew, if he had turned, he might have prevented the disastrous confrontation with the gunmen on the roof. But Omar Yussef had made his way quickly home that night and, though he hated to think of it that way, it was what he decided to do now.

Khamis Zeydan came out of the house and walked wearily toward the jeep. Omar Yussef came to the side of the vehicle.

'Can you drop me at the school?' he said, quietly.

Khamis Zeydan yawned. 'I thought you retired from teaching.'

'You already said that. I don't know where you heard it.' Omar Yussef said, raising his voice.

'Are you telling me it's not true?'

'Where did you hear it?'

'It's going around. Someone I know has kids in your class. He spoke to the American at your school, Steadman, about his kids. He was told you retired.'

'Someone who went to complain about my lack of support for the intifada? My criticism of the martyrs?'

'Why else would anyone take the time to go to

see a school director these days? And why else would your name come up?'

Omar Yussef climbed into the back of the jeep. He grunted as he pushed up with his injured ankle. 'I'm going back to the school,' he said.

Khamis Zeydan looked at him. There was suspicion and power and knowledge in his eyes, and they made Omar Yussef look away. Khamis Zeydan slammed the back door of the jeep.

As they jogged up the hill and came around toward Dehaisha, Omar Yussef watched the side of Khamis Zeydan's face. The officer stared out of the front of the jeep. *Is he thinking about Dima's murder?* Omar Yussef wondered. *Or is he contemplating the role he played in it? Can he really have passed details to Hussein Tamari about what Dima told me? Have I been so blind to the real character of this man I considered my friend?* It occurred to Omar Yussef that there might be many more of his friends who were guilty of terrible things, but he couldn't believe any of them would have taken part in a murder. It surprised him that it was so easy to conceive of Khamis Zeydan's involvement in a slaying.

Omar Yussef stepped from the jeep in silence outside the UN school. It pulled away down the uneven, puddled road, leaving the scent of gasoline, alluring and poisonous in the damp cold. Omar Yussef held his breath until the wind cleared the air. He stopped outside a classroom window to listen to children reciting a multiplication table.

He smiled when they stumbled over nine times eight: that always tripped them. At the entrance he greeted the janitor and noticed that the man, surprised to see him, sat hastily upright, as though a senior military officer or a forbidding uncle had passed.

Or a ghost.

Through the glass in the door of his classroom, Omar Yussef saw a young woman sitting silently at his desk while his students worked in their notebooks. He couldn't see the woman's face, because she was bent forward over a book. The substitute teacher wore a white headscarf and a loose mustard robe, but he could tell from the clear skin of her hands that she was probably in her early twenties. He paused and considered entering, but the class was quiet and concentrated. He would not disturb them.

Omar Yussef went to the end of the corridor and smiled at Wafa.

'Morning of joy, Abu Ramiz,' the school secretary said.

Omar Yussef noticed that Wafa's lips showed a mischievous pleasure at his arrival. 'Morning of light, Umm Khaled,' he said. He nodded at Christopher Steadman's office and Wafa gave him a be-my-guest shrug. He entered.

The heat felt stifling in Steadman's room, even though Omar Yussef had frozen once again without his coat on the ride back from Irtas. The air seemed thick with dust. The American looked up from his papers. His face flushed, but he said nothing. He tilted his head quizzically to the left, as though he had trouble remembering the identity of this man with the gray moustache and flat, beige cap.

'I have changed my mind,' Omar Yussef said. He pronounced each word crisply and precisely in English.

Christopher Steadman merely increased the inclination of his head. He pursed his lips and looked angry.

'I no longer wish to retire.'

'You have until the end of the month to decide,' Steadman said.

'I don't need that long. I already decided.'

'I would prefer that you take until the end of the month. In any case, I've taken on a replacement. She has been paid until the end of the month, so you have nowhere to come.' Steadman lifted his head so that it was straight and jutted forward on his neck. 'Until then, at least.'

Omar Yussef could see that he would have to wait a few weeks before he could take over his classroom once more. He decided on a delaying tactic. 'I must insist that you do not tell people that I have retired. It is damaging to my reputation.'

'I haven't told anyone.'

'I believe you have.'

'I have not.'

'Perhaps you forgot.' Omar Yussef paused and

looked very hard at Steadman. He forced himself to approach the American constructively, with the kind of argument that might overcome Steadman's apparent dislike of his history teacher. 'You have to understand something about Arab culture, Christopher. If you allow me to retire on my own terms, it's quite possible that I will decide to go. If, through no intention of your own, you make it appear as though I have been forced out, I shall have to remain in my job to counter that impression.'

Steadman looked thoughtful, rolling his tongue about his mouth. Omar Yussef saw that the director understood he had made a tactical error.

'It's a cultural matter, Christopher. You see, it would reflect badly upon me. But I don't expect that to concern you. No, the important thing from your point of view is that it would make you look very culturally insensitive and other people would find it hard to trust you. You know, I have many friends and my clan is one of the most prominent in Dehaisha camp.'

'Are you saying that you want to retire, after all?'

'I am tending toward that course.' Omar Yussef enjoyed the sound of the English words. It made him happy to talk his way around Steadman in the American's own language. 'I can't say anything definitive. I only ask that you consider the cultural implications of my position. I know that you are sensitive to these things. Your reputation in the camp is for exactly this kind of sensitivity. I wish to help you protect that good name.'

Steadman took off his glasses. Omar Yussef had him confused but not yet beaten. Now was the time for his ace.

'To appear to force me out of the school during the holy month of Ramadan . . . Well, this would be a great insult to all the Muslims of the camp.'

Steadman looked up with the hint of a frown. *Got him*, Omar Yussef thought.

'Very well, Abu Ramiz. I shall wait until the end of the month,' Steadman said. 'Until then, I shall tell everyone that you continue to teach here.'

'Actually, it would be wiser to wait for the end of Ramadan itself.'

'That's three more weeks.'

'Then there's the *Eid*. The *Eid al-Fitr*.'

'The holiday after Ramadan?'

'Yes, it marks the new moon.'

'I know that.' Steadman flipped his eyeballs upward in irritation. 'So you won't decide until the new moon?' His voice was sarcastic.

'It would not be appropriate for a Muslim to make such a decision during the holy month. It is a time for communing with the Master of the Universe, not for trivial, earthly matters like employment or retirement decisions.'

You can look that up in the hadith *of the Prophet titled Fuck You, Steadman.*

Wafa gave him a knowing nod as he passed her desk on his way out. Omar Yussef left the school. He had arrived only a few moments earlier and experienced a nostalgia for the sound of children

141

reciting in unison. He had been determined to take up his old job and abandon his investigation, but the hiring of a replacement teacher forced him to reconsider. Now there were three weeks before he would have to tell Steadman what he wanted to do about retirement.

Omar Yussef came out onto the muddy street and turned past the black granite statue of the map of Palestine toward his home. He wasn't sure that he could just sit around the house brooding on his decision. To retire or to continue in his work? He would know the answer when the moment came. Until that time, there was something else that he must decide. He remembered the murdered body of Dima Abdel Rahman. He still couldn't tell if his overwhelming feeling was of determination to expose her killer or fear that by investigating he had already exposed himself to too much of the reality of life in his town, too much danger.

The wind came colder along the empty street. Nayif skipped toward Omar Yussef, wearing a filthy white T-shirt. He hugged himself with his bare arms, but smiled at Omar Yussef. 'It's still raining, uncle,' he called out, as he jumped into a puddle.

Omar Yussef listened. There was the sound of the helicopter, resonating through the clouds still. He wondered if it were the only noise the boy could hear, ringing inside his misshapen head. Omar Yussef smiled back and looked up at the blustery sky. He lifted the collar of his jacket to keep the chill from his neck and wondered if his herringbone coat would be enough to keep George Saba from dying of the cold in his cell.

CHAPTER 13

As he approached his house, Omar Yussef felt filthy. He recalled the touch of Dima Abdel Rahman's eyelids on his fingertips, delicate and caressing like the wings of a butterfly, but still and dead. The mud of the street sprayed gray-brown splashes on his loafers and the cuffs of his chocolate-brown trousers. He sensed people staring at him and wondered if they were angry parents, resentful that he taught their children to be freethinking outcasts. Perhaps they already knew what Dima's death and George's arrest had led him to suspect: to study with Omar Yussef was to make yourself so dangerous that society would have to blot you out. He was so uncomfortable by the time he opened his front door that he had decided to do nothing more about George Saba's case for that day at least, and perhaps ever.

'Grandpa, you look very cold.' Nadia came to Omar Yussef as he entered. She took one of his hands and began to rub it and blow on it comically.

Omar Yussef glanced at the wall mirror. He looked like a vagrant. His hair stuck out spikily from beneath his flap cap. His skin was sallow and, though he was indeed very cold, he seemed to be sweating. His eyes were bloodshot. He wondered if he were sick. He managed to smile for his granddaughter and asked her to bring him some tea. He went into the salon and sat in front of the gas heater. It was like sinking into a warm bath.

Maryam came to the door. Omar Yussef glanced at her, assuming that she brought the tea he had asked Nadia to make. But there was something else in her hands which made him look up a second time from the soothing, orange glow of the heater.

'Omar, are you crazy?'

Maryam brandished the old Webley revolver that Omar Yussef had hidden in the bedroom closet.

'There are children in this house. You can't bring a gun in here,' she said. 'What on earth do you want it for?'

Omar Yussef reached out his hand. It shook as it always did, but more so now from the cold and the shock of seeing George Saba's antique gun in his wife's small hands. 'Give that to me, Maryam.'

'No, I'm throwing it out. Tell me why you brought it into our house. Imagine if the Israelis came in here and found it. They would take you away. Or Ramiz. They would take away our son.'

'Stop it, Maryam. You're overreacting.'

Maryam looked truly angry now. 'Omar, you don't know what things are like in this town now.

145

You get up every day and you go to the school. You teach the kids about the past. You stop in at one of your friends' offices for a coffee, and then you come back here and read all night. I go to the market and I hear people, and I see things. And Ramiz tells me of the events he knows you don't want to hear about.'

'What does he keep from me?'

'He doesn't like to upset you.'

'Upset me, how?'

'With reality,' Maryam yelled. She waved the pistol at Omar Yussef. 'This gun is real, and I found it in our closet. So it's time for you to tell me what this gun is for.'

Omar Yussef patted his hand on the sofa. Maryam came, reluctantly, and sat.

'It was George Saba's. It *is* George Saba's gun.' Omar Yussef thought of telling her about his investigation. He saw how her anger slipped away at the mention of George's name. But the truth in its entirety would include his decision to investigate, and his present doubts about the dangers of continuing in his detective work. He decided to tell a half-truth. 'Habib Saba gave it to me yesterday, when I went to see him. It is an antique pistol that George was going to sell in his shop. Habib gave it to me as a gift. I put it in the closet because I don't want the children to see a gun around the house, even if it is a gun that no longer works. I'm sorry, Maryam. I should have told you.'

'I'm sorry that I was angry.' Maryam substituted for her anger with fussiness. 'Omar, you're cold. Where is your coat?'

He waved away her question.

'You need to warm up. I'll make you some tea.'

She stopped at the door and held up the gun. 'I'll put this back in the closet. For now.'

Wearily, Omar Yussef nodded.

As Maryam turned, Omar Yussef heard the front door open. He saw his wife hide the gun behind her back. Ramiz came in from the street.

'Hi, Mother.'

Maryam greeted him as she left the hallway to hide the gun. Omar Yussef noticed guiltily that her voice shook as she said hello to her son.

Ramiz stood in the doorway, watching the spot where his mother had been with a look of mild contentment. He looked into the salon and, when he saw his father, his expression became serious. He unzipped his parka and joined Omar Yussef on the couch.

'Dad, I have to talk to you.'

Omar Yussef sensed a tone of warning in his son's voice. *He must know something about what I've been doing*, he thought. *I'm supposed to be the detective, but everyone's investigating me.* He tried to divert his son. 'Halloun the accountant tells me you're expanding your business. I'm happy that trade is good for you.'

Ramiz stopped a moment, as though he wanted to address Omar Yussef's comment, but he shook his head and ignored it. 'The Martyrs Brigades people came to my shop this morning.'

Omar Yussef sat up sharply.

Ramiz noticed his motion. 'I see you know what I'm talking about. They know that you're trying to clear George Saba. On the one hand, I assume that the fact they want you to stop is a sign that they're involved in the killing for which George is being blamed. On the other hand, if guys like that want you to stop, you simply have to do so.' He put his hand on Omar Yussef's forearm. 'Dad, these men are really evil. They'll do anything.'

Omar Yussef tried to speak, but he needed to clear his throat first. What Ramiz had told him made him more nervous than he would have expected. He coughed. 'What did they say?'

'It was Hussein Tamari who came to see me. The big boss. He made threats, Dad. Threats against my business, that he'd burn it down. Threats that he'd do something to this house.' He paused. 'He didn't say it directly, but I got the impression he would hurt you physically, too.'

'He said he'd kill me?'

'No, but he implied he'd beat you up. If those guys beat you, Dad, it'd take you a long time to recover, if you ever did.'

'At my age, you mean?'

'I didn't say that. But you aren't in the best shape, are you? I'm just worried about you.'

'If you're so worried about *me*, why did you mention the threats to your business first?'

'Because I know you. I know how stubborn you are. If I said they made threats against you, you'd just say "Fuck them." If I told you the threats affect the rest of your family, I figured maybe you'd think twice.'

'In other words, you're on their side.'

'No, Dad.' Ramiz sounded exasperated.

'Yes, you are. You're trying to make sure that I give in to their threats. That's how they run this town, isn't it? They turn up at your shop. They look tough. They sound mean. Then you run off and get me to stop investigating.'

'Don't make me sound so cowardly. It isn't like that. I'm trying to be realistic.

'Realistic?'

'Yes, and responsible. We have a big clan. It's big enough that it gives us more protection than most people might have. Tamari doesn't come directly to you and hurt you, because he'd be starting a war with the Sirhans in Hamas and Fatah, and with the rest of us, too. But the clan can only protect you so much. If you carry on with your detective nonsense, eventually Tamari will act.'

Omar Yussef looked down at his hands and pressed them together. They felt powerful. Maybe he didn't look strong; perhaps he even seemed a little frail for a man of his age, but he knew that there was a force within him that couldn't be seen by anyone, even the son who knew him best. He sat up straight. 'I went to see George Saba this morning.'

'At the jail? How did you get in there?'

'It doesn't matter. Anyway, George doesn't have your option – of being realistic.'

'But *we* have an option. I have a problem, and I've come to you. A problem that threatens everything we have. Most of all it threatens to take my father from me.' Ramiz's voice caught. 'I don't know how I'd live without you, Dad.'

Omar Yussef put his hand on his son's shoulder. Ramiz shook slightly and covered his face with his hand. He wiped a fingertip beneath his eyes and tried to smile. He was chubbier than his father. His facial structure made him look like Omar Yussef's mother. His cheekbones were wide and high, and his eyes had a lazy glibness that concealed his sharp intelligence. The things Ramiz said were the words of a normal, decent man. *He's worried about his kids, about his business, about his own father*, Omar Yussef thought. *He's planning for the future by building his phone stores, rather than risking his life for the sake of his legacy, for the way in which people will remember him. I'm trying to find out who killed Dima Abdel Rahman, a person who's dead and gone, and to save George Saba, a man who's as good as dead. It's all so people will look back and see that I was someone who made children into worthy adults. What will they say if I ruin my family in the process?*

It was no good, though; that was how he always had been and he wouldn't change that, even if he could. He only had to look at the expensive cars driven about town by the dumbest of his ex-pupils to know that integrity and knowledge were worthless in the world. But they were precious to him. If he had a soul, he thought, its core would be warmed by the love of his sons and his wife and his grandchildren. But its fringes were insulated against the slime of Bethlehem by his morality and his principles. If Ramiz didn't see that now, he would understand in the end.

Omar Yussef went to the coat rack by the front door. He put on a beige parka.

'Dad, where are you going?'

Omar Yussef opened the door and felt the freshness of the cold air. 'I'm going to talk this over with someone.' He stepped outside.

CHAPTER 14

Omar Yussef walked up the hill toward the *souk*. He felt at once furious and calm. These gunmen scum of the Martyrs Brigades threatened him, but they chose not to do so to his face. They went to work on his son, instead. Why was everyone going behind his back? The gunmen went to Ramiz; Steadman connived with the schools inspector. It seemed to Omar Yussef that if anything was to be brought out into the open, it would be up to him to accomplish it. Naturally, he would do so alone.

In spite of his anger, Omar Yussef felt a sense of composure. It was based on the strength of belonging. He belonged in this town more than these gangsters. Hussein Tamari's clan was living in filthy tents on the periphery of the desert back when Omar Yussef's dear father was an admired figure whose opinion the leading families of Jerusalem respected. In his father's world, there was law and gentility. But in the desert, the traditions by which life was lived were as absolute and harsh as the sun. Tamari's people now congregated in the village of Teqoa, just south of

Bethlehem, but they were still as brutal as their nomadic fathers.

'Peace be upon you, *ustaz*.'

Omar Yussef stopped. 'And upon you, peace.'

'How are you?' The greeting was from one of his old pupils who worked now as an architect. Omar Yussef couldn't remember the name of the man, who was in his mid-twenties.

'I'm as well as can be expected,' Omar Yussef said. 'How is your business?'

'Well, not so good. In all this fighting a lot of buildings are being knocked down, but not many are being built.' The man laughed. 'Times are bad for architects. And I can't get into Jerusalem to my office, of course. All the checkpoints are closed and I have no permission to pass through them.'

Omar Yussef parted with the man and savored the friendly simplicity of the exchange. He remembered his name now – Khaled Shukri. His father had been killed in crossfire outside the hospital two years earlier. He wished he had remembered the name sooner, so that he might have inquired about his former pupil's mother. He had heard that she became chronically depressed after her husband's sudden death.

The calmness Omar Yussef had sensed in himself, the feeling of belonging in Bethlehem, was overwhelmed by his anger at the gunmen. Here was a boy who had worked hard at the Frères School and become a professional. Khaled Shukri's intention was to build his hometown into something lovely, to replace the neglected refugee slums with functional new homes and to refurbish decrepit Ottoman mansions as hotels and restaurants. The curfews and gunfights had destroyed his career, murdered his father and made his mother suicidal. This was the reward for his goodness. Yet the gunmen thrived, they whose accomplishments and talents were of the basest nature, they who would have been obliterated had there been law and order and honor in the town. Perhaps Bethlehem was their town, after all, and it was Omar Yussef who was the outlaw interloper here, peddling contraband decency and running a clandestine trade in morality.

As Omar Yussef approached Manger Square, women filled the streets of the *souk*, buying the food with which they would prepare the evening *iftar*. The village women sat in the shade at the side of the street with plastic baskets of coriander and tomatoes. Their breasts were massive and low, their black robes embroidered on the front with scarlet in the patterns specific to the Bethlehem area, and their faces were mauled by the sun and the dust so that their cheeks hung like the jowls of a bulldog. This was the tradition, the authenticity that Omar Yussef loved about his town. Yet the women sat in the dirt, desperate for a little shade while they traded for a few shekels. Afterwards they would bypass the checkpoints, crossing the stony hillside to their villages. Prosperity was reserved for those who scorned all tradition and toil. For Hussein Tamari and his men, this town was no different from the empty wastes of the desert they came from. It was a place that belonged to the one who would use the greatest force, and if there was an oasis within it, then it was they and no one else to whom access would be given.

Omar Yussef crossed Manger Square. As he passed Khamis Zeydan's police station, a woman went by him with a baby. He remembered then that Maryam had told him Khaled Shukri had become a father. No wonder he was so cheerful. Omar Yussef wondered why his former pupil hadn't mentioned the birth. Maryam had told him about it more than a month ago, so perhaps Shukri no longer considered it news. Omar Yussef descended the steps at the side of the Church of the Nativity, resting his hand on the mottled, brown stones of the basilica wall as he did so because the steep flight made him dizzy, and went down the hill. He must stop in and see Khaled Shukri to make it clear that he hadn't forgotten about the birth. No doubt he would find a young man, doused in thin vomit, still too happy with the new arrival to wonder how he would provide for it in a destroyed town that no longer needed an architect.

Omar Yussef saw the row of expensive cars parked on the roadside. They belonged to the Martyrs Brigades. He approached the building next to the cars.

It occurred to him that, with his first baby, Khaled Shukri would still be at the stage of laughing each time his child vomited. A baby is happy after it spews up, smiling with a sense of relief. *Perhaps that ought to be our natural, unconstrained reaction to the world around us*, Omar Yussef thought. *We learn to restrain ourselves, because we are taught that there is something disgusting about vomit. Imagine all the bile I should have heaved out that instead sat inside me, entering my bloodstream, carried to my brain and through my heart. It's becoming too much for my system. I will have to heave, to cleanse myself of all the hate and frustration and disgust.* He thought of Shukri's baby once more. It would vomit and scream. Both were genuine, wild, real. *Yes*, he thought, *it's time for me to scream.*

Omar Yussef stepped into the stairwell. Two gunmen looked toward him from the landing. The sign on the wall, which bore an official crest with a standing eagle and a national flag, said that this was the office of a government ministry. Like everyone else in Bethlehem, Omar Yussef knew that this was where the Martyrs Brigades spent their lazy days.

'Who are you?' said the older of the two guards, who was in his thirties, lifting his Kalashnikov and slinging it over his shoulder.

'I'm here to see Abu Walid.'

The younger gunman leaned against the banister. He regarded Omar Yussef sullenly. Omar Yussef recognized him as the boy who had tried to prevent him from parking his car outside George Saba's house the previous morning.

'Oh, you're the detective,' the young man said. 'Are you here to investigate Abu Walid?'

Omar Yussef wondered if the gunman had checked up on him and discovered that he was only a schoolteacher. He couldn't tell if the youth's tone had a sarcasm aimed directly at him, or if he was merely insolent to everyone.

'Well, I'm not here to check the records of the Ministry of Planning and International Co-operation,' Omar Yussef said, gesturing to the sign on the wall. He mounted the steps.

The other gunman, who seemed disconcerted by the rudeness of his colleague toward an older man, stopped Omar Yussef politely. 'Let me see your papers, uncle.'

Omar Yussef made his choking, spitting laugh. 'Is this an Israeli checkpoint? Abu Walid will recognize me.'

The gunman stepped aside and Omar Yussef entered what had been the foyer of the government office. There were a dozen men on a series of low, black sofas. They sprawled uncomfortably, as only men who spent most of their nights awake would do at one in the afternoon. It was cold in the unheated room and the men wore their olive parkas and camouflage jackets zipped up. Their weapons lay on the shiny coffee tables and on the floor next to the couches. The air smelled of cigarettes, a scent carried constantly in the men's clothing.

Omar Yussef noticed Hussein Tamari in the corner. He leaned on the arm of a sofa, talking quietly to Jihad Awdeh. The gray Astrakhan hat obscured Awdeh's face. He was looking at his hands, rubbing his fingernails against his knuckles.

As Omar Yussef picked his way past the extended legs of snoozing gunmen, careful not to step on their rifles, Hussein Tamari looked up.

'Greetings, uncle,' he said.

'Double greetings,' Omar Yussef said.

'Who are you?'

'I am Omar Yussef, the history teacher at the UNRWA Girls School and the father of Ramiz Sirhan, who had a visit from you today at his cellular telephone store.'

Hussein Tamari's eyebrows rose. His broad, tanned cheeks rolled, as he dropped his jaw. He sat upright and rubbed the narrow crown of his head in surprise.

Omar Yussef noticed Hussein Tamari's MAG machine gun. It lay beside the sofa. It had been hidden by Tamari's slouching torso, until Omar Yussef's arrival made him sit up. His tongue was dry, but he wouldn't let it stop him from talking.

'I came to see you because I want you to know that I am available any time you have anything to say. You don't need to go to my son. You can come to me at home or at the school.'

The Astrakhan hat lifted. Unlike Hussein Tamari, Jihad Awdeh was not taken aback by Omar Yussef's appearance in the room. 'At the school? I thought you retired.'

Damn Steadman, Omar Yussef thought. 'The information about my retirement is as flawed as the story you told my son today.'

Hussein Tamari put a hand on Jihad Awdeh's shoulder and addressed Omar Yussef. 'Don't be angry, my brother. We only wanted to be sure that everyone understood the situation. Please sit, Abu Ramiz. I wish I could offer you coffee, but in view of the holy month . . . I hope you will sit and talk in friendship.' He stood and held out his hand.

This man surely wants me dead, but he can't attack me in front of all these people, even if they are his gang, Omar Yussef thought. *It would leak out and he would find himself at war with all my relatives among the Sirhans. How real is this handshake, though? What does it mean? Is it really only a sign of hospitality, a formal requirement upon him to welcome a man who has come into his domain, even if he considers him an enemy? Or is he somehow drawing me onto his side?* Omar Yussef decided he had defused the immediate threat by his direct approach to Tamari. It had been easier than he expected.

Then it occurred to him that this could be the hand that killed Dima Abdel Rahman. There might be traces of her skin under those dirty fingernails where Hussein Tamari had scratched at her buttocks. But he couldn't decline to shake that hand without making things worse than they had been before he entered Tamari's headquarters. He took Tamari's hand. It was thick and the skin was gritty with dirt, but Tamari's grasp was mild. It carried no unusual strength, no attempt to intimidate. He asked Omar Yussef to sit beside him on the couch and kept hold of his hand as he questioned him about the effect of the curfews on the school.

As they talked, Omar Yussef saw that Jihad Awdeh watched him keenly. Awdeh slouched low on his sofa, his hips balanced at the front edge and his shoulders nestled deep and flat in the back cushion. He rested his elbow on the arm of the sofa and held his head with his hand, spreading his fingers into the curls of the Astrakhan hat so that his face could barely be seen.

Omar Yussef almost forgot the tension with which he had entered the room. He found it hard to maintain his anger toward Hussein Tamari. The man was stupid and brutal, but he behaved with a traditional politeness that appealed to Omar Yussef. It was as though Omar Yussef came to Tamari's tent in a previous era, emerging from the desert and begging the hospitality that tribes commanded of each other in emulation of the Prophet's generosity to strangers.

Tamari repeated the report that Omar Yussef had retired. With an ingratiating smile, he said he hoped it wasn't so, because Palestine needed to educate its children well and good teachers were in short supply.

'It's true that I told the American director I might retire, but I haven't made a decision,' Omar Yussef said.

'Why did you tell him that?' Jihad Awdeh's voice was low. He spoke without removing his hand from his face, so that the words seemed to come from the dark, hard eyes that looked out from between his fingers.

Omar Yussef realized that he could think of no good excuse for his talk of retirement. He had been carried away by the formal warmth of Hussein Tamari. Certainly he couldn't say that it was because he wanted time to clear George Saba of the charge of collaboration in murder. 'It's not a matter of any importance,' he said. 'Once you have been a teacher as long as I have, you will teach until you die.'

'In that case, if you are planning retirement from teaching, perhaps that means you are planning to die,' Jihad Awdeh said.

Hussein Tamari looked at Awdeh quickly.

'I only meant that once you begin to teach, you will always be a teacher,' Omar Yussef said. He sharpened his voice. 'Just as once you have killed, you will always be a killer.'

Jihad Awdeh took the hand away from his face. He smiled, but his eyes were lidded. 'You mean that they are both ways of life, teaching and killing? Things that we do for money?'

'Do you kill for money?' Omar Yussef said.

He saw Hussein Tamari sit forward as if to

interrupt, but Jihad Awdeh seemed to relish the opportunity to flourish his own nastiness. 'I kill for money when it's strictly a matter of business between strangers.' Awdeh lifted himself out of his slouch and reached a finger toward Omar Yussef. 'But you're my brother, so I'd have to kill *you* free of charge.'

Hussein Tamari turned aside Jihad Awdeh's finger. He gave Awdeh a glance of annoyance.

Omar Yussef realized that he couldn't allow Awdeh to intimidate him. If they saw his weakness, they would soon come after him, in spite of the necessarily pleasant reception tradition demanded Hussein Tamari give him now. He had to punch back.

'I want you to see to it that George Saba is freed,' Omar Yussef said. 'I believe you know that he is not a collaborator. He is a friend of mine and I have come to you to ask that you free him.'

'That's a matter for the courts,' Hussein Tamari said.

'Let's be realistic, Abu Walid,' Omar Yussef said. 'George Saba confronted you and Jihad Awdeh on his roof. Two days later he was arrested. There is a connection that I prefer not to spell out. I ask only that you use the same influence with which you put him in jail to get him out of there.'

Omar Yussef was surprised that Hussein Tamari didn't respond, nor did he seem upset at the accusation. Perhaps he considered framing George Saba a minor infraction compared to his other activities and thought it was nothing to get angry about.

'How could you know that he's not a collaborator, unless you were working with the Israelis?' Awdeh said.

'How is it possible that *you* discovered he is an Israeli collaborator, unless *you* are working for the Israelis?' Omar Yussef said. He felt the strength that he had sensed in himself earlier when he had sat with Ramiz growing, and he pressed his hands together. 'An innocent man's life is at stake. Don't waste my time with your cheap accusations.'

'No one's time will be wasted any longer,' Jihad Awdeh said. 'In fact, it'll all be sorted out tonight.'

'What do you mean?'

'The trial of your friend George Saba is set for tonight at eleven o'clock.'

'When was this scheduled?'

'You'd have to ask the judge. Apparently, he became interested in moving quickly.'

Hussein Tamari rested his hand on Omar Yussef's arm, and this time he gripped it tightly, with command. 'You see that this matter is out of my hands.'

Omar Yussef rose. What use was the strength he had felt? He was powerless in the face of the world. Even if he believed he carried some inner, moral toughness, it was no use to his friend. As he walked to the door, he felt the gunmen's eyes burning the flesh on his back.

CHAPTER 15

Attorney Marwan Natsha decorated the entryway to his office with gaudily framed Koranic calligraphy and copies of his diplomas. Omar Yussef stopped to cast his eye over them, welcoming the opportunity to catch his breath after three flights of stairs. The degrees were in thick, black Gothic script. They were from Hebron University and issued in the mid-eighties. The segments from the Koran were in slashy kufic characters, curling the names of the Prophet and his followers around the edges, as lush as the stitching on an embroidered cushion. The extracts from the Muslim holy book suggested to Omar Yussef that the man might be religious, perhaps even a supporter of Hamas. It gave him some hope. Omar Yussef was no believer, but he had observed that, among his compatriots, the more a man followed the way of Allah, the less likely he was to accede in the corruption of the law. Maybe this lawyer would put up a good defense for George.

The quiet anteroom was dark and cold as twilight came on. Omar Yussef flicked the light

164

switch. There were more framed pages from the Koran and a tan leather couch so worn that it looked as though someone had passed a bad night's sleep on it in sandpaper pajamas. A desk lamp cast a dim glow from within the back office against a frosted glass door. Omar Yussef opened the door.

A long, thin man looked up from a file of papers through a cloud of cigarette smoke. There was a guilty cast to his gray face. The religious calligraphy was decorative and nothing more, Omar Yussef realized. Hamas supporters didn't smoke Rothmans during Ramadan. Omar Yussef left the frosted door open to create a fresh draft in the blue air, so that he might breathe a little.

Marwan Natsha lifted himself from his chair. He moved like a man with a hangover dragging himself out of bed. He gestured questioningly with his cigarette. Omar Yussef waved that it didn't offend him. There was relief in the attorney's sad, wet eyes. He flopped back into his seat and pushed the papers away from him across his desk with a bony hand.

'I am Omar Yussef. I am a friend of George Saba.'

Marwan Natsha dropped his thin shoulders forward. His slack chin rested on the knot of his gray tie, and his melancholy face became even more desolate.

'I understand you are to defend George at the hearing tonight. I have information that will help you.'

'Oh, dear.'

Omar Yussef paused.

Marwan Natsha looked up and sighed. His voice sounded like it ached in his throat, as your legs might on the day after a long walk. 'Uncle, you don't understand.'

'What is there to understand? This is a capital trial. I want to save George Saba.'

'Nothing can save him, sir.'

Omar Yussef pulled his chair closer to Marwan Natsha's desk. The lawyer edged back into his chair as though he were threatened by the advance of the man across the cherrywood from him.

'I have known George since he was a boy. I was with him a few nights ago when he went to his house to confront some Martyrs Brigades people. He forced them away from his home, but they threatened to return. When they came back, it was to make allegations of collaboration. This whole case is a matter of revenge on their part.'

There was no sign in Marwan Natsha's gray face that he found anything encouraging in what Omar Yussef said. If anything, he seemed deeply discomfited.

'I also discovered information at the site of Louai Abdel Rahman's murder that convinces me Hussein Tamari took part in that killing. I believe he returned later to kill Louai's wife, because he discovered that she gave me information about his role in the shooting. Tamari is also the man who has framed George Saba.' Omar Yussef waited for

166

Marwan Natsha to ask a question. 'Are you not interested? We don't have very long.'

'We have until eleven tonight.'

'That's only six hours.'

'Six hours. Six days. It makes no difference. I'm afraid he's going to be found guilty.'

Omar Yussef was angry. 'I found a bullet from Hussein Tamari's gun at the place where Louai was killed.'

Marwan Natsha lit another Rothman with a shaky hand and was silent.

'That means Tamari was there,' Omar Yussef said.

'But it doesn't mean he shot Louai Abdel Rahman.' Marwan Natsha curved his spine slowly forward over the desk as though testing each vertebrae and picked a photocopied sheet of paper from the file. 'This is the ballistics report on Louai Abdel Rahman's death. The two bullets that killed him were from some kind of American sniper rifle the Israelis use. It's called an M24, apparently. I don't really know much about it, but you can read the report if you like. It's rather technical. In any case, I don't think that's the kind of gun Tamari has.'

'No, it's not.'

'Well, that's that, then.'

'No, it isn't. What motive did George have to collaborate in the death of Louai Abdel Rahman? None. But Tamari had a motive. He wanted to get Louai out of the way so that the family would

167

no longer have anyone among the resistance factions to protect them. As soon as Louai was killed, Hussein Tamari's brother simply took over the Abdel Rahmans' autoshops.'

'And the Israelis didn't have a motive to murder Louai? He killed a settler recently, I gather.'

'Of course the Israelis have a motive. But what motive did George have to be their collaborator? Hussein Tamari had a motive to collaborate, but not George.'

Marwan Natsha cleared his throat with a rattle like a snare roll. 'If you think I'm going to enter the court and tell the bench that the head of the resistance in Bethlehem is an Israeli collaborator, you'd better think again, Abu . . . ?'

'Ramiz.'

'Abu Ramiz.'

Omar Yussef felt himself growing hot. 'Then there is the death of Louai's wife. She was killed after George Saba's arrest. He couldn't have been involved.'

'Who said he was?'

'No one. I just mean that it's more likely that Louai and his wife were killed by the same person.'

'Why is that more likely?'

'Do you think there are two people out there who'd want to kill someone from the Abdel Rahman family? Two random, unconnected people who decide to murder someone in the same family? The two deaths are connected. If George Saba was part of the first death, he couldn't have been involved in the second since he was in jail. Therefore, George is not the connection. Someone else is. That makes George innocent of Louai's death.'

'As I heard, the lady in question was raped. Clearly there are many men in this town who, to put it bluntly, would have an incentive to do that, particularly to a woman with no husband to protect her. In any event, it's not my case, and I couldn't bring it up tonight with the judges. It wouldn't be admissible.' Marwan Natsha shuffled through the pages before him on the desk. 'Do you read Hebrew, Abu Ramiz?'

'No.'

Marwan Natsha gave Omar Yussef a pitying look. 'This is a report in *Yediot Aharonoth*. It's an Israeli newspaper. It's dated two days after Louai Abdel Rahman's death. It's the story of how the Shin Bet used a Palestinian collaborator to guide them to Louai and to identify the victim. There's a lot of stuff about Louai's resistance activities in the article. It calls him one of the most dangerous terrorists in the Bethlehem area – that's the precise wording. Then it goes on to detail the role of the collaborator in making sure that the Israelis killed the right guy. Apparently, it's absolutely essential to these kinds of assassinations. Without a collaborator on the ground, they can't assassinate anyone from the resistance. So, the article says, there was a collaborator up close to Louai Abdel Rahman who identified him to the Israeli sniper. You see?'

'Yes, I understand that.'

'I don't think you do. Someone has to be guilty here. There is a collaborator. Even the Israelis admit it in their newspaper. Now, our police don't seem to be capable of producing such strong detective work as you've done on this case. But I'm sure they'd tell you that if the results of an investigation led them to the most dangerous man in town, Hussein Tamari, they'd let the fall guy – take the fall.' Marwan Natsha opened his bony hands wide. 'That's George Saba.'

'You're telling me you don't even believe George Saba is guilty?'

'There isn't so much evidence against him. It's true.'

'Then your job is simple.'

'Well, that's also true. But not in the way you mean. My job would be simple whether the case against George was weak or strong. My job is to keep my head down. In State Security Court, defense attorneys are, by definition, supposed to consider the state and its security first. If a collaborator gets away with it, the Israelis will find it easy to recruit more. If someone is seen to be punished for collaboration, it makes it harder for Israel to get others to betray their comrades.'

'Even if the man who pays the penalty isn't really a collaborator? He just dies as a symbol of all the real collaborators who're out there but can't be detected by our security forces? You can't be serious?'

Marwan Natsha shrugged.

Omar Yussef pulled off his flat cap and ran a hand across his wisps of hair. 'You're not from Bethlehem, are you, Mister Natsha?'

'No, I'm from Hebron.' Natsha smiled at the mention of his hometown. He seemed relieved, as though the conversation had moved on from the tiresome business of the trial to polite smalltalk.

'Then imagine how you would feel if some gang took over *your* town. Would you not do what George Saba did?'

'My brother Abu Ramiz, they *have* taken over my hometown. That's why I don't care what they do in Bethlehem. It's the same everywhere in Palestine. It's too big to fight.'

'Then we all have the same problem. It should unite us. We have a common cause, all Palestinians against these gunmen.'

'It's only in the most superficial way that we Palestinians manage to be united even against the Israelis. Do you think we're capable of unity at all? People aren't like that. I ran away from what the gunmen are doing in my hometown of Hebron. Why would I make a stand against them in Bethlehem?'

Omar Yussef pitied this man. He wondered what made Natsha flee his home. With what outrage might the Martyrs Brigades have sucked the will out of him?

'I'm very sorry, uncle,' Marwan Natsha said, 'but I have to lock up and go to an *iftar* now.'

'Will you pray for George Saba, before you break the fast?'

'No, I'll be thinking of the food, because I'm hungry, and I'll be trying to forget that I have to go before this damned court later tonight. *You* can pray for George Saba.'

'I'll be praying for you.'

Marwan Natsha held Omar Yussef's gaze a moment, as though he were weighing whether he was, after all, a more promising recipient of someone's devotions than a condemned man. Coughing, he stood and gathered the papers from his desk. He stubbed out his cigarette and picked up his briefcase. He was down the stairs so quickly on his long legs that he left Omar Yussef behind in the dark.

In the corridor, Omar Yussef lifted one of Marwan Natsha's legal diplomas off the wall. The frame shook in his hand. He flung it down the first flight of stairs. The glass shattered against the wall. Three flights below, Marwan Natsha's steps halted for a moment, then he moved on.

Omar Yussef listened to Natsha's cough receding along the empty road. He walked down the stairs and picked up the broken frame with the attorney's diploma and carried it back to the office door. He leaned it against the window. There was a smear of dirt on the parchment and he was sorry for that. Slowly, he went down the stairs.

Across the street, the hill dropped quickly. Omar Yussef looked beyond the agricultural fringe of

Bethlehem and into the Judean Desert. The shallow folds of the sterile hills below rippled down to the Dead Sea. In the first reflected light of the night, the desert was illuminated a bright, milky blue. It looked like the cratered surface of the moon. Omar Yussef felt as though his own existence traveled a more distant orbit than that dead satellite, gliding silent above the impossibly frenetic, cynical reality of the rest of the planet. He wondered if there was any place as barren anywhere on earth.

CHAPTER 16

In the State Security Court, the crowd murmured with the animated tenor of a theater audience before a first night. As he found himself a seat, Omar Yussef felt that this was, indeed, a staged drama, scripted and contrived, a tragedy that would run forever in his own distressed mind. The hall was large and plainly painted, with a low ceiling. It was lit by fluorescent tubes that stuttered through a floating layer of cigarette smoke to cast a sickly blue flicker over the people crowded into the rows of chairs. Omar Yussef figured there must be about a thousand spectators packed into the plastic seats and jammed along the aisles at the sides of the hall. A dozen policemen guarded the front of the court. Khamis Zeydan paced behind them, murmuring orders. Acquaintances of Omar Yussef smiled and waved to him through a screen of excitable, bobbing heads.

The only people in the room who seemed quiet were Muhammad and Yunis Abdel Rahman. The father and brother of the man in whose death George Saba was accused of collaborating leaned against a square pillar at the side of the room. The father looked sad, but Yunis Abdel Rahman's bony face was flushed and indignant as he stared at the empty bench where the judges would sit. The father glanced at Yunis, but the boy refused to acknowledge the older man's presence. Omar Yussef detected something desperate and lost and ashamed in the way Muhammad Abdel Rahman tried to catch his son's eye.

Though the windows of the courtroom were closed, Omar Yussef felt cold. It was as though all these bodies exuded such animosity toward the accused that they were incapable of generating warmth. He checked his watch. The hearing was due to begin in five minutes and he had been lucky to find a seat. As he settled into his place, the jostling spectators in the aisles argued with the press of new onlookers shoving their way through the door. It was late at night and they were excited and irritable, like children allowed to stay up past their bedtime.

Omar Yussef overheard the stupid rumors of George Saba's evil passing through the crowd. It was all he could do to keep quiet. There would be no point in defending his friend before these people. It disgusted him that there were, among his neighbors, so many who would gladly see a man condemned to death, for it was not an acquittal that the crowd had come to witness. He felt saddened that his town was so beaten down and full of hate that its highest pleasure would be the punishment of what it perceived as a single, small element in the machine of oppression. He looked about for Habib Saba, but couldn't find him in the crowd.

The lawyers came to their places at the tables facing the bench. Some of the people in the front rows leaned between the officers in the cordon of policemen to shake hands with the prosecutor. They were handshakes of congratulations, and the prosecutor smiled broadly, as though everything were already finished and the case were settled in his favor. Omar Yussef knew that collaborators received unfair trials in Gaza, but he had thought that in Bethlehem there was more decency than that. Marwan Natsha sat alone at his table. In the fluorescent light, he was grayer than when Omar Yussef visited him that afternoon. His height, which should have made him commanding, only highlighted that he was too thin, unhealthily so. It seemed as though he might easily be snapped in half, like a tall, withered flower that had already shed its few melancholy buds. Natsha brought no documents that Omar Yussef could see, not even the file that had lain upon his desk. The only objects he placed on the table before him were a pack of Rothman's and a tin ashtray, which he seemed absorbed in filling.

Khamis Zeydan moved behind his policemen and broke up the congratulatory handshaking. He spoke a curt sentence that swiftly replaced the prosecutor's smile with a look of hurt and slight embarrassment. Omar Yussef watched his old friend, who turned a stern glance on the spectators crowded behind the prosecutor. At least the police chief was ready to remind people that this was not an entertainment, that a man's life was in the scales of whatever kind of justice might prove to be on display. There was a tension in Khamis Zeydan's jaw and an intensity about his eyes that suggested he was suffering at this moment. By this time of night, he was usually fairly well drunk and it could merely be the strain of maintaining his sobriety that showed on his rigid visage. Omar Yussef hoped that it was simply because, as a lawman, Khamis Zeydan couldn't bear to see justice turned into a popular circus. Then it struck him: it was because the police chief knew the truth behind Louai Abdel Rahman's death, knew the identity of the true collaborator, an identity that Omar Yussef only suspected.

Omar Yussef reconsidered his suspicion that Khamis Zeydan had tipped off Louai's murderer to the fact that Dima Abdel Rahman knew of 'Abu Walid.' No one else outside of Omar Yussef's immediate family could have known what Dima had told him, except Khamis Zeydan. If he had realized who he should warn about the clue Dima had given Omar Yussef, it was surely because Khamis Zeydan also knew the details of Louai's murder. Omar Yussef knew better than to expect the police automatically to arrest a killer, the way things were these days, particularly if that murderer were the head of the Martyrs Brigades.

But he hadn't considered that the police chief would protect the guilty man at the cost of endangering another innocent person. Perhaps Khamis Zeydan hadn't known that Hussein Tamari would kill Dima. Maybe he expected him to warn her to stay quiet, to frighten her, even to beat her. But Zeydan knew with whom he was dealing, and it would surely have occurred to him that, if he passed on damaging information, Hussein Tamari might silence Dima for good.

Omar Yussef wondered how much Khamis Zeydan had told Hussein Tamari. The Martyrs Brigades chief had issued his warning to Omar Yussef earlier that day through his son Ramiz, because the gunman feared angering Omar Yussef's entire clan. A direct approach or a physical attack would prompt a small war. But maybe Tamari didn't know that Omar Yussef was the one to receive Dima's tip about 'Abu Walid.' If Tamari thought only that Omar Yussef was agitating for George Saba's freedom without any real information, he might feel less threatened. Omar Yussef figured Khamis Zeydan would've told Tamari what Dima revealed, but the policeman might not have given away his old friend's identity. Perhaps it was because Khamis hadn't said *who* Dima told that Tamari had made do with the mild warning through Ramiz. In that case, he wouldn't feel threatened enough by Omar Yussef to kill him. Not yet.

Omar Yussef didn't want to believe that Khamis

Zeydan had fingered Dima, and anyway, he had to consider that someone might have killed her for some other reason. It might not even have been Abu Walid. She could have gone outside to meet someone, a secret lover, for all Omar Yussef knew. Or, as Khamis Zeydan suggested, her in-laws may have decided that she was carrying on an affair and murdered her to preserve the family honor. But maybe he was just making excuses for his old friend. Whatever decency he believed he detected in Khamis Zeydan's comportment at the front of the courtroom had to be balanced by the fact that the police chief was presiding over a terrible distortion of a legal proceeding. If he would stand by, organizing his troops, as the court prepared to legitimize the murder of an innocent man, what would he not do?

At 11:05 P.M., Hussein Tamari entered with a phalanx of armed men. The crowd gave way and the people in the front row rose in haste to give up their seats. Tamari's guards shoved those who were slow in moving. Tamari smiled, acknowledging greetings benignly, like a monarch. When Tamari was already seated, Jihad Awdeh slipped along the side of the room. He wore the Saddam Hussein-style hat again and didn't respond to any of the salutations from the crowd. He allowed himself one sneering smile as he passed Muhammad Abdel Rahman. The dead man's father looked down at his feet, but his son glared back at Awdeh, who only seemed yet more amused by the boy's defiance. As though he had been waiting for Tamari's contingent to arrive before he began, one of the policemen called out for the crowd to rise, and three judges entered from the door behind the bench.

A thin silence came over the thousand men in the hall, as the head judge slammed down his gavel. He was a portly man with skin the color and softness of coffee cake and gray hair that puffed high and back like a French crooner. His mouth was set and angry, but his eyes shifted with fear. He was a man Omar Yussef knew to be upset with the workings of the government. They had met at a UN function only a few months previously. The judge had enjoyed spilling scandalous details of the legal system's powerlessness in the face of the Martyrs Brigades gangsters and their cohorts in the government. It occurred to Omar Yussef that perhaps this would be the time for the judge to declare that he would no longer be pushed around. But, when he saw the way the judge averted his eyes from the Martyrs Brigades people in the front row, he sensed that this was a vain hope.

The judge announced that the State Security Court for the Bethlehem District was in session. He called for the accused to be brought into the court. George Saba came through the same door by which the judges entered. The crowd immediately called out its own sentence, demanding the death of the man they saw before them and doing

180

so in Allah's name. Indeed, George Saba seemed a little dead already and made no sign that he heard the eruption of hatred accompanying his entrance. He wore Omar Yussef's herringbone coat, which appeared much smaller than it had in the cell that morning. His hands were cuffed in front of his belly and his hair stood wildly. It astonished Omar Yussef that it was only fifteen hours ago that he had sat in conversation with George. Even from halfway back in the big room, he could see that his friend had a black eye and a bruise on his cheek. George stood against a table with a policeman on either arm. He hunched his shoulders and let his head flop onto his chest.

Omar Yussef felt his vision clouded by tears. He wiped them away with his fingers. He tried not to listen to the specific words of those around him as they cried out against George Saba. He heard nothing but their animal, blood-thirsty tone. He sat and leaned his forehead on his hand, while the spectators shouted.

The judge quieted the crowd with repeated slaps of his gavel that seemed to vibrate through his smooth, chubby face. He read the docket, which pitted the government against the lonely, battered man in Omar Yussef's coat. He asked the prosecutor to outline his case.

The prosecutor stood and turned sideways, so that his voice would carry through the still crowd. He flipped his black court robe dramatically along his arm so that it seemed to Omar Yussef to rise like the looming cape of some terrible, dark sorcerer. When he lowered it, perhaps George Saba's swaying carcass would have disappeared magically from the dock.

'Your Honors, the case is simple. The accused guided an Occupation Forces special unit to Police Officer Louai Abdel Rahman, whom the accused knew to be wanted by the Occupation Forces. Callously he pointed out Officer Abdel Rahman, who was immediately martyred by the Occupation Forces. The accused has confessed repeatedly to the charges. The State demands the death penalty, which must be imposed upon all those who collaborate with the Occupation Forces and participate in the assassinations of the martyrs who struggle for the freedom of Palestine. Thank you, Your Honors.'

The prosecutor lowered his arm. George Saba had not been spirited away by magic. He remained standing, but it would have been better for him had he disappeared through a showman's trap-door. The crowd resumed its shouting once more, mingling it with applause for the statement of the prosecutor, who turned to nod gravely in acknowledgement.

The judge called on Marwan Natsha, who stubbed out a cigarette, raised himself from his chair and spoke quickly in a strangled, high voice. 'The accused pleads guilty, Your Honor.' The defense attorney then sat, before he had quite yet stood straight, and lit another smoke.

Even the crowd seemed surprised that there was to be no defense. The judge stared at Marwan Natsha for a moment. It was in these few seconds, Omar Yussef decided, that a man's morality takes a big gulp of air before plunging beneath the surface of the sea of iniquity on which Bethlehem wallowed. The judge said nothing to Natsha. He was holding that breath. Instead he turned to George Saba.

'George Habib Saba, this court finds you guilty on all counts . . .'

Applause began and a cheer.

'. . . and sentences you to death by firing squad at a date to be determined by the president.'

The cheer blasted from the crowd with such force that it seemed to drive it to its feet. Omar Yussef rose with it, to see George Saba pulled limply out of the door by his two guards. The judges waited embarrassedly for him to pass along the narrow space behind their bench, as though he were a cripple or a pensioner who must be allowed to pass along a crowded bus. In the doorway his legs gave way and the head judge stepped backwards to avoid a collision with the condemned man. The judge went as pale as George Saba. *Still the judge is holding his breath*, Omar Yussef thought. *He'll breathe out when he comes into contact with someone like me at another UN function, someone he thinks is sympathetic enough that he can expel some of the self-disgust he feels at his participation in this charade. He'll blame the system and take no responsibility for what happened here. I hope he tries it with me. I'll tell him I was in the courtroom, and I'll tell him that he has blood on his hands just as surely as the firing squad detailed to pull the trigger on George.*

Omar Yussef sat, exhausted. It was 11:15 P.M. The trial had lasted no time at all. Spectators shoved along the rows of chairs to leave, chatting about the scene as though it were a sporting occasion. Most had looked forward to a resolute defense that would draw the prosecutor to reveal more shocking details of George Saba's collaboration, in order to prove the case beyond all argument. Yet they satisfied themselves that at least the man would die.

When the crowd was gone, Omar Yussef stood and prepared to follow. He looked back toward the door. In the last row of chairs, a man wept on the arm of a priest. It was Habib Saba, whose shaking head rested against the black robe of Elias Bishara. Omar Yussef went slowly through the jumble of chairs and sat beside the old man.

'I had to wait until everyone left, Abu Ramiz,' Habib Saba said. 'I had to wait, or they would have noticed who I was.'

'They *should* have seen you. They should have been forced to acknowledge that George has a father who weeps for him. They treated him like someone who isn't human, Abu George.'

'It's all over for him, Abu Ramiz. They'll kill him now.'

'It takes some time for the president to sign the death warrant. We will clear his name in the meantime. Don't worry.' Omar Yussef pulled a monogrammed handkerchief from his trouser pocket and gave it to Habib Saba. 'Now that we know that we are working on a deadline, it will only make our efforts more forceful.'

'It can't be done, Abu Ramiz. It just can't. They don't need evidence against him. How can you prove that a case is false when they didn't even need to *make* a case? He was guilty automatically, because he's Christian, because he's not one of them.'

'I refuse to accept this.'

Habib Saba looked up. His red eyes seemed suddenly surprised and fearful. He looked pleadingly back and forth between Omar Yussef and Elias Bishara. 'Abu Ramiz, are you going to make more trouble for us?'

'More trouble? I want to aid you in saving your son.' Omar Yussef would have been appalled, if the long years of their friendship hadn't made him forgiving of Habib Saba's desperation and helplessness.

'Don't try. They will kill George, and then they will come and kill me and his family and destroy our house. You'll see. If you force them to cover their tracks, they'll obliterate everyone.'

'So you would let George die? He is to be a martyr to save your house?'

'Abu Ramiz.' Elias Bishara raised a cautionary

eyebrow at his old schoolteacher. 'We are all too emotional.'

Omar Yussef immediately regretted his harshness. He thought of Dima Abdel Rahman's body, face down in the pines with her buttocks scratched. Habib Saba was right. Dima was probably a casualty of his attempt to investigate the truth behind Louai's murder and to clear George of the charge of collaboration. He felt a flash of fear, as though the Martyrs Brigades might be waiting for him at that moment, to add his name to the list of corpses. He looked about the courtroom, but saw that it was empty, except for a single policeman stationed at the door.

Habib Saba collapsed against Omar Yussef's sleeve. 'I know you love him, Abu Ramiz. You've been a better guide to him than his father ever was able to be. I've been selfish and weak, and I still am. I don't deserve a son like him.' He raised his voice and cried out: 'I want them to shoot me instead of him. I want them to shoot me.'

Omar Yussef put his arm around Habib Saba's back and slipped it beneath his arm. He lifted him with difficulty to his feet. Elias Bishara took most of the weight. The three men went slowly to the door.

The policeman at the exit stepped hesitantly forward. 'Abu Ramiz,' he said, tentatively, as though he hardly dared speak to Omar Yussef. 'I have a girl in your class. Khadija Zubeida.'

Omar Yussef thought a moment. 'You are

Mahmoud. Khadija told me about you.' He remembered how the girl had come into the classroom with her father's exaggerated, hateful account of George Saba's arrest. He wanted to tell the policeman that he was a participant in a disgusting travesty and that he was breeding the ugliest strain of his people's wickedness into his daughter. Then he felt the heaviness of Habib Saba against his shoulder and heard the old man sob. He thought of how Habib suffered for failing his child. Omar Yussef nodded at the policeman. 'Khadija is a bright girl,' he said.

The policeman smiled broadly. 'Thank you, *ustaz*,' he said. As Omar Yussef and the priest took Habib Saba through the door, the policeman turned out the lights.

CHAPTER 17

The sentence of death on George Saba was five hours old when the bulldozer came to Omar Yussef's house. He heard its approach, through the most silent hour of the night, as he sat sleepless in his salon, his blank stare fixed on the sideboard where he kept the bottle of Johnny Walker for Khamis Zeydan's visits. He wanted a taste of the whisky now, raw and scorching in his throat. Because it was forbidden. Because it would damage him and he didn't care. Because it would make him numb. So he sat through those five hours, alone, choked and stifled by the absolute stillness outside and the chaotic frenzy of his frustration. He looked toward the dark window and wondered why the streets weren't full of people as angry as him, so that he could join them and cry out that an innocent man was condemned to die.

The electricity went out at 4:00 A.M., but Omar Yussef remained in his seat. He welcomed the darkness, because it let him forget the room, the town, the land in which he lived. He pulled his jacket around him as the deepest time of the night chilled the house. He touched the MAG cartridge casings in his pocket. They had been heated by the pressure of his hip. How could things that were components to an instrument of death be warmed by his body, when he felt so cold? He stood and moved toward the sideboard. He would have that drink.

In the dark, he hit his shin against the coffee table and cursed under his breath. He stepped to the sideboard, but the pain in his leg had cleansed him of the desire for the whisky. The shooting tremors from the nerves in his leg told him what was good for him. He must feel everything now, not dull it with alcohol. He had to remain aware, clearly and fully, knowing how important it was that he should not lose heart nor become distracted. He must be the opposite of Habib Saba. He could not be weak, self-centered. If he was lonely and miserable here in his dark, chilly living room, how much more sad and frozen must George Saba be in his cell, huddled in Omar Yussef's small overcoat against the night winds blustering through the bars in the windows? How much colder still in the ground where Dima lay buried? The thought of her undignified end, her body exposed and violated, filled him with a desire to avenge her and to preserve his own self-respect. He turned away from the sideboard.

Omar Yussef rubbed his shin and sat down, wincing. He worried about his physical fitness at the best of times. Now he would have a bruise across the bone for a week or two. It would bite into his nerves every time he took a shaky step. Nevertheless he was grateful for the pain, because as long as he suffered he was sure to be alive.

Then the Israelis came. There was a low growl along the hilltop above Dehaisha. Omar Yussef heard it and knew immediately that the soldiers had cut the electricity so they could operate without being seen. He wondered if he should wake Maryam, or Ramiz and his family downstairs in the basement apartment. He moved closer to the window and watched from the shadows.

A tank and an armored personnel carrier came along the road, churning the blacktop with their metal tracks. A massive digger followed. It was the height of two tanks stacked on top of each other. The tank and the APC set themselves on either side of the street at the corner a dozen yards before Omar Yussef's house. The digger came between the two, lowered its arm to cut into the tarmac and started to slice a trench across the main road. Its impact on the paving and the rocky earth beneath sounded like the noise you hear inside your head when you crunch a handful of peanuts with your mouth closed.

'Omar?' Maryam called to her husband, sleepily, from the bedroom at the back of the house. She came into the salon, wrapping herself in a woolen dressing gown. She pushed her ruffled hair from her face and peered into the darkened room.

'Don't come near the window,' Omar Yussef said. 'There are tanks outside.'

'What are they doing?' She walked toward his voice. He knew that she couldn't tell exactly where he was.

'I told you not to come to the window. Stay there. Go back to bed.'

'Are you crazy? How can I go to bed when the army is at the front door?'

'Then just stay there.'

'What are they doing?'

Omar Yussef looked back toward the digger. Its trench was halfway across the street already, perhaps six feet deep and two yards wide. 'They're digging a hole across the road.'

'Why?'

'I assume it's so that people won't be able to drive between Bethlehem and Dehaisha.'

'But why?'

It would surely be so the army could cut the Martyrs Brigades and Hamas into smaller pieces, making it harder for explosives and weapons to be transported. To move about, the gunmen would have to bring their rifles and explosives and mortars across the trench by hand. If they had to take their weapons into the open, there was a greater chance that they would be spotted and intercepted. In which case, the spotting and intercepting would be done outside Omar Yussef's front door, perhaps by snipers or helicopter missiles or tank shells, and it might be done when he or his grandchildren happened to be crossing the street. He didn't want Maryam to think about that. 'Just because they can, the bastards,' he said.

Even in the dark, he realized that Maryam didn't believe him. It was he who always told her that blind hatred of the soldiers led to misunderstanding of the army's tactics. People saw them as nothing more than cruel animals, and that was the first step to becoming just as vicious oneself.

'You usually don't talk about them like that, Omar.'

'Fine, then I don't know. I don't know why they're doing it. I just want them to go, so that we can fill in the big, damned hole in the road.'

Maryam moved across the room. Her eyes were accustomed to the dark by now. Anyway, she knew better than Omar Yussef where the furniture would be to obstruct her, because it was her role to clean it every week. She put her hand on her husband's shoulder and he reached up to hold her fingers.

'I thought they were coming for Jihad Awdeh,' she said.

The sound of that name caused Omar Yussef to shudder. He pictured Jihad Awdeh emerging with his grim, sneering smile from the darkness in the corners of the room. Why did Maryam mention Awdeh, though? It struck him that she might somehow have meant that the Israelis knew her husband was investigating the Martyrs Brigades; that the soldiers came to his house, aware that they would catch Awdeh there, stalking his kill.

'Why would they come to our house to look for Jihad Awdeh?'

'Not our house. Across the street. He just moved into the apartment building right there.'

'Which one?'

'The one where Amjad and Leila live.'

Omar Yussef looked out at the building. It was a four-story, square block with a dozen apartments and a tall television antenna in the shape of the Eiffel Tower on the roof. He searched the darkened windows for a malevolent face or a trace of the Saddam Hussein Astrakhan hat. 'I haven't seen him there.'

'He moved in two days ago. Leila told me yesterday. She's very worried that the soldiers will come and blow the place up or that there'll be a gunbattle. She already told Jihad not to let his men sit around in the hallway with their guns when her kids are around.'

'What did he say?'

'She said he was very polite and promised to keep the guns inside his apartment.'

'How nice of him.'

'His family moved in, too. Leila says he brought his wife and his two kids.'

Omar Yussef hadn't thought of Jihad Awdeh as a husband or father before. It seemed strange to imagine him sharing intimacies with a wife or dandling his children. He could even picture Hussein Tamari, burly and boisterous, playfully wrestling his young son. But he couldn't conceive

193

of Awdeh engaging in such innocent, homely pleasures.

Omar Yussef wondered if Jihad Awdeh knew he lived across the street from the UN schoolteacher who had confronted his boss Tamari only yesterday. Somehow, the thought of such a close proximity to Awdeh made him feel tenser than he would have if Maryam had told him that Hussein Tamari had moved in. There was something more unpredictable about Awdeh and, despite what he knew about Tamari's part in Louai's murder, Omar Yussef thought the senior Martyrs Brigades man was bound by codes of tribal honor that Awdeh would scorn. There was something basic and lupine about Awdeh that made Omar Yussef's mouth dry. When he entered Hussein Tamari's headquarters, he knew that at least there he was safe. Tamari wouldn't dishonor himself and his family by killing a guest. Omar Yussef considered what he would have done had Jihad Awdeh been in charge. He concluded that he would have been compelled to take the same action, but he wasn't sure that he would have left the gunmen's lair alive.

The digger reached the edge of the road. Omar Yussef moved away from the window a little and wondered if the driver intended to keep digging right through the middle of his house.

'Omar, your gun. The army might come in and find it,' Maryam said.

'It's not *my* gun. Anyway they aren't searching the house. Not with a mechanical digger, at least.'

As the digger pulled its tray up from the trench, there was a gush of water.

'They cut the pipes,' Maryam said.

The water shot into the air a moment, catching the faint, leaden light of the moon that filtered through the cloudy sky, then disappeared into the trench. The digger hovered for another plunge into the dirt, but then it turned and moved away. The APC moved out in its wake. The tank was the last to leave, spinning with a roar toward the hill that would take them over the back of Dehaisha to Beit Sahour and the army camp.

Maryam's grip on his hand remained tight until the sound of the tanks almost disappeared, then it loosened and Omar Yussef stroked her palm, silently. There was a moment when he almost felt calm, in the dark and the quiet with his wife. Then her strong grip returned and broke his reverie.

'What's that smell?' she said.

There was a damp rankness in the cold air. At the moment they smelled it, there was noise downstairs. Ramiz's children began to cry out and Omar Yussef could hear his son speaking urgently to his wife. The door opened at the bottom of the stairs and the children ran up them. Omar Yussef stood and went to the hallway. The smallest girl was crying. Nadia held her arms around her little sister's neck. Omar Yussef noted that Nadia was calm and quiet. He smiled and touched her cheek. Ramiz came up the stairs with little Omar, who was sniffling and not quite awake. He put the boy down on an armchair and gave a quick look at his parents.

'The basement is flooding,' he said, rushing back down the stairs.

Omar Yussef followed his son. At the foot of the stairs, the last two steps were already submerged. The water was black in the darkness, but Omar Yussef knew from the stink that it was sewage. The pipe the digger broke was spilling its contents into his house. He took off his loafers and socks, rolled the socks into a ball and placed them inside the loafers on the fifth step, and waded into the slimy water. Ramiz and Sara hurried past with the children's thin, foam mattresses and Ramiz's laptop.

Omar Yussef went to the back door, opened it and began to bail the sewage out into the night with a saucepan. His back hurt, bending to the water and flipping the pan up the basement steps. The cold swill rose almost to his knees. Its iciness soothed the bruise on his shin, but the smell made him want to puke. It seemed appropriate that he should be throwing filth out of his home with hopelessly insufficient tools. It was what he had been trying to do ever since George Saba's arrest. His mind had been full of anger and fear, frustration and intense focus since the Zubeida girl came into his classroom with the news of the raid on George's home. Now the ordure of his own town was right here, physical and disgusting, crawling up his legs and making him nauseous.

He stopped bailing and slowly straightened his back. He looked out into the night. Tomorrow they would mend the pipes. They would clean the basement and his grandchildren would sleep there again soon enough. But that would not be the end of the smell. The reek would remain in his nostrils, and he knew that in his dreams he would feel the ooze rising over his skin.

CHAPTER 18

Omar Yussef came down with a flu. It started in his legs, after the night's freezing immersion in the sewage downstairs. By the time the municipality cut off the flow of effluent through the pipes and Omar Yussef had tossed the mess out of his back door with a saucepan, his knees were stiff and burned feverishly to the touch. His back ached. His face was clammy. His pulse was fast.

Maryam sent her husband upstairs to rest and called in their neighbors to shovel out the remaining few inches of sewage from the basement and to scour the tiles until the stink of effluent receded. He lay on his bed. His back throbbed as though a small child were kicking it in time with his heartbeat. He would have to take off a day or two from his investigation to organize the repairs to the pipes and to his home. He would need to recuperate from the night's damp exertions. It was time that he didn't have to waste, and neither did George Saba. He tried to sit up, but his back rebelled and he fell, feeling very cold, though Maryam had lit the gas heater. Yet it was hot in the room, too, and he undid his shirt down to his belly. There was sweat in the hair about his navel. Still, he felt cold. Cold, when he should have been hot, and weak and feverish when he should have been forceful, standing strongly against the wrong done to George. He imagined his friend in the freezing cell at the police headquarters. He wondered what he would say if he could see Omar Yussef lying on his back with his shirt open over his slack, perspiring stomach and the heater turned on full.

There was a knock at the door. His neighbor Leila Salman looked in. She was a cheerful woman who worked for the head of the local university as a secretary. Omar Yussef enjoyed her company, because she was one of the few people he knew who was less interested in the intifada than in the history of art, recipes for stuffing dumplings with ground meat to make *kubbeh*, and archeology. She was not yet forty, and she had become quite fat after giving birth to her last child four years ago. She had a fulsome, motherly roundness that made Omar Yussef wonder what it would be like to touch her, to hold her. He often played with what might ensue if she were to enter his bedroom, but those fantasies typically didn't include his incapacitation through fever and a strained back. She bustled through the door in an old gray sweatsuit and pink dishwashing gloves and held out a small cup of coffee toward him.

'I made it *sa'ada* for you, Abu Ramiz, as you like it,' Leila said.

Omar Yussef tried to sit and accept the coffee, but his back gripped him and he collapsed. Leila put the coffee on the bedside table and placed her knee on the bed. She clutched Omar Yussef under his arms and pulled him upright. His cry of pain was muffled farcically by her large breasts. Omar Yussef cursed the pathetic figure he must make before a woman to whom he felt attracted. She sat on the edge of the bed and handed him the coffee.

'Umm Ramiz asked me to come over and help,' she said. 'Such a terrible mess down there.'

When she mentioned his wife, Omar Yussef felt ashamed and silly for his fantasies about Leila. He drank the coffee and breathed heavily.

'Leila, thank you for everything.'

'What are neighbors for these days, Abu Ramiz?'

The coffee had the delicious grittiness that Omar Yussef loved. He finished drinking and handed the cup to Leila on its gold-leaf saucer. 'Speaking of neighbors, I hear you have a new arrival in your building,' he said.

'Not just in our building. In the apartment right next door. It makes me shiver to think that those men and all their guns are just on the other side of the wall from the room where my children sleep.'

'Is it only Jihad Awdeh and his family?'

'The family, yes. There's his wife and two children, I think. But at all hours there are so many men, with all kinds of guns and I don't know what.

Last night I was sure the tanks that tore up the road outside had come to get him, or to destroy our entire building. I am just waiting for that night, and I'm certain it will come.'

'I'm sure it won't happen, Leila.'

'Then you're the only one who feels such certainty. Even the Martyrs Brigades are preparing for it.'

'What do you mean? They're fortifying the apartment?'

'No, they're planning where they'll run and hide. I went to Jihad Awdeh and asked him to keep his guns inside the apartment, so that my kids don't see them in the hall when they're out playing. He was very nice to me. He told me he'd keep the weapons out of the way. He seemed to like me, so I asked him if he wasn't worried that the Israelis would come for him.'

'What did he say?'

'He said, "I can see that you are worried I will draw the Jews down on your head, my sister. Don't worry. If they invade our town, I will leave the apartment. My family is here, after all, and I want them to be secure, too. I plan to take refuge inside the Church of the Nativity. The Jews won't dare enter, and so I'll be safe."'

'He would hide inside the church? He has no respect.'

'I don't think it's a matter of respect with him, Abu Ramiz. He's fighting them to the death, by the looks of all the weaponry in his apartment.

201

He'd do anything to get away from the Israelis, even if it means hiding in the very crypt where Jesus was born.'

'Would the monks let him in?'

'I suppose that depends whether he holds a gun on them or not, doesn't it? Not everyone wants to be a martyr.' Leila stood and took the coffee cup away. 'The monks would also have to consider whether barring the gunmen from the church would make it look like all the town's Christians were against the resistance. Everyone calls the Christians collaborators. Here would be their proof, right?'

Omar Yussef heard Leila's footsteps receding to the kitchen. The coffee cup tinkled as she set it down, then she descended the stairs to help with the clean up.

So Jihad Awdeh would run to the Church of the Nativity when the Israelis came for him. If he had a few minutes warning, the gunman could quickly be into the narrow streets of the *souk*. From there, he would only have to cross Manger Square and he'd be at the church. One of the most important churches anywhere in the world. Unless the priests closed the Gate of Humility before he got there, Awdeh would be inside. Then he would be safe. The soldiers wouldn't dare follow him into the dark, brown church. Omar Yussef imagined how the world would condemn the Israelis if they fought out a gun battle inside the Byzantine basilica, or if they finally shot down Jihad Awdeh on the fanlike staircase to the cave where Jesus was born.

It was a plan that might save Jihad Awdeh, but it would be a disaster for Bethlehem. Perhaps the Israelis would attack the church after all. Some of the priests might be killed. Or they might kick Jihad Awdeh out of the church and the town's Muslims would turn on the Christians. Omar Yussef wondered if he ought not to pass on the information to someone in the church hierarchy. With warning, they might be able to lock the gates and keep the gunmen out. He would go to Elias Bishara and warn him. When his back was better.

Omar Yussef wanted to lie down again, but he was stuck in the upright position in which Leila had left him. He edged a little lower in the bed, but only succeeded in sliding his back into a painful curve. With a great effort, he dropped onto his side and lay panting, his heavy breathing rasping in time with the throbbing in the small of his back.

It was in this position that Khamis Zeydan found him in the early evening. Omar Yussef heard the police chief's hearty voice downstairs and Maryam's answering laughter. She was enjoying the crisis, her anger at what the Israelis had done mitigated by the generosity with which her friends came to her aid. Omar Yussef knew that Khamis Zeydan would come upstairs to see him. He struggled to roll onto his back, but he couldn't move. He was sweating thickly when the police chief entered.

'Abu Ramiz, you look terrible.' Khamis Zeydan pulled a chair to the edge of the bed. He was about to sit when he decided to shift Omar Yussef into a more comfortable position. 'Let's get you sitting straight.'

'I can manage,' Omar Yussef said.

'Even so.' Khamis Zeydan lifted his old friend and sat him with a pillow behind his back against the center of the headboard.

Omar Yussef shoved him away. 'Leave me alone.'

Khamis Zeydan retained the good humor he had shared with Maryam and the crowd downstairs. He waved his black-gloved prosthetic hand, playfully. 'This reminds me of the time I was shot in the back in Damascus, after I escaped from Jordan during Black September. Did I ever tell you about that? I was almost arrested by King Hussein, and I had to escape across the Jordanian border to Syria with Abu Bakr, you know, my friend from Majdal who's now down in Gaza working for General Intelligence. But we knew someone was following us. In the end, they got to me when I was about to leave for Lebanon. The doctors said I was very lucky the bullet didn't hit my spine, or I'd be in even worse health than you now. Of course, I imagine the only thing that *could* make anybody's health worse than yours is a bullet in the spine.'

'Is someone planning to put a bullet in my spine?'

Khamis Zeydan's jaunty bedside manner disappeared. 'It's quite possible.'

'Did you come here with a message from them?'

'I'm not their messenger boy.' The police chief was angry now.

'You seemed content enough after you carried the message to them that got Dima Abdel Rahman killed.'

'Are you still thinking that way? I can't believe it. Do you really think I'd pass information from you to people who would commit murder? Even if I knew for sure who murdered Dima Abdel Rahman, I would never have led her killers to her.'

'You know who the killers are.'

'No. If I had proof, I'd arrest someone. As I told you, I suspect it might be an honor killing. The father or brother may have believed she was sleeping with someone and killed her to prevent her dishonoring her dead husband. Or she might have been meeting a man in the woods at night; someone whose lust got a little out of hand. But I can't prove any of that. Not yet.'

'You told me when we went to see her body that there was more to this than I knew. What is it you aren't telling me?'

'Only what's not good for you.'

'Get out of here. If you can't be honest with me, I don't want you in my house.'

Khamis Zeydan stared at the bedridden schoolteacher. Quietly, he spoke again: 'I came to tell you that the president signed the order for George Saba's execution. They've set a date.'

Omar Yussef was silent and still.

'George will be executed at noon, the day after tomorrow.'

'No, that's too soon.'

'Too soon for what? For you to clear his name? You can't help him, Abu Ramiz.' Khamis Zeydan put his good hand on Omar Yussef's leg. 'You need to think of yourself, to protect yourself and your family. George is beyond your help.'

I am protecting myself, *Omar Yussef thought.* If George dies in this disgusting way, they may as well blindfold me and tie me to the same execution post, so much of me will be gone with him.

'You need to get fit and go back to the school.'

Omar Yussef looked curiously at Khamis Zeydan. 'Didn't you hear I'm retiring?'

Khamis Zeydan shook his head. 'Your boss the American, Steadman, has been telling everyone that he wouldn't dream of letting you retire. I mean, really, he's telling absolutely anyone who'll listen. He even came into the police station this morning to announce it. I don't know what you said to him, but if he wanted you to resign before, he sounds now like he'd do anything to keep you on the job.'

An appeal to cultural sensitivity can have an amazing effect on a clueless, liberal snob, Omar Yussef thought. If he hadn't felt so miserable and suspicious, he would have loved to share the joke with Khamis Zeydan, but the fever and the impending execution froze the smile lines around his eyes.

'Steadman even said that your temporary

replacement was no longer working and that he was teaching your classes himself until you returned.' Khamis Zeydan stood and slapped Omar Yussef's leg. 'Well, I have to go. May Allah help you to feel better. And go back to work at the school.'

'I will,' Omar Yussef said. 'I will be at my old desk in the morning.'

Khamis Zeydan smiled and left.

Omar Yussef willed his back to recover. He had less than two days to save George Saba. Perhaps he could persuade the judge to change the verdict. He would take the old Webley pistol and the MAG cartridge cases to the judge. He had his vague personal connection from their meeting at that UN function a few months back. Maybe the judge would remember him.

The president already had signed the order. No one except Omar Yussef appeared to want to stop the execution. But he had to try.

It was dark and cold. The digital clock on the bedside table glowed red through the gloom. It was 7:00 P.M. precisely. George Saba was condemned to die in forty-one hours. It seemed a matter of seconds, so short was the time Omar Yussef had to work with. He rubbed his face and looked back at the clock. It was 7:01 P.M., and yet it seemed as though the executioners must already be preparing George for death. At 7:02 the crowd would have gathered, a drum roll sounded at 7:03, and by 7:04 Omar Yussef felt it was all over for his friend. Every minute of the next two days he knew he would live through George's judicial murder, again and again. Those would be the last minutes of George Saba's life. Unless Omar Yussef could stop the clock.

He wondered how he might push on with his investigation. Perhaps there would be a clue in the way George was arrested, something that would definitively show that Tamari was responsible for framing him. He'd been told repeatedly that George had confessed. That couldn't be. So far Omar Yussef had heard only the girl Khadija Zubeida's twisted account of the arrest on that first morning in the schoolroom. What truly was said when the policemen went to George's house? Khadija's father was a part of the arresting squad. Omar Yussef would go to the school in the morning and ask the girl where he might find her father. Then he would go to Mahmoud Zubeida and get him to recount the story of George's apprehension. He must piece together the details of what happened, and who had led the operation.

CHAPTER 19

The rain threatened, darkening the dawn and squeezing cold licks of ice onto Omar Yussef's face as he hunched along the main road to the UNRWA Girls School. He had fallen asleep early and without dinner, so exhausted was he by the flood in the basement and the night without sleep. He awoke early and showered, spraying hot water on his strained back. It surprised him that he felt so much better than he had when he lay on his bed the previous evening. Even the cold wind and the darkness of the early morning couldn't dampen his resolve. His deadline was short to save George Saba, and for the first time in days he felt that his body was up to the task. He almost would have said that he felt younger after his long night's sleep.

It was just before 7:00 A.M. The children would arrive in a quarter of an hour. If Khamis Zeydan's information was correct, Steadman would be in the history classroom now, looking up a few unknown phrases in an English-Arabic dictionary, preparing to lecture the students in his strange pidgin. The poor idiot was prepared to put himself through the excruciating task of talking to the kids in Arabic and, worse, struggling to comprehend the slurring slang of teenagers, just to avoid the impression of cultural insensitivity. Well, by the end of the month, he would know that it had all been a waste of effort. Omar Yussef would be back at his desk, ready to teach for another decade. He would still be instructing the girls of Dehaisha in the meaning of their history and culture when Steadman had moved on to the kind of distant United Nations posting in which Omar Yussef always imagined him, sweating it out at some hinterland Somali schoolhouse, or teaching Arabic to Bosnian Muslims. Yes, that would be the man's specialty. Omar Yussef smiled. Steadman would think of himself as an expert on things Arab now.

Omar Yussef crossed the road to the school. The tall, gray column carved into the shape of the map of Palestine blended into the oppressive sky, so that at first glance he wondered if it had been obliterated by some nighttime Israeli raid. When he was able to pick it out in the gloom, he wished it had disappeared. He stopped to look at it. He couldn't help it; each time he saw the sculpture, he fixed his gaze for a moment on the spot where he was born, his father's village. That was the purpose of the sculpture, of course, to perpetuate the desire for a return to those places, communities that had ceased to exist, memorialized in the sentimental recollections of the old people and weighted around the necks of the youngsters in this massive stone. Omar Yussef hated the sculpture.

The blast pounded like a heavyweight fist into Omar Yussef's chest. It dropped him onto his backside in the mud outside the school. He was dazed a moment, sitting on the cold ground. A billow of black smoke wafted out of the school entrance with the scent of charcoal on it. Omar Yussef tried to calm himself. At first he thought he must have been in the center of the explosion, so strong was the blow. It felt as though the shock wave had collapsed his ribcage. But his heart continued to beat. He saw that the detonation had been inside the school. Who would be inside now? It was too early for Wafa. The janitor might be in there cleaning – his chair next to the entrance was empty.

Omar Yussef stared into the smoke. He watched the empty plastic chair. Then he heard someone coughing in the corridor, approaching the entrance. The janitor crawled out of the black cloud. Omar Yussef got to his feet and bent over him. He felt a stiffness where his back had throbbed with pain the day before, but he ignored it. The janitor's face was black with smoke and his nose was bleeding.

'Abu Ramiz, you're here?' the janitor said, surprised.

'What happened?'

The janitor coughed and spat. 'It came from your classroom, Abu Ramiz. Mister Christopher is in there.'

Omar Yussef pulled the janitor out onto the street and left him with two young girls who had come early to school. 'Go to the bakery over there,' he said to one of the stunned children. 'Tell them to call for an ambulance.' Then he went into the smoky corridor.

The windows of Omar Yussef's classroom were blown out along the left-hand side of the corridor. His feet crunched on glass. He pulled his handkerchief from his jacket pocket and covered his mouth and nose. With each breath the bitter smell of burned wood overcame the *eau de cologne* he doused every morning on the handkerchief. He coughed.

The door of the history classroom hung from one hinge at a forty-five-degree angle. Omar Yussef pushed it aside and peered into his classroom. The bookshelves were aflame and some of the children's desks in the front row lay on their backs. His own desk was splintered into so many parts that only the barest frame remained. Beyond it, Omar Yussef saw a hand. Its fingers were bent, as though it were trying desperately to grip the floor, driving its nails into the linoleum. Omar Yussef dropped his own hands to his sides in shock, and choked on a sharp, involuntary intake of breath that was caustic with smoke. He lifted the handkerchief again to his mouth and breathed hard. It was a hand, severed, there on the floor of his classroom. It must belong to Steadman. The janitor had said he was in here, and Omar Yussef, too, had expected that the American would be preparing for his class at that desk.

Omar Yussef stepped past the remnants of the desk. Beyond the hand, the smoke billowed and then cleared, revealing what remained of Christopher Steadman. The American's shirt was scorched away in the front. His pale chest and stomach were smeared with black and scraped bright red by the blast. He was half upright against the beveled bottom of the burning bookshelf, his head tilted back. He looked as though he might be resting, snoring gently through his slightly open mouth. Omar Yussef thought that perhaps he was alive. He hurried to him and knelt beside him. He must get him away from the bookshelf before it burned down to his head or the smoke suffocated him. He hooked his arms around Steadman's torso and shuffled toward the door. The American was heavy. As Omar Yussef struggled, he averted his face. The scalp was singed away on the left, which was also the side on which he had lost his hand. Steadman's eyes jarred open. They were blue and glassy. Omar Yussef almost dropped the American, when the head rolled toward him, the eyes gazing with the emptiness of a drowsy calf. He realized that the man was dead, but he pulled him toward the corridor anyway. Sweat ran into his own eyes and it mixed with the smoke, stinging them.

Three teenage boys rushed into the room and helped Omar Yussef haul the corpse to the corridor and toward the entrance.

'What happened, *ustaz*?' one of them asked. 'Is he dead?'

They lay Christopher Steadman flat on the step of the school's entrance. Omar Yussef felt hopelessly for a pulse in the man's neck. He took off his coat and laid it over the naked torso, the abraded scalp, and the handless arm, so that the other children would not see. That was the second coat he had given up in two days. The first he'd surrendered to a man who was as good as dead. This time it was for an actual corpse. Omar Yussef's sweat chilled now that his exertions were over and he was away from the heat of the fire. This was too much death for him to have clothed. It was as though his overcoats had become shrouds. He wondered if his last remaining coat, back on a hook by his front door, would be his own winding sheet. It was a black anorak, a good color to die in.

The siren of the camp ambulance wailed to the front of the school. Three medics cut through the gathering crowd of children. They were about to remove the coat from the corpse, but Omar Yussef stopped them. 'Wait until he's inside the ambulance,' he said. 'For his dignity.'

The medics nodded and slipped Steadman's body onto a lightweight orange stretcher. Two of them took him to the ambulance, while the other checked the janitor's wounds. Omar Yussef wondered that death caused him to consider Steadman's dignity. The dead man felt his own pride too much when he lived, so Omar Yussef

214

hadn't cared about it then. Now he was the only one who would protect it.

The fire truck arrived. The firemen took a hose down the corridor and began pouring water into the history classroom.

A few of the children cried, though most were morose and silent. Omar Yussef stood on the step of the school. 'Director Steadman has been killed. We can't say yet what happened, but as you can see the school cannot operate today. Go home now, and tell the children from the afternoon shift not to come to school today.'

As the crowd of children slowly cleared, Khamis Zeydan arrived with two jeeps. Omar Yussef watched the police chief approach him. Something in the way Khamis Zeydan looked at him suggested that he hadn't expected to see his old university friend standing at the entrance to the school issuing orders to the children. Then Omar Yussef understood. Someone had intended to kill the teacher in the history classroom. There was no reason anyone would have wanted Steadman dead. The bomb – and this surely had been a bomb – was intended for Omar Yussef.

'Abu Ramiz, what happened here?' Khamis Zeydan said.

'There was a bomb. It exploded in the history classroom. Steadman was preparing to take my class. The explosion killed him. The ambulance took him away just a minute ago.'

'Why was the American taking your class?'

Omar Yussef thought Khamis Zeydan spoke with a hint of disappointment. He remembered that he'd told the police chief yesterday that he would be back in the classroom this morning. Could it be that Khamis Zeydan had set the bomb? Or that he had passed on the information, just as Omar Yussef suspected he did in the case of Dima Abdel Rahman's death? Omar Yussef felt the smoke in his throat again and coughed until his eyes wept. Khamis Zeydan reached out to touch his arm, but he pulled away.

'He was taking my class,' Omar Yussef spluttered, 'because I told him it would be an insult to me in the eyes of the camp if he continued to employ a replacement.'

'He was in the classroom at your request?'

'No, not directly. But partly, yes.'

'Is that so.' Khamis Zeydan stared at him, hard, his head turned to the left, but his eyes looking straight at Omar Yussef.

'Are you suggesting that I had him killed?' Omar Yussef was furious.

'He was trying to get rid of you, wasn't he? Despite his recent public denials, he still intended to force your retirement.'

'You're insane.'

'Listen, Abu Ramiz, you've been getting involved in some crazy things lately. I don't know with whom you've been associating or what they're doing for you, but I do know that you went to Hussein Tamari's headquarters two days ago.'

'Are you having me watched?'

'I keep an eye on who goes in and out of Tamari's hideout. What were you doing there?'

'You know perfectly well that I was trying to help George Saba. Do you really think I went to Tamari to arrange for the American to be killed? Why don't you arrest the people who killed Louai and Dima Abdel Rahman? They're the ones who framed George Saba, and they're the ones who set this bomb. Can't you see they wanted to kill me? They thought I'd be in that classroom. You, in particular, know that very well.'

'What do you mean?'

'Because I told you last night that I'd be teaching this morning.'

'I didn't believe you for a minute. I didn't even think you'd be on your feet this morning. You're tougher than I thought.' Khamis Zeydan stepped aside as the firemen came out of the corridor. He stopped one of them. 'Is the fire under control?'

'Yes, you can go in now.'

'Look, Abu Ramiz, we shouldn't suspect each other,' Khamis Zeydan said, quietly. 'We should be calm. Why don't you take control of the staff, of the school, and arrange the cleanup? I'm going to start investigating the scene of the explosion.'

Khamis Zeydan went into the school with half of his squad. The others stood in a semicircle around the entrance, surrounded by a dozen curious pupils who remained nearby. Omar Yussef noticed that Khadija Zubeida's father was among the policemen who stood in the mud with their Kalashnikovs. He had come to the school that morning to ask the girl how to find her father, and here he was. He put his hand out to him in greeting.

The policeman was friendly. 'Morning of joy, *ustaz*,' he said.

'Morning of light,' Omar Yussef replied. 'Mahmoud, I need to talk to you.'

Omar Yussef passed along the corridor with Mahmoud Zubeida behind him. The policeman glanced blandly into the broken classroom, where his colleagues were assessing the size and source of the blast. *He's seen this kind of destruction many times*, Omar Yussef thought. *It doesn't even concern him that this is his own daughter's classroom.*

The two men went into Steadman's office. Omar Yussef closed the door and gestured for Mahmoud Zubeida to sit. The man tried to rest his Kalashnikov across his lap, but the arms of the chair got in the way, so he laid it on the floor. He rubbed the back of a finger nervously across his black moustache. He swiped off his beret and gripped it in front of his chest, like a medieval peasant doffing his cap to the seigneur. Omar Yussef remained standing behind the desk.

'First, Mahmoud, thank you for allowing me to remain in the courtroom a little late the other night,' Omar Yussef said.

'It's nothing, *ustaz*. May I ask, was that the collaborator's father? The old gentleman who was crying?'

218

'Yes, he's an old friend of mine.'

'Even if he did raise a collaborator, one must have respect for the grief of a father. God knows it isn't necessarily the father's fault if the child is bad.'

'Of course.' Omar Yussef leaned forward. 'Mahmoud, I need you to explain for me what happened during the arrest of George Saba. Khadija told me you were there when Saba was taken in. I found her description very interesting. Would you mind telling me?'

'Why? I mean, how does it interest you, *ustaz*?'

'Mahmoud, something terrible happened here this morning, in the very classroom where Khadija studies. I hope you'll understand that I can't tell you everything right now, though I will share all I know with Brigadier Khamis Zeydan. But I believe there's a possible connection between what happened to Director Steadman and the incident with Saba.'

'Why would a collaborator be involved in the death of the UNRWA school's director?'

'It's not as simple as that, Mahmoud. But, look, for the sake of your daughter, please tell me about the arrest.'

Mahmoud Zubeida seemed nervous. His face was puzzled. *He's a simple man*, Omar Yussef thought, *and he doesn't know if he's going to get himself in trouble with Khamis Zeydan, or even Hussein Tamari, by talking to me. He's also simple enough that anyone standing behind a desk intimidates and commands him.*

'We went to Beit Jala early,' Mahmoud Zubeida said. 'There were three jeeps. We blew in the front door. We couldn't wait to knock, because our commander told us that George Saba was dangerous. He might attack us or kill himself with a cyanide capsule. The Israelis give poison to their collaborators in case they are caught, you know.'

'Who was the commander?'

'Major Awdeh.'

'Jihad Awdeh?'

'Major Jihad, yes.'

'He's a major?'

'In Preventive Security. We were assigned to work with his detectives that morning.'

'What happened once you were inside?'

'We got the Christian against the wall.'

'Did he resist?'

'No, he was very cowardly and frightened.'

'Did he confess?'

'Immediately. He said, "I know what this is about."'

'Did Major Jihad tell him the charges?'

'Yes, he told him he was accused of collaboration with the Occupation Forces in the death of Louai Abdel Rahman.'

'And George Saba confessed to that?'

'Yes.'

'Jihad Awdeh told him the charge and Saba said, "I know what this is about."'

Mahmoud Zubeida paused. 'No, he confessed even before the major told him the charge.'

'So he might have been confessing to something else?'

'I don't understand.'

'He said that he knew why you came to arrest him. But he could have been wrong about the reason. Did he look surprised when Major Jihad told him the charges?'

'I don't remember, *ustaz*. I'm sorry.'

'Did Major Jihad say anything else?'

'Not that I remember.'

'You took Saba out to the jeep?'

'Yes. I rode with him back to the jail.'

'Did he go quietly?'

'Yes, he was very cowardly and scared, like I said.' Mahmoud Zubeida smiled. His teeth were the color of old ivory, from chewing betel. 'Major Jihad really frightened him.'

'How?'

'On the way out of the door, he did like this.' The policeman mimed the act of slitting a throat. His laugh came through his stained teeth slow and deep, like a cartoon cretin. 'The Christian went quite white.'

Omar Yussef remembered the gesture George Saba had described in the cell. Jihad Awdeh had drawn his finger across his throat when George drove him and Hussein Tamari from his roof late at night. So he had repeated the gesture when Tamari sent him to arrest George for collaboration. Omar Yussef remembered how disquieting it was to talk to Jihad Awdeh at the gunmen's headquarters two days ago. He couldn't imagine the terror George must have felt as Awdeh gloated over the gunmen's revenge.

'Thank you. Mahmoud.' Omar Yussef sat in Steadman's chair. 'Perhaps you had better return to your guard duty before Brigadier Zeydan gets annoyed that you're gone.'

'You're right, *ustaz*.' The policeman stood, pulling his beret down to his eyes. 'Thank you.'

When Mahmoud Zubeida left the room, the school secretary came to the doorway.

'Greetings, Abu Ramiz,' she said.

'Double greetings, Wafa.'

'Are you here to help clean up the school?'

Omar Yussef put his palms flat on the rough wooden desktop. He couldn't spare the time to organize workmen and teachers. In twenty-eight hours, George Saba's execution was scheduled to be carried out. But he couldn't see how to proceed. He needed the police to help him, yet Khamis Zeydan was either dismissive of his concern with the matter or even involved in the cover-up. There was no use in rushing all over town talking to lesser officials. They would simply refer him to Khamis Zeydan or tell him to keep his head down for fear of incurring the wrath of the Martyrs Brigades. Well, that wrath was already thoroughly incurred. There was a charred school-room and a dead American to prove it. It might be better to remain close to the policemen for a while as they sifted through the bombsite. Though he thought Khamis Zeydan was in touch with the killers, no one would try to murder him while the school was full of investigators, workmen and teachers. Perhaps he should stay here and think things through.

'Wafa, tell all the other teachers to check their classrooms for damage. I'll call the Jerusalem office and arrange for them to send workmen to repair everything.'

Wafa nodded. 'Do you think they will send another American to be in charge of the school, Abu Ramiz?'

'I haven't thought about it, Wafa.'

The secretary smiled. 'I suppose you don't have to retire now, anyway.'

'Wafa, you're terrible.'

Wafa laughed and closed the door.

Omar Yussef sat in the quiet room, listening to the dim sounds of the policemen in the destroyed classroom. Wafa was right: he no longer faced a boss who wanted to get rid of him. The hateful government schools inspector would have to start working on the new director all over again, and this time Omar Yussef would prepare to defend himself more thoroughly. Suddenly his career prospects were brighter than they had been for months. For the first time since Steadman began to push for him to leave the school, he once again had something to lose. He considered for an instant that his attempt to clear George Saba risked that new security. He was immediately

ashamed of the selfish thought, but he acknowledged that it was there.

He turned on the small stereo Steadman kept
on a shelf behind his desk. He tuned the radio to
the government's local news channel. Perhaps
there would be an announcement of clemency or
some other change in the case of George Saba.
Even if there were some news for the worse, he
would want to hear it as he sat in the office
wondering what to do next. There might even be
a report about the bomb in the school. He picked
up the phone and dialed the UN office in
Jerusalem.

CHAPTER 20

ethlehem Radio broke into its morning discussion program with news of a martyrdom. This martyr sacrificed himself, the radio announcer intoned, when he detonated a bomb he carried to Jerusalem. He died in a street by a market called Mahaneh Yehuda. There was no more detail, but the announcer said he would be back with news of the martyr's identity and the number of dead as soon as it was available. The gravity in his voice couldn't quite disguise the excitement.

Omar Yussef waited in Christopher Steadman's office for the UN's Jerusalem headquarters to call him back and tell him when the workers would arrive to fix the classroom damaged in their own bombing that morning. The police finished rummaging through the destroyed schoolroom and, with all the students sent home, the place was quiet.

The discussion program switched to speculation about the likely origin of the bomber. One of the commentators believed that presently it was easiest to enter Jerusalem from Ramallah, so the bomber had probably come from there. Bethlehem, on the other hand, seemed to him unlikely, because so many soldiers were watching the edge of the town, where the gunmen fired across the valley from Beit Jala, and it would be impossible to sneak past them. The announcer came back with a death toll. He said eight occupiers were reported killed. Omar Yussef snorted. Occupation bargain shoppers. On military operations to buy fresh fish and a bunch of cilantro and two-dollar underpants.

Omar Yussef remembered his one visit to the market where the bomber had died. He had found it unpleasant, dirty and noisy, crowded with people who seemed to have a greater than usual dislike of Arabs. That was years ago, but the people there when the bomber came would have had the same faces, lives identical in their ordinariness. He couldn't categorize them as occupiers, no matter what their government did to him and his own people. He hated these phrases. They made it so simple for his compatriots to ignore the horror of what one of their own had done to someone's wife or grandfather. He knew that when the bomber's name was announced, the dead man's family would be expected to celebrate. The people who sent the kid to die would mob the family house and shoot their Kalashnikovs in the air. What was there for the family to cheer? The loss of a son? The imminent destruction of their home in an army reprisal?

The wall in front of Omar Yussef was obscured by four filing cabinets. Government gray, they were almost as tall as he was. When he had come to see the director in the past, he had always sat with his back to the cabinets and hadn't much noticed them. Now he thought they must loom uncomfortably over the director. The cabinets seemed to threaten to spit out years of worthless paperwork, deluging the desk.

Omar Yussef ran his finger down the titles taped to the front of each drawer. The first two were the educational records of the students. The third was filled with the school's financial accounts. Omar Yussef stopped at the last one. It was marked: 'Personnel.' He bent his knees with a small groan and opened the bottom drawer. He flipped his fingers along the top of the files. Typed along the pink edge, he read his name: SIRHAN, OMAR YUSSEF SUBHI. He wondered what he would do if Wafa entered and saw him looking through confidential personnel files. It wouldn't matter. Wafa didn't seem so sad to see Steadman out of the picture, and if someone else came in, they wouldn't know immediately what was in this drawer.

Omar Yussef lifted his file. It was four inches thick and he needed two hands to wrench it from the crowded tray. The edges of the file were blackened by the dirt of many fingers, more soiled, he thought, than the rest of the staff files next to it. He shoved the drawer shut with his foot, took the grubby file to the desk and dropped it with a deep thud.

The first few pages contained Omar Yussef's application for the job at the UNRWA Girls School and his references from the Frères School. There was a black-and-white passportsized photo attached to the corner of the application with a rusting paperclip. Omar Yussef noticed that his moustache had not quite been fully white back then. It was only ten years ago. He stroked the moustache in the photograph and then ran his finger through the bristly hair on his upper lip. Perhaps he ought to shave it. It surely made him look older than he really was, particularly as the remaining hair on his head was white, too. Steadman might have had the idea for him to retire simply because he looked old enough to be a pensioner. If he shaved the moustache and dyed his hair, the next director wouldn't think of him as an old codger who ought to make way for younger blood. With a pencil he filled in the moustache in the photograph to the gray color of the skin. He took a pen and stroked in dark hair. He looked at the man in the photo. With the new hair and clean lip, he could pass for forty-five years of age, just about. Then he remembered that the man in the old photo was, in fact, only forty-five, and he was thankful that he had cleaned up his lifestyle since then. He put a finger beneath his eye and felt the slack skin there, then he leaned close to the photo and decided that his eyes were baggier a decade before, when he was always up late and sometimes couldn't sleep at all, so charged up had he been with whisky. He would ask Maryam to buy some hair dye and he would get rid of the moustache.

Omar Yussef read the reference from the principal of the Frères School. The headmaster, who had worked with Omar Yussef for twenty years, blamed his departure on budget cuts, for which Omar Yussef quietly thanked him as he sat in the UN director's chair. Old Brahim hadn't reported that he was forced to get rid of Omar Yussef by the government schools inspector, Abu Sway.

Then Omar Yussef glanced over the reports written by his first director at the UN school. He was an Irishman named Fergus whom Omar Yussef had liked. They were excellent assessments. But he came to a halt when he read the reports of the next director. This had been a Spanish lady. Pilar had preceded Steadman, and Omar Yussef always remembered her four years at the school fondly. She was a little younger than him and he had enjoyed a flirtatious exchange of humor with her. He remembered how she would laugh like a teenager when he told her how elegant she looked with her Gucci scarves and Fendi sunglasses. She was unmarried and often came to dinner with his family. Yet her annual appraisals of his teaching skills were damning. She wrote that he was too old to learn modern techniques of teaching and that he hadn't adapted to the new syllabus issued by the president when the government took over the schools system from the Israeli Civil Administration.

Omar Yussef flipped through the other papers. There was another negative assessment by Pilar and then a letter she'd left in the file for Steadman, when he took over a year ago. It said that Omar Yussef was a difficult employee and that she had begun the process of securing an order from the government schools inspector for his dismissal. His dismissal. Perhaps Abu Sway had used the letter to try to force Steadman to fire him and, instead, the American had attempted to offer Omar Yussef an honorable way out. The rest of the file consisted of letters from parents complaining that he spoke negatively about political life in the town and that he kept too many students behind for detention at the end of the day. There was no appraisal from Christopher Steadman.

Omar Yussef closed the file. He was astonished. He had been wrong about Steadman. He immediately regretted the joke about not washing on Ramadan and all the heated words he had spoken to the poor man. Aloud, he asked for the American's forgiveness. The man was dead, and Omar Yussef knew there would be no opportunity to correct the lack of respect he had shown Steadman while he lived. Every hostile sentence he had growled at the American seemed to come back now to smack him in the mouth from which he uttered them. He considered searching the gray cabinets for a personnel file on Steadman. Perhaps he would call the man's parents in the United States to inform them of his death, but then he figured the headquarters in Jerusalem would have someone do that.

The sadness Omar Yussef felt at misunderstanding Steadman fed his anger about the Spanish woman. What had made her treat him with such duplicity? He always thought it was people like Khamis Zeydan and Hussein Tamari who had to be alert to double games. Duplicity and bluff surrounded them, occupied their every thought. But he was a schoolteacher. Why should he be forced to guard against the possibility of betrayal? It disgusted him. It was bad enough that his investigation of the George Saba case led him down dark, dirty paths where there were hidden threats against him. He thought of writing an angry protest to the Spanish woman. But he wasn't supposed to have seen his personnel file, so how could he respond to its content? If these appraisals were any judge of her true nature, Pilar would use this infraction as a pretext to get him fired. Maybe his flirting had secretly annoyed her. Or perhaps she felt rejected because he never followed up with a genuine sexual advance. It was possible. Though Omar Yussef would have considered it indecent, these European ladies behaved according to a morality that even a broadminded Arab man might find shocking. He acknowledged that, with a wife as good as Maryam, he had never been forced to confront a woman who concealed a deep anger, nor had he needed to understand the desires of an unmarried lady.

Omar Yussef quickly ran through the file and pulled out each of the blue sheets on which the Spanish woman had written her appraisals, as well as the letter she left for Steadman. He ripped each of them into eight pieces, crumpled the shreds into a ball and dropped them in the wastepaper basket. He stared down at the paper, bitterly. He picked it up, pressed it firmly in his fist and hurled it hard into the empty wastepaper basket once more. It rolled around with a tinny sound. He felt a little better.

Omar Yussef took his file to the drawer and knelt unsteadily. He jammed it among the other files and pushed the drawer closed. He stood and shook his head.

The tone of the radio changed. It cut to a static-riddled phone connection, catching Omar Yussef's attention. A reporter was calling in new information about the Jerusalem suicide bomb. '. . . The Aqsa Martyrs Brigades announces in a leaflet distributed to news media that the martyrdom operation in Mahaneh Yehuda market was carried out by Yunis Abdel Rahman, who is from the village of Irtas in the Bethlehem district. The martyr was nineteen years old. The Martyrs Brigades sends its congratulations to the family and to the village . . .'

Omar Yussef leaned against the edge of the desk and gasped. The studio host repeated the information. The commentator, who had speculated that the bomber must have come from Ramallah, said the Israeli army would surely now descend on Bethlehem. Certainly, he said, the new policy of destroying the homes of martyrs' families would bring destruction on the heads of the Abdel Rahmans, but the people would stand steadfast with them. Omar Yussef turned the radio off.

Why did Yunis Abdel Rahman give his life in this way? Omar Yussef ran over his conversation with the boy outside the family house, when Dima's body was found. Yunis had been angry and hostile. But these Martyrs Brigades people, for whom he had carried out this final mission, were the same men who stole his family's auto business as soon as his powerful elder brother was murdered. Omar Yussef had felt sure that Yunis knew Tamari was responsible for the deaths of his brother and his sister-in-law. He remembered the way the boy glared at the Martyrs Brigades leaders when they arrived at George Saba's trial. To kill oneself in one of these bombings was always unfathomable to Omar Yussef, but this seemed stranger than all the others whose cases he knew from around the camp. There were factors common to most of the Dehaisha youths who died like this, as far as Omar Yussef deduced. Usually they had something to prove. Sometimes they were mentally unbalanced after they had witnessed the death of someone close to them in an Israeli attack. But most of the bombers wanted to show everyone that they were not the person people believed them to be, that they were selfless and honorable and brave. Their lives generally were worthless, or had become so, because of some social transgression or indiscretion, and they tried to redeem themselves and the reputation of their families through martyrdom. What did Yunis Abdel Rahman want to prove? Perhaps he was simply unhinged by the deaths of his brother and sister-in-law in the cabbage patch outside his home. But the boy had seemed to be eaten by revenge, not desperation, when he had spoken so angrily to Omar Yussef two days ago. Then he remembered Yunis's look of shame. Had the boy murdered Dima and blown himself up to end the guilt? Or was he involved with Tamari in his brother's death outside the family home?

Omar Yussef needed to think this through. His pants were muddy from the fall he had taken when the bomb exploded in the schoolroom. He considered walking home to change and consider the meaning of this new development in his comfortable salon. Then he thought about the announcement that Yunis Abdel Rahman's bombing mission was organized by the local Martyrs Brigades. The Israelis might come to Bethlehem to take revenge on the gunmen. When that happened, Jihad Awdeh's plan was to take refuge in the Church of the Nativity. Before going home to change, he decided he would walk to the church. He would warn Elias Bishara of the gunman's plan. Elias would have to figure out a way to keep Jihad Awdeh from entering the church.

Omar Yussef put on his jacket and his flat cap. He bent to pick the blue wad of paper from the wastebasket. He squeezed it and felt as though he were grasping the neck of the Spanish UN school director. That woman had touched these pages. Now she was gone, Omar Yussef had destroyed her deceitful traces. Everything could be wiped out somehow. Yunis Abdel Rahman had been full of anger when Omar Yussef had seen him, and now he was empty, a husk, broken, ready to rot, without leaving any sign of himself in the world. He had strapped a belt of explosives to his torso, but the detonation was inside him.

Wafa looked up when Omar Yussef opened the office door. She was on the phone and put her hand over the receiver. 'It's the maintenance director in Jerusalem,' she said. 'They're coming in one hour. Do you need to speak to them?'

Omar Yussef shook his head. He waved to Wafa and went down the corridor, crunching over the broken glass by the blasted classroom. At the entrance, Mahmoud Zubeida sat on a plastic chair, on guard, his Kalashnikov leaning against the wall. He straightened a little when he saw Omar Yussef. 'Peace be with you, *ustaz*.'

'And with you. Allah lengthen your life,' Omar

Yussef replied, squinting into the wind and pulling up the collar of his jacket.

The air was cold and blustery after the stuffiness of Steadman's office. Omar Yussef crossed the muddy street. The chopping baritone of an Israeli helicopter growled from somewhere up in the clouds. Omar Yussef looked about to find Nayif, but no one was around except a dappled goat with its head in a trash can. Omar Yussef turned his back to the wind. He tossed the blue ball of paper as far as he could. The coming gale took it and dropped it into a pool of dirty water behind a brimming garbage dumpster.

CHAPTER 21

A Greek Orthodox priest leaned against the smooth edge of the altar, keeping watch over the entrance to the cave where Jesus was born. He stroked his long black beard, gathering its thickness repeatedly in his fist like a girl fixing her ponytail, and stared as Omar Yussef came across the floor of the empty Church of the Nativity. His eyes were hooded, ringed with a black as vivid as his short mitre and long gown, and his face was immobile with a lazy hostility.

'Greetings, Father,' Omar Yussef said, when he reached the corner of the church by the cave.

The priest mumbled something that probably wasn't loud enough even for him to hear it.

Omar Yussef restrained his irritation. The priest was a Greek. The other denominations allowed locals to rise in the priesthood, but the Greek Orthodox almost always shipped men from Athens to minister to a people about whom they knew nothing. The imports ended up alienated, resentful, and churlish like this one. Omar Yussef figured there were no tourists today for the priest to bully, so he must be in a bad mood.

'I'm looking for Father Elias Bishara.'

The Greek priest looked at Omar Yussef's muddy, damp pants. He lifted a languid hand and, with a crooked finger, angled his wrist toward a small door in the north transept. The hand went back to stroking his beard and Omar Yussef had been dismissed.

Beyond the door was St Catherine's Church. The Franciscans built it onto the side of the Nativity Church in the nineteenth century. Its white marbled interior was quiet, so Omar Yussef went into the cloister. The granite medieval columns had been restored to a grayness that shone unnaturally in the blank light from the cloudy sky. At first the cloister seemed empty. There was a statue of an old man in a monk's habit at the center of the courtyard. Then, behind the statue, Omar Yussef saw a kneeling priest, his head bowed in prayer. He recognized the thinning, curly black hair as Elias Bishara's.

The priest rose as Omar Yussef crossed the flagstones and smiled. 'Abu Ramiz, welcome.'

'How are you, Father Elias?'

'Don't call me "Father." It sounds strange in the mouth of a man who has instructed me since childhood,' Elias said. 'Am I supposed to call you "my son"?'

'Aren't you cold out here?'

'Well, that's the point, really.' He looked around

the cloister. 'The discomfort concentrates my prayers. So does this old bastard.' He gestured to the statue.

Omar Yussef looked up into the bearded face of the carved figure. He detected nothing spiritual in it. It was as blank as if it were set in a supermarket jello mold. 'St Jerome?'

'Yes, our local saint and martyr,' Elias Bishara said. 'I was meditating on our friend George Saba earlier. I realized that I felt hatred toward the Muslims of our town for what they have done to George. I hate them for their unthinking orthodoxy and their crazy compulsion to martyrdom. I came here, to the feet of Jerome, to be reminded that we Christians have had our share of lunatics, fanatically rejecting those who thought and worshipped differently.'

'Not to mention those who worshipped the martyrs almost above God himself,' Omar Yussef said.

'You're right, Abu Ramiz. This fellow Jerome's translation of the Bible into Latin was the official version of the Roman Catholic Church for sixteen hundred years. It was a great achievement for a man who lived as a hermit in Bethlehem. But he destroyed the careers and lives of other theologians who dared to challenge his orthodoxy, and he decorated the tombs of martyrs with so many candles that people said he was a pagan worshipping the light, instead of God.'

Elias Bishara dusted off the front of his robe

where his kneeling had soiled it. He looked at Omar Yussef's muddy trousers. 'Did you fall, *ustaz*?'

The mud had dried to a dusty cake on the outside of Omar Yussef pants. Underneath, his legs were wet and cold. 'It's nothing,' he said.

'Let's go inside, anyway. There's no need for you to join me in scourging yourself out here.'

'I wouldn't say that.'

The two men went into the quiet, white chapel. From the small door to the Nativity Church, the Greek priest watched them, his fingers still brushing his beard. Elias Bishara took Omar Yussef's arm and led him to the rear pew.

'Elias, I must warn you of a danger to the church,' Omar Yussef said. 'There was an attack, a suicide bomb, this morning in Jerusalem.'

'Yes, I heard.'

'It was carried out by the Martyrs Brigades. The operation was organized from Bethlehem. I fear the Israelis will come tonight to capture or kill the leaders of the group. They will need to exact some kind of revenge for the deaths in their market-place.'

'How does this involve the church?'

'Jihad Awdeh, who is a leader of the Martyrs Brigades, has become a neighbor of mine. He told someone that if the Israelis came to take him, he would flee to the church.'

Elias gasped.

'You understand, of course, that if he enters the

240

church, it could draw the Israeli soldiers inside, too. There might be a gunfight in the church. Who knows how it would end? But it would be bad for the town, and bad for the Christians, either way. Your shrine could be damaged, even destroyed, if the gunmen enter. If they are denied sanctuary by the priests, the Muslims of the town will rise up against the Christians for abandoning the so-called resistance heroes to the Israeli army.'

Elias glanced toward the watching Greek priest, who dodged behind the stone lintel of the door, out of sight. 'Abu Ramiz, I can't believe it has come to this,' he said.

'Why do you think the Martyrs Brigades has its headquarters right around the corner? They could be out of their hideaway and inside the church in a minute. You must close the doors early tonight.'

'I can't, Abu Ramiz. It isn't my decision. Even if I can persuade the Latin patriarch to shut the church, the Greeks won't allow it. They'll be suspicious. They'll think we're trying to change the operating arrangements of the church. Nothing has been done differently here for hundreds of years. You're a history teacher, so you know all about it. Remember how the French empire ended up at war against Russia a hundred and fifty years ago because the priests here argued about a new decorative plaque on the spot where Jesus was born? Even today, a Catholic priest sweeps some steps that are supposed to be cleaned by the Greek

Orthodox and he gets a punch in the face. It's hopeless even to ask about locking up early.'

'Surely they'll understand the threat?'

'It doesn't matter. There's such stubbornness in this church, there are priests who'd rather see the place destroyed by Muslims and Jews than concede a point to another Christian denomination.'

'Then there's nothing you can do?'

'Maybe there's something.' Elias looked down the aisle toward the figure of the crucified Christ on the altar. 'I'll be here. I'll stop them.'

'Elias, they'll just kill you. How will you stand up to them alone?'

'Abu Ramiz, I'm not a hero, of course. I fear these gunmen. But I hope that I fear them less than I love this church. This building *is* the history of Christianity in the Holy Land. You always taught me that history was the essence of life, that its study gave us the key to a better future. Even if these stones were to be destroyed, the spirit of their history must be protected. This place represents a past when Muslims and Christians lived together peacefully and the chance that it could be so again, when all of this madness is over. I will be here tonight, and I will pray for the church. I will stay here even when the Martyrs Brigades come, and I will pray for them too.' Elias laid a warm hand on Omar Yussef's leg. 'Thank you for the warning, Abu Ramiz. Now I will be ready for them when they come. But you must go home and change into dry clothes, before you catch your death of a cold.'

'I'm beginning to think that would be a blessing.'

'Do you want to be an influenza martyr?' Elias Bishara laughed. 'They will give you seventy-two cups of hot cider in Paradise.'

Omar Yussef laughed, too. But as he left the church, he noticed that Elias Bishara was back on his knees. The priest's gaze was stern, fixed on the cross.

CHAPTER 22

Omar Yussef lay flat on his bed, waiting for Maryam to call him to the table for the *iftar*. The throbbing in his back that began when he bailed the floodwater from his basement had returned. The trek from the school to the church and then home had tired him, but the fear that the young priest would put himself in danger truly exhausted him. After sitting down to drink a cup of coffee, the chill crept into his lower spine and his muscles seized up, clenching him like the familiar fist of an awful, recurring nightmare. It seemed curiously appropriate to Omar Yussef that on an evening when he should have been rushing around Bethlehem, unearthing clues and persuading people of George Saba's innocence, he instead passed a fruitless five hours prone in his bedroom. The silence of the broody, featureless sky outside his window taunted him like the blank stare of a sadist. He would lie here the remaining eighteen hours until George Saba's execution, gaping hopelessly at the heavy clouds. Then it would rain, and he would know that George was dead.

Omar Yussef wondered if he were depressed. Perhaps he was in some state of traumatic stress. He had read about such things happening to those who were close to a bomb when it went off, as he had been. He put his hand to his breastbone and felt that it was a little bruised from the impact of the shockwave that had knocked him onto his backside that morning at the school. Traumatized he certainly was by the sight of Christopher Steadman's body. He hadn't thought of it while he sat at Steadman's desk or as he walked home. There had been other things to ponder. Once he was home, though, the American's lifeless limb came back to him. All afternoon, he had examined his own hand, holding it before his face in the same position in which he'd seen Steadman's, seeming to scratch itself along the floor tiles, like a scorpion, scuttling to catch up with the director's charred body. Omar Yussef wondered how often Khamis Zeydan thought about his lost hand. Would that not turn anyone to drink? The loss of the hand, the horrors of soldiering, the loneliness of a man whose closest companionship was with the dead of his old battles. Omar Yussef had barely managed to conquer his own compulsive drinking and smoking, and he struggled against nothing more than the frustrations of life under occupation. How much harder must it be for his friend? Yes, he still thought of Khamis Zeydan as his friend. He felt suddenly very forgiving, as he pictured him lying on his back in Lebanon, fainting, searching desperately about him for his severed hand in the dirt, oblivious to the bullets flying around him, hoping he could simply slot the limb back into place and flee forever from the battlefield. Omar Yussef imagined that might have been the very moment when the idealistic young man he had known at university had turned into the bitter, melancholy, apathetic drunk who now headed Bethlehem's police force. But he wondered if the darkness that had shrouded Khamis Zeydan's life for many decades was deep enough that it might also obscure the police chief's judgement of right and wrong. Could his friend be so contaminated that he would have tipped off Tamari about Dima? Omar Yussef hated to think it, but he couldn't see how else Tamari would have known that he needed to kill the girl.

Nadia entered her grandfather's bedroom carrying a cup of coffee. Darkness ringed the twelve-year-old's eyes and her diaphanous skin was blued by the veins beneath. Omar Yussef understood that she had barely slept since the flood descended on her family's apartment in the basement. The guest room on the ground floor was crammed with Ramiz's entire family, and it was fearfully cold at night. Everyone around her, her parents and her grandmother and the relatives and neighbors who came to help clear out the basement, they all spent the day wailing or bitching about the occupation, the destruction, the mess of everything. Nadia was quiet. Omar

Yussef looked across at her from where he lay on the bed. If she put on a little weight, it would be almost like looking at his mother, he thought. Her eyes sloped down, giving them a melancholy cast. Her hair was a black frame to the pale, unblemished face. Omar Yussef's father always said his wife looked and walked like a Turkish princess, the old pure Turks of the Caucasus, from before the Ottoman conquests. Nadia carried herself with the same slender authority as Omar Yussef's mother had. She had the same sensitive personality. She was withdrawn, as though something made her feel the world couldn't be trusted. She was knowing, too, as only an unhappy child can be.

Omar Yussef remembered his mother's funeral. It was 1965 and he was seventeen. It was a cold day that threatened rain, like this one. Omar Yussef's father, who never criticized his wife, took his eldest son aside that day. 'My son, you're mourning your mother, and I acknowledge that she was a good mother to you and you are right to be sorry that she passed on. It's not easy for me to tell you, but I want you to understand: it is better that she should go, because there was no way for any of us to help her. You see, after we left the village, when you were a newborn, she was never the same. You never saw her really happy. I wish you had. I don't want you to feel that your experience as a son was not a happy one, nor that you didn't give her the joy a mother derives from a son. But she was different after we left the village. She couldn't stop thinking about what life was like there, or how much harder it was here. She never spoke about it very much. She thought it would make me ashamed that I was able to provide only a lesser life for her than the one she expected when we married. Of course, I wouldn't have felt that way, and even now I tell you this without bitterness. Don't let the way life is for us rob you of your happiness, my son. Remember your mother. When you have children and grandchildren, I hope they will return to our village. But if they don't, then be sure that they leave it behind for good. Don't allow them to be pulled in both directions as your mother was, between the village of the past and the camp of today. If so, they truly will live in neither place.' If anyone else had spoken that way to Omar Yussef at that time, he would have rejected him as a pathetic defeatist. How much more did Omar Yussef understand what his father meant now? Now that he saw Nadia before him, tentative and tired, Omar Yussef wanted to banish all thoughts of Khamis Zeydan, of George Saba and Dima Abdel Rahman, and of the Martyrs Brigades. This girl was his responsibility.

'Hello, my darling. Come and sit here.'

Nadia put the coffee on the nightstand and sat at the edge of the bed.

Omar Yussef held her hand. It was cold as a frozen cut of beef. 'Are you tired?'

Nadia nodded.

'Life is quite difficult here, my heart. But I want you to know that things are much worse for people elsewhere in the world.'

'Yes, Grandpa.' Nadia stared at her feet.

'No, really. It's true. Imagine if we lived in Russia. There would have been a century of horrible suffering under Communism, and now there would be enormous criminal mafias, and diseases like AIDS that no one tries to halt. It's true that things are bad here, but they could be much worse. Even the weather in Russia is worse.'

Nadia giggled.

'Yes, there'd be a foot of snow for six months outside our door, if we lived in Russia,' Omar Yussef said. 'So never mind that we had a foot of water in the basement for one day.'

'Snow is fun, Grandpa.'

'When it comes only once a year, as it does here, but not when it snows for months at a time. And anyway it was fun to see all the neighbors come in and help clean up. It shows that we have good neighbors. And it was fun to bail out all the water. You remember how you helped me throw the water out of the back door.'

'Yes.'

'That was fun. And we didn't even have to go to the beach to play in the water. The beach came to us.'

'It was smelly.' Nadia laughed.

'The beach is smelly too. Haven't you seen all the sewage they pour into the sea nowadays. Yes,

yes, it was much better to stay here and not go to the beach. This way we could enjoy Grandma's cooking *and* play on the beach.'

Nadia smiled and hugged her grandfather. His eyes teared up. Her shoulders were narrow and the bones in her back were hard against his hands. She felt so small and brittle. He held her close until he was sure that she wouldn't see tears in his eyes; then he let her go.

'Thank you for my coffee, my darling.'

The phone rang in the salon.

'Will you answer that, Nadia?'

Nadia ran out of the room. Omar Yussef sat up, slowly, listening to the slap of her sandals on the flagstones of the hallway. The pain in his back made him purse his lips and puff. He drank the coffee Nadia left him. She came back with the cordless phone.

'It's Abu Adel,' she said.

Omar Yussef put down his coffee. Nadia left the room.

'Greetings, Abu Adel.' Omar Yussef could hear shouting voices near Khamis Zeydan's phone.

'Double greetings, Abu Ramiz,' Khamis Zeydan said. 'How are you?'

'Thank Allah,' Omar Yussef said.

'I'm down by Shepherds Field. An Israeli helicopter missile struck Hussein Tamari's jeep. He's dead.'

'Hussein is dead? Are you sure he was in the jeep?'

'I was following him. I know he was in there.'

'Why were you following him?'

'I was pretending to be a policeman, just for a change of pace, you know. The Israelis must have got him in revenge for the bomb in Jerusalem this morning. You heard the Martyrs Brigades sent Yunis Abdel Rahman to blow himself up.'

'Yes. Why did they send *him*?'

'I don't know.'

'It doesn't matter anyway. The important thing is that now George Saba can be freed.'

There was silence from Khamis Zeydan.

'I mean,' said Omar Yussef, 'that now the police can acknowledge that Hussein Tamari was the man who either killed Louai Abdel Rahman or who led the Israelis to him, and that he was also the man who killed Dima Abdel Rahman.'

'First, Abu Ramiz, you don't know that.'

'I know it.'

Khamis Zeydan raised his voice. 'You don't know it for sure, and you certainly don't know that he killed Dima. Second, Hussein Tamari is a martyr now, a big, big, big fucking martyr. Do you think Bethlehem would swap a big martyr for a dirty little collaborator? Does that sound like a good trade to anyone but you, Abu Ramiz?'

Omar Yussef's forgiving feelings toward Khamis Zeydan for the loss of his hand disappeared. He felt desperate. How could he clear George Saba if the police chief wouldn't help, particularly now that the real killer was dead and could never be made to confess? His suspicions returned. Khamis

Zeydan was following the dead man's jeep when the missile struck. Perhaps *he* was a collaborator. *The* collaborator. Maybe he'd called in the details of Hussein Tamari's whereabouts to his handler in the Shin Bet and enabled the Israelis to strike, just as he might have done in the case of Louai Abdel Rahman's death in the pines outside his home. But why would Khamis Zeydan have left a cartridge from a MAG behind at Louai's murder scene? It wouldn't benefit him to tag the murder on Hussein Tamari. He would have picked a more powerless fall guy, like George Saba. In any case when Omar Yussef had told Khamis Zeydan that Hussein was Louai's killer, the police chief had said he should forget about it. He wasn't eager to pin the murder on Tamari, so clearly he hadn't tried to frame him, either.

'I called you, Abu Ramiz, to let you know that now there's nothing more you can do for George Saba,' Khamis Zeydan said. 'If it was going to be hard for you to pin the blame on Hussein Tamari when he was alive, it's impossible now.'

'You can't just let George die. It's disgusting. It's a stain on our entire town.'

'Every house has its sewers, Abu Ramiz.'

'Don't quote proverbs at me. You have to help me.'

'I'm telling you: Hussein Tamari is untouchable. By you, *and* by me. The only thing that's going to happen if you speak up now is that you'll get yourself lynched. There's already a crowd here that you can probably hear in the background and they're very angry. If they find someone they want to accuse of collaboration, they'll beat him to death on the spot. So I don't advise you to speak ill of the dead tonight.'

'We only have until tomorrow at noon to prove Tamari's guilt and to save George.'

Khamis Zeydan waited a moment, took a breath. 'No, *George Saba* only has until tomorrow at noon. We don't have such a deadline.'

'You're right. Your time was up a long time ago.' Omar Yussef punched the button on the phone that terminated the call.

In the quiet of the night, Omar Yussef strained to hear the sound of the army helicopter. He recalled the noise of its engine, reverberating above him all week. It rained a deafening rotor thump onto the handicapped boy Nayif. It mirrored the beating of Omar Yussef's anxious heart when he came out of the school to toss his old personnel reports into the puddle. It must be there now again, the blaze of Hussein Tamari's destroyed vehicle a flickering spot below it in the blackness of the earth. It hovered above Bethlehem like the famous star that announced the birth of Jesus. It doomed each man it tracked, just as surely as that ancient messianic sign destined the child born in the manger to crucifixion. The sky was silent, but Omar Yussef knew the chopper was up there. Not even if George Saba could fly like a bird would he find escape and safety.

Omar Yussef couldn't give up now. He must find someone who would refuse to let an innocent man die just for the sake of preserving the memory of this scum Tamari. No one in the police or the judiciary or the government would take that risk. He had to think of someone who might be even more powerful than the memory of Tamari. There was only one person who could possibly chance slurring the martyr's image. It was risky. Khamis Zeydan was right: they might lynch him. Well, then he would die before George Saba's execution and his worries would be over. He would go to Jihad Awdeh.

CHAPTER 23

At the door of Jihad Awdeh's apartment building, there were two guards. One of them tucked his cigarette into the corner of his mouth to free his hands and, with his eye squinting against the smoke, patted down Omar Yussef. As he was searched, Omar Yussef glanced back across the street at his own house. Silhouetted in the window of the living room he recognized his granddaughter Nadia. It was the stillness of the outline that told him it was her, watchful and tense as her grandfather went into danger. A few moments before, it had seemed to him that he had nothing to lose by this desperate attempt to influence the new head of the town's most wicked gang of killers. That silent, unmoving shadow in the window of his home gave him a pang of doubt. Perhaps he ought to make an excuse, tell the gunman searching him that he had forgotten something and head home. The search concluded. The guard took a long drag on the cigarette and told him to go up the stairs. If he turned to leave now, they would be suspicious.

On the staircase, it occurred to Omar Yussef that

the Israelis might try to assassinate Jihad Awdeh tonight, just as they had killed Hussein Tamari. He wondered if the helicopter missile would blast through the window even as he sat with the new chief of the Martyrs Brigades. From the window, Nadia would see the streak of orange from the tail of the missile as it roared in to kill her grandfather, and then the puff of gray smoke from the window, the vaporized remains of the glass and concrete and of Omar Yussef's body. He breathed deeply as the door of Jihad Awdeh's apartment opened for him.

The boy who held the door for Omar Yussef was about Nadia's age. He pulled the laquered cherrywood door back and stepped aside, giving Omar Yussef a brief glance of contempt and hostility. Across the living room, Jihad Awdeh sat on a sofa. He was surrounded by Martyrs Brigades men. There were at least a dozen and the room seemed very crowded. Omar Yussef was surprised and relieved that Jihad Awdeh appeared to be in good spirits. He had expected that the death of Hussein Tamari might have made Awdeh fearful or angry. Instead, he seemed to be enjoying his new status as the boss of the gang. He laughed loudly at a joke, took a small square of baklava from a tray his daughter carried around the room, and scooped a handful of sunflower seeds from a bowl on the coffee table.

Jihad Awdeh glanced across the room at the open door. His eyes darkened for a moment when he noticed his visitor, but the smile remained in place and he beckoned Omar Yussef forward. *You are my brother. I would have to kill you free of charge.* Omar Yussef wondered if that generous offer remained valid. As he approached, Jihad Awdeh whispered to the man on the couch next to him, who vacated his seat. Jihad patted the sofa and the man who had stood came to usher Omar Yussef to his place next to the chief.

'I'm happy that you have come, and I wish your welcome to be a good one,' Jihad Awdeh said. He moved very close to Omar Yussef, who sat on the edge of the couch.

'I'm happy to be welcomed at your home,' Omar Yussef muttered. It seemed strange to speak the formulas of politeness in these circumstances.

Jihad Awdeh picked a piece of baklava from his daughter's tray and handed it to Omar Yussef, dripping honey and syrup. The sweetness seemed deceptive, excessive, sickly. He told himself to be on his guard against this man's sudden charm.

Jihad Awdeh smiled and spat the empty pods of sunflower seeds into his hand. He dropped them in a crystal ashtray and stuffed another couple of seeds into his mouth. His jaw worked on the seeds, pressing their edges between his molars to open the pods, so that his sustained smile seemed to want to consume, like the threateningly bared fangs of an aggressive dog.

Omar Yussef tried to ease the memory of their confrontation at Hussein Tamari's headquarters two days ago. 'My condolences on the death of the brother Hussein,' he said. 'May Allah be merciful to him.'

Jihad Awdeh nodded and let his smile fade into seriousness for a moment. Then he put his hand on Omar Yussef's knee and leaned close. 'You didn't like him, Abu Ramiz, did you?' he whispered.

Omar Yussef stared at the powerful hand on his leg. The nails were long and yellow, like the claws of a wild animal. He said nothing.

Jihad Awdeh laughed. 'Neither did I.' He nodded. 'I didn't like him at all. Now what do you want, Abu Ramiz? My time is limited, as the funeral of the martyr Hussein and his bodyguards is to be held in half an hour.'

It surprised Omar Yussef that Jihad Awdeh would admit to his dislike of Hussein Tamari, even in a hushed voice. He remembered that Khamis Zeydan had told him Hussein's men would often scorn Jihad, even to his face, as a member of a small clan of refugees. Hussein had born the confidence of a man who belonged, whose entire village would back him against any threat. Jihad Awdeh's clan was not powerful, even in the refugee camp on the northern edge of Bethlehem where most of his relatives lived. Omar Yussef wondered if Jihad Awdeh might not be less aggressive toward him tonight because he finally had Tamari's clan where he wanted them. In that instant, he thought of the Abdel Rahmans, who lost their protection with the death of Louai in the pine grove. Jihad Awdeh still needed to make a show of bereavement, because most of the Martyrs Brigades men belonged to Tamari's clan, but he had taken over the gang just as surely as Hussein Tamari had robbed the defenseless Abdel Rahmans of their autoshops.

'Perhaps we should talk privately, Jihad,' Omar Yussef said.

Jihad Awdeh nodded and, taking Omar Yussef's hand in his, he led him onto the small balcony at the back of the living room. 'I won't turn on the light, Abu Ramiz, in case there are snipers watching for me.'

Omar Yussef looked out into the darkness, nervously. A rocky slope descended from the next houses to the base of the apartment building. The rocks, white in the moonlight, seemed to move about on the dark earth. Omar Yussef felt the stones scrutinizing him, stalking him, but he knew that the tension he sensed when he looked into the dark was all because of the man who stood beside him.

Jihad Awdeh lit a cigarette and spat the last of his sunflower seed pods over the balcony. He held his palm upward, gesturing for Omar Yussef to speak.

'Jihad, I know that Hussein was the one who collaborated with the Israelis in the death of Louai Abdel Rahman.' Omar Yussef waited for a reaction, but Jihad Awdeh took another drag on his

259

cigarette and was silent. Omar Yussef smelled the acrid exhalation and wished he could have taken a smoke himself. 'I went to Irtas after Louai was killed. I found a MAG cartridge on the ground. It was in a patch of grass that had been flattened by a man lying there. Louai's wife Dima told me there had been someone waiting for her husband. She heard Louai say hello to someone called Abu Walid. Then something like a red laser dot appeared on him and he was shot. You know that Hussein was called Abu Walid and that he used a MAG. No one else in Bethlehem has that kind of gun.'

Jihad Awdeh flicked his cigarette onto the slope behind the apartment building. Its orange tip rested in the darkness a moment. Omar Yussef watched it disappear. He waited again, but Jihad merely rested his elbows on the balcony rail and looked into the darkness.

'You remember how angry Hussein was when George Saba forced you both off his roof that night, when you went there to fire at the Israelis?' Omar Yussef continued. 'Well, I believe that Hussein led the soldiers to Louai, and then had his revenge on George Saba by tagging him as the collaborator. That way he'd also prevent anyone from suspecting that he himself was, in fact, the collaborator. But when he found out what Dima told me, he killed her, too.'

'How did he discover that she spoke to you?'

Omar Yussef decided not to mention his suspicion

260

that Khamis Zeydan passed on the details of that meeting to Hussein. 'I don't know.'

'So someone else could've killed her.'

'I suppose so, but I don't know why anyone else would have done so.' Omar Yussef turned toward Jihad Awdeh. The man's face was obscured, silhouetted against the light emanating from the room behind them. Omar Yussef didn't want to touch him, but he needed to make some kind of contact in the darkness. He put his hand on Jihad's shoulder. 'I need your help, Jihad. George Saba is an innocent man. He'll be executed in seventeen hours. His blood would be on my hands, if I didn't come here and beg you to help me. The law counts for nothing in this town. You are the power. You are the one who can save a guiltless man.'

'Do you think someone who holds a gun on me and Hussein when we are resisting the occupation forces is a guiltless man?'

That's a trap, Omar Yussef thought. *Be careful.* 'George was desperate. He knew that your presence on his roof would draw Israeli fire. He feared for his family. He didn't know that it was you and Hussein on his roof.'

Jihad Awdeh lit another cigarette. 'Who will be ready to listen to the notion that the martyr Hussein was really a criminal and a collaborator?'

'You said that you didn't like him.'

'That doesn't mean I believe he was a collaborator. Or that I believe George Saba is innocent.'

261

'I told you the evidence.'

'Hussein Tamari risked his life against the Jews many times. Even this morning, he organized the martyrdom mission in the Jerusalem market. These are things that outweigh your evidence.'

'Then don't pin Louai's murder on Hussein. Let Hussein's name remain clean, let him be a hero. But set George Saba free, anyway.'

'Someone has to pay. If it isn't Hussein, it'll have to be the Christian.'

Omar Yussef moved closer. He smelled Jihad Awdeh's sweat beneath the aura of his cigarettes. 'I came to you, Jihad, because I know that you aren't one of *them*. You haven't become leader of the Martyrs Brigades just because you happen to be a member of the right family. You're clever. You've made it to the top of the Martyrs Brigades, in spite of the fact that the others treat you as an outsider. For the rest of them,' Omar Yussef gestured beyond the glass door to the gunmen milling about the living room, 'Hussein was some kind of hero and saint, because he's their blood. But you're able to think independently. You can see what he really was. Don't let George die for the sake of someone else's image. This is flesh and blood that will be destroyed tomorrow, not someone's reputation.'

Jihad Awdeh was silent.

'Look, you have to admit that George Saba can't be the collaborator,' Omar Yussef said. 'Hussein was assassinated tonight while George was in jail.

Could he have led the Israelis to Hussein from inside his prison cell?'

'Since the Israelis killed Hussein,' Jihad said, 'doesn't that prove that he was no collaborator? Your accusation against him doesn't make sense. Why would they kill their own agent?'

The Martyrs Brigades leader looked about him, as though making sure no one could overhear. It seemed to Omar Yussef that a tinge of regret passed over Jihad Awdeh's face as he looked at the crowd of gunmen inside. Quietly, he spoke. 'Just before Hussein left his headquarters for the *iftar*, Khamis Zeydan was with him. Hussein told the police chief where he was going.'

Omar Yussef remembered Khamis Zeydan's phone call from the side of Hussein Tamari's burning vehicle. The policeman had told him that he knew Hussein was in the destroyed jeep because he was following him when the missile struck. Omar Yussef felt a deep horror. Already he suspected his friend of betraying Dima Abdel Rahman. Certainly he knew that Khamis Zeydan hated the Martyrs Brigades boss who scorned and humiliated his authority as police chief even to his face. He had wondered why Khamis Zeydan was at the scene of Hussein's death when he received the phone call. Jihad Awdeh wondered, too.

Jihad opened the balcony door. Voices spilled out. The living room was filling with gunmen who would depart from here to Hussein Tamari's funeral. 'I have to go now. We're burying the martyrs.'

Omar Yussef nodded. He shook the hand that Jihad Awdeh proferred. It was cold, but Omar Yussef, too, found it chilly on the balcony. He passed through the crowd of burly men in their sweaty camouflage jackets. They carried their Kalashnikovs, which they would fire into the air as they took what was left of the martyr Hussein to his final rest.

Omar Yussef ran his suspicions about Khamis Zeydan through his head again as he went down the stairs. If Jihad Awdeh believed the police chief was guilty, Khamis Zeydan was in danger. Omar Yussef wanted to call his friend immediately. But if Khamis Zeydan was prepared to let George Saba die for something he hadn't done, could Omar Yussef count him as a friend any more? Was he even a man whose life was worth protecting?

As he crossed the street Omar Yussef briefly saw the silhouette of his granddaughter Nadia, still watching from the window of his house. Then she was gone.

CHAPTER 24

When Nadia stepped away from the window, Omar Yussef wanted to hold her, comfort her, strangle the worry that kept her on watch for him the entire time he was with Jihad Awdeh. He felt that urge almost as a physical force, lifting his feet toward home and raising his arms to clasp her. But he knew he must make one last attempt to free George Saba from jail. He wondered if his granddaughter might have a better grasp on reality and the dangers he faced than he did himself.

Omar Yussef turned right along the main road, cut up toward the *souk*, and headed for Manger Square. The streets were empty, except for occasional jeeps filled with Martyrs Brigades men heading toward the funeral. They poked their rifles out of the windows and fired into the air. Each report from the guns made Omar Yussef jump. It was as though they wished to be certain that their celebration of Hussein's martyrdom should jar him to his very soul. He breathed heavily as he labored up the hill to the *souk* and down through the empty alleys of the old town toward the church.

At Manger Square, there was silence. The broad piazza, resurfaced with a pattern of pink and white bricks a few years before for a visit from the pope, glowed faintly in the moonlight and the dim aura of the faux-Parisian gaslamps erected during the renovation. The firing continued in the distance. They would be burying Hussein now at his village, a few miles to the east, near the conical hill of Herodion. Omar Yussef was glad to be in the quietness, instead of the fury that would eat through everyone at the funeral, biting into their core with the irresistibility of pure, communal hatred and vengefulness. He crossed the northern edge of the empty square toward the police station. He glanced over at the Church of the Nativity. Two priests in brown Franciscan surplices bowed their way through the Gate of Humility. They passed along the front of the church, keeping close to the foot of the wall, where it curved inward like the base of a massive fortress.

The guard at the entrance to the police station greeted Omar Yussef. The policeman's face was bony and undernourished. His eyes were jumpy.

'Is Abu Adel here?'

'Yes, go up to the top of the stairs. His office is there.'

'I know.'

Omar Yussef needed to make one last appeal to Khamis Zeydan. Perhaps his friend did pass information about Dima Abdel Rahman to Hussein Tamari. Maybe he had caused her death. He might even be an Israeli collaborator who had engineered the killing of Tamari, as Jihad Awdeh suggested. But he was the only contact Omar Yussef had. He was the sole person he knew who held the key to the jail in his hand. There must be some way to persuade him to turn that key in the lock and look the other way while Omar Yussef smuggled George out of Bethlehem.

Khamis Zeydan's office was dark, except for the light from a single desk lamp. The pool of yellow light illuminated the police chief's gloved prosthesis. It lay so still on the desktop when Omar Yussef came to the door that he wondered if Khamis Zeydan had detached the hand and left it there out of forgetfulness. The police chief's pistol lay in the light next to the hand. When he saw the gun, the scene immediately made Omar Yussef think of suicide, the quiet drunken moment of self-contempt in the darkness that would precede death at one's own hand. He spoke, doubtfully: 'Abu Adel?'

The glove lifted and turned the lamp toward Omar Yussef. He raised his hand to block the glare.

'Abu Adel, I've come to ask you to forgive me.'

There was silence from the desk. The lamp turned downward, deflecting the light away from Omar Yussef's face. Its beam guided him to a chair on the other side of the desk. He sat on the edge of the seat.

'I apologize for my earlier anger. I should not have accused you when you called to tell me about

Hussein Tamari's death. I've been desperate with worry about George Saba.'

'You ought to think about someone other than George for a change.' Khamis Zeydan's voice was thick and slurred and self-pitying. Omar Yussef knew that the darkness in the office was intended to prevent any subordinate who might blunder in from witnessing the boss with his whisky bottle.

'You're right. Abu Adel, you've been a good friend to me. I mean that. Right up to this very moment, you've been a great friend, and I haven't always responded. But please understand that it's only because I'm not used to dealing with the dangers and deceits of these kinds of events. I'm just a schoolteacher.'

'Stick to teaching, I told you.'

'Yes, you did, and you were right.'

'Yeah, I told you, all right. Stick to—'

'I just spoke with Jihad Awdeh.' Even through the darkness of the room, Omar Yussef sensed a change in Khamis Zeydan's alertness. The mumbling stopped. He was waiting.

Omar Yussef went around the desk. 'Jihad believed me when I told him how Hussein Tamari killed Louai and Dima, and how he framed George.'

The shades snapped open. The cloudy moon-light cast strips across Khamis Zeydan's face. He was upright in his seat with his hand on the cord of the shades. His eyes were intense, narrow,

268

vicious where the light caught them. The shadows looked like tattoos or camouflage.

'You listen to me, Abu Ramiz,' Khamis Zeydan said. He coughed and gathered himself. Omar Yussef saw that the policeman was still drunk, but desperately trying to control himself. 'Don't trust a word Jihad said to you. He's a crook and a liar. Don't trust a word. Not a word.'

'He's the only hope I have.'

'Then you're lost.'

'I would have preferred to rely on you.'

'There's nothing I can do.'

'So don't tell me not to appeal to Jihad, if you won't help. You have the key to the jail. Let's go and free George now. We can hide him somewhere until we convince the court that he's innocent. Maybe Jihad will help us.'

'I don't know which part of what you just said is the most idiotic. First, I'm still a policeman, so I won't release a convicted man from his cell. Second, you won't get into the courtroom, let alone convince them that Hussein Tamari was really the collaborator and killer. Do you think the judges are as eager to get themselves killed as you appear to be? Third, Jihad isn't going to help you. He helps himself. He blew you off, that's all, Abu Ramiz, stalling until he gets a chance to finish you off quietly.'

Omar Yussef struggled to think of a way to persuade the police chief. He could grab Khamis Zeydan's gun from where it lay on the table. With the gun held on him, Khamis Zeydan would lead him to the cells and release George. But Omar Yussef knew it would be an empty gesture. He had heard of something called a safety catch and he wouldn't know how to disengage it. Even if he did, he could never use the gun on his friend. Khamis Zeydan would simply take it out of his hand and he would let him do so.

The police chief glanced toward the window. He stood and slid the glass open. Omar Yussef suddenly heard what his friend's keener ear had detected. The gunfire was growing nearer.

'Is the funeral coming here?' Omar Yussef asked.

'The burial was in Teqoa. This noise must be something else.'

The firing grew more intense. It approached up the hill behind the Church of the Nativity. Omar Yussef leaned out of the window. A row of jeeps pulled around the corner and stopped in front of the police station. There must have been more of them out of sight, by the entrance, because even as the armed men piled out below, he heard heavy footsteps on the stairs behind him. Khamis Zeydan turned.

'They're coming up here,' Omar Yussef said.

'No. They're going down. To the jail.'

Khamis Zeydan picked up his gun from the desk and holstered it. 'Stay here, Abu Ramiz.' He went to the door.

'Why are they going to the jail?' Even as he spoke, Omar Yussef knew the answer. *George*. 'I'm coming with you.'

Khamis Zeydan was already on the stairs. Omar Yussef could see how shaky the police chief's legs were from the drink. Both men descended the steps slowly, despite their despairing efforts to move quicker. Omar Yussef cursed his aging body and Khamis Zeydan muttered about the whisky in his bloodstream. At the entrance, the guard stood against a wall with his hands in the air. Two Martyrs Brigades men held their Kalashnikovs on him. There were at least a dozen of them in the small hallway, and more outside.

From below came the sound of an explosion. Falling metal rang through a corridor. They must have blown the door off George's cell.

'What the fuck do you think you're doing?' Khamis Zeydan walked straight to the gunmen holding his nervous guard against the wall. He pushed their rifles aside. 'You should be ashamed of yourselves. Get out of here now, or you'll pay a terrible price.'

Khamis Zeydan's determined arrival seemed to puncture the resolve of the gunmen in the lobby. But they were revived by the sight of their leader a moment later. Jihad Awdeh came up the stairs with a raised Kalashnikov in one hand and George Saba's hair grasped in the other.

George's eyes were closed by fresh bruises and his nose wept blood. As Jihad Awdeh hauled him up the steps by his scalp, blood rolled across George's forehead and he bawled in pain.

Omar Yussef made the last few steps, clinging

to the banister. In his panic, he wasn't sure if he would be able to stand without support. He called out to George Saba, but the gunmen chanted that they would revenge the martyr Hussein Tamari, and George didn't hear his old schoolteacher.

Jihad Awdeh let go of George's hair long enough to lift his rifle butt and club Khamis Zeydan in the face. The police chief crumpled. The policeman who had been guarding the door bent to catch his commander. Khamis Zeydan appeared to be out cold. Jihad Awdeh called above the laughter and cheers: 'This way the godless bastard achieves oblivion without having to waste all his whisky.'

Omar Yussef jostled with the gunmen as they pushed toward the small doorway. He caught sight of George wearing his small herringbone coat. Its shoulders were drenched with blood. The gunmen took swings at the prisoner whenever they were close enough.

Omar Yussef was almost the last through the door. Outside on the sidewalk, he saw Muhammad Abdel Rahman. The gunmen must have brought the old man to see them exact their justice on the Christian who had led the Israelis to kill his son. Muhammad's face was blank, deathly. Omar Yussef wondered what it was that he knew about the way Louai died, about Abu Walid, about the killing of Dima, his daughter-in-law. Then he thought that the knowledge of having lost two sons in a few days, one to an assassination and another who took his own life in the act of destroying ordinary people with a bomb strapped to his midriff, would be enough to make a man seem almost dead himself. Muhammad noticed Omar Yussef stumbling out of the police station at the back of the crowd. He turned away and wrapped his face in the end of his *keffiyeh*.

The mob of gunmen moved to the edge of the square. From the center of the crowd, someone tossed a rope over the arm of one of the fake gaslamps. *Oh, God, it's happening*, Omar Yussef thought. He rushed toward the group, barely able to breathe. How could he stop them? He would get to the center of the crowd and throw himself over George. He reached the back of the melee. He shoved between two of the gunmen, screaming to them to make way.

There came a cheer and Omar Yussef saw George hauled halfway up the lamppost by his ankles. The tails of the herringbone coat fell over his face, so that at first Omar Yussef believed he was dead already. Then his arms moved, flailing desperately toward the crowd below as though he might catch hold of it and anchor himself to the earth. The gunmen yanked him higher until he was almost at the top of the post. Then there was a single shot, and it unleashed a full volley from the crowd of men. George Saba's body jerked with each fatal impact.

Until it stopped. The deafening noise of the guns ended, and it seemed to Omar Yussef that there was perfect silence everywhere. No one seemed to move, even though the crowd of gunmen was joined by others coming from the funeral. They chanted the glory of God for the death of the traitor and their joyful, jostling number grew every moment. But Omar Yussef was alone on the square, staring above him at the swinging corpse of George Saba. He shoved into the center of the crowd, but they were not men surrounding him; they were empty of humanity and he was solitary among them with all he had lost. Below George Saba there was a slick of blood on the new cobbles. Omar Yussef felt the blood in the air, as though it were a light drizzle that would begore the surface of everything. Then he realized that it was rain.

The crowd moved away. Someone called out that they were going to the traitor's house to destroy it, as the Israelis would obliterate Hussein Tamari's house and the home of Yunis Abdel Rahman, the suicide bomber.

In only a few moments, Omar Yussef was almost truly alone beneath the corpse of George Saba. He reached up, but the body was strung too high for him to touch. The rain came more heavily. It was the downpour that had threatened for a week. Omar Yussef looked at his shoes. The rain washed them until the buckles were bright in the light from the lamppost. The water took the pool of blood and swirled it across the cobbles to the drain in front of the dark Church of the Nativity.

Omar Yussef turned from the shadows of the

church's spartan façade toward George Saba on the lamppost. The dead man looked as though he might be descending from the light, his hands above his head in a dive from the radiance of a star to the hard earth. George had brought that brightness to Omar Yussef, who had watched him transform from a little boy to a grown man to a punctured sack of meat. Omar Yussef spun away, looking back toward the church.

The body is like this Church of the Nativity, he thought. It's warmed by some divine breath at first, but sustained by worldly impulses. All the time this breath slowly chills, until death. Every exhalation is an expulsion of some part of our finite store of life, and also a sigh of relief that the grave is closer by one tedious, depressing pulse. The body is abused and renovated and squabbled over, like this church, where they say Jesus was born. But there is only a crypt where that famous birth is supposed to have taken place. There is nothing there, just as we find nothing but an emptiness left to mark where each of us was alive. Here in Bethlehem there was a Messiah who left the job unfinished. In this church, there's no glowing spirit, no redemption. Each time we breathe, we fear that it's our last breath and it will chill us all the way to the void.

There was only one reason not to feel over-whelmed by that fear and that was the belief in the legacy we leave, the positive changes we bring to the world. Omar Yussef had hoped George Saba would be his legacy, living after him as proof that the schoolteacher made the world better. He had hoped that Dima Abdel Rahman would be part of that gift, too. As he looked at the body swinging above him, he fought against the urge to feel that all his life's work was just so much destroyed hope and goodness befouled. Instead, *he* could be George Saba's legacy, giving the dead man life in his every decent, kind, intelligent deed.

He picked at the big knot the gunmen had tied around the base of the lamppost to secure the body high in the air. The corpse dropped a little. As he freed the knot, he lost his grip on the wet rope and it slipped from his hands. He reached out to grab the falling body. George's elbow caught him painfully on the side of the head as the body came down. Omar Yussef grabbed the shoulders to break the fall and went to the ground on top of the dead man. He lay still. If he was going to weep, now would be when it would happen, he thought.

There was a hand on his shoulder, lifting him. When he came up, Muhammad Abdel Rahman stood beside him. Both men were bereaved, but Omar Yussef thought perhaps he would be the one who might draw the greatest strength from these terrible days, not the man before him.

Shots came from the west, distant, their reverberations threading between the raindrops.

'They are firing up at Beit Jala,' Muhammad Abdel Rahman said. 'They are destroying this Christian's house. In revenge.'

'For the death of your son?'

Muhammad Abdel Rahman shook his head. He looked no more alive than the corpse at their feet. 'No, my son wasn't their concern, truly. They are taking revenge for Hussein Tamari, the martyr.'

Omar Yussef felt angry, despite the frailty of the old man who had lost his sons. Hussein Tamari was a murderer and gangster. He was no martyr. Omar Yussef pointed at George's body. 'There is your martyr,' he said. 'There. There is your martyr.'

A police jeep squealed around the corner, throwing up spray from the rain that rushed down the slope. Six policemen jumped out at the entrance to the station. Omar Yussef saw a staggering Khamis Zeydan step among them. They rushed across the square toward George Saba's body. Four of them picked up the corpse roughly by the legs and arms, and hauled it toward the police station. The others shoved the few onlookers who remained and told them to clear the square.

One of the policemen pushed Omar Yussef with his rifle butt and told him to go home.

'Fuck you,' Omar Yussef shouted. He pushed the policeman back. 'Where were you ten minutes ago, when they were killing your prisoner? Don't touch me.'

Khamis Zeydan came to Omar Yussef. He thrust the policeman aside and took his old friend by the arm. The police chief's upper lip swelled beneath his nicotine-stained moustache, and his teeth were bloody from Jihad Awdeh's blow. The two men stared at each other. Omar Yussef wondered if Khamis Zeydan felt shame, or simply confusion after the impact of the rifle-butt on his head and all the whisky.

Khamis Zeydan looked up when a shot sounded through the rain. There were more percussions, spattering randomly through the air like the first raindrops of a storm. 'What the fuck is that?'

'The Martyrs Brigades went to Beit Jala. They've gone to destroy George's house,' Omar Yussef said.

'He has a wife and family, doesn't he?'

'Yes.'

Khamis Zeydan took Omar Yussef by the arm and pulled him toward his jeep. 'Let's go.'

CHAPTER 25

Omar Yussef climbed stiffly from the back of Khamis Zeydan's jeep. The rain penetrated his coat and seeped through his flat cap. It washed over the tops of his loafers. His bare fingers were icy and swollen. He shook himself to get the blood moving through his arms and legs, as he looked toward George Saba's home.

The Martyrs Brigades surrounded the house. A half dozen of them kneeled on the roof. With their assault rifles, they aimed at the Israelis across the valley. It was hopeless to expect that they would hit anyone except by the most random of chances at this distance and with their view obscured by low rainclouds. Omar Yussef followed the Israeli tracer as it came toward the gunmen on the roof, striping the stormy valley, slapping into the side of the Saba home or over-shooting it and striking the house across the street. Between Omar Yussef and the Saba house there were a dozen Martyrs Brigades men. Some of them watched the arrival of Khamis Zeydan's police jeep, but most were intent on the doorway and windows of the house. From where they milled about, they must be able

279

to see inside, Omar Yussef figured. Sheltered from the gunfire by the walls of the house, the gunmen seemed to find something highly amusing about whatever was happening in the bedroom that fronted the street.

The policemen advanced toward the house with Khamis Zeydan at their head. They dashed across the exposed gaps between buildings. When they reached the cordon of gunmen, Khamis Zeydan ordered them to let him through. Someone called out an insult about the police chief's sister. The police and the gunmen shoved each other. As they jostled, Omar Yussef passed along the edge of the street. In the darkness, he sidled past the gunmen on the steps by the entrance. To his surprise, the sound of gunfire was louder within the house.

The lights in the living room had been extinguished. From the entrance, Omar Yussef saw that the gunmen had removed the sandbags from the windows. They clustered around the shattered frames, shooting toward the Israelis. The noise was terrifying. It echoed about the high ceilings and off the thick walls. One of the men at the window turned toward the door. His face was manic with the ecstacy of the fight. Omar Yussef recognized him. It was Mahmoud Zubeida, the policeman whose daughter had brought him the news of George's arrest. His eyes were as dark as his betel-stained teeth, but they radiated a chilling energy. When he saw Omar Yussef, his grin faded.

He looked embarrassed and ashamed, but also angry. The presence of the schoolteacher broke the anonymity that allowed him to free the ugliness he would otherwise have hidden deep within himself.

Omar Yussef looked away from Mahmoud Zubeida. He took a step forward and turned to his left. George Saba's family cowered against the wall. Here was the evidence that George had taken the wrong path, if you wanted to see it that way. George was dead, because he'd tried to defend his family, but here they were, unprotected, because of his death. Then Omar Yussef decided that if his former pupil had acted differently, George Saba too would be shivering with fear on the floor, and maybe he hadn't been wrong to do as he did. The wrong was done against him, not by him.

Sofia looked up. Tears laid crooked fingers of mascara across her cheeks. She held her two children under her arms. Habib Saba sat next to them. The old man was quiet and motionless. He cradled something black in his lap, perhaps a book. Its square edge jutted from beneath his arms like the tail of a stricken ocean liner going down. Omar Yussef was about to speak to Sofia, when he noticed a movement on the other side of the bedroom.

Jihad Awdeh sat in an old Damascened armchair next to the big vanity by the bed. He uncrossed his legs and stood, flicking his cigarette out of the open window. He smiled at Omar Yussef and lifted his gun.

Omar Yussef thought of jumping back toward the entrance, but he couldn't do it. Something held him in place there, despite the gun trained on him. He thought it might be the memory of George Saba, who had refused to buckle before wickedness, that now kept his old teacher steady. So he stayed where he was, turning to face Jihad Awdeh.

'We're taking care of the traitor's family, as you can see, Abu Ramiz,' Jihad Awdeh said. 'But I'm happy to see you here, too.'

'Jihad, you know that if you harm me, you'll be starting a fight with the biggest clan in Dehaisha. Even you should think twice before taking on all my people,' Omar Yussef said.

'There are bullets flying as wildly here as those accusations of murder and collaboration you made about the martyr Hussein. Who knows if one of those bullets might happen to strike you? I believe your clan would agree that an Israeli bullet killed you. Most people are happy with an excuse to avoid trouble.'

'But not you.'

'Nor you, evidently.'

Jihad Awdeh walked across the room with his gun on Omar Yussef.

'You don't think you're really protecting the reputation of Hussein Tamari by what you're doing here,' Omar Yussef said. 'This is evil. You shoot from inside this house, because you know the Israelis will destroy it in return.'

Jihad Awdeh lifted a concurring eyebrow. He fed a bullet into the chamber of his Kalashnikov and raised it to his chest.

This is it, Omar Yussef thought. *At least I didn't have to be hung upside down in the square.* The image of Nadia, her face sad and eyes lowered, flickered through his mind, but he fought it away. He felt proud that his last moment would be defiant, and he stared into Jihad Awdeh's black eyes.

The blast came with a whoosh like a jet plane passing low. Jihad Awdeh looked up momentarily. Then Omar Yussef's ears went dead, as though he was underwater, and the wall of the bedroom came down. Omar Yussef felt himself tumble out of the doorway and down the steps. He hit his head against the railing, then struck something soft.

He found himself upside down on top of two gunmen. The men wriggled frantically as though they thought he might be dead and they wanted no contact with the corpse. They rolled him off them and into a puddle. The cold water roused him and he was already on his knees when Khamis Zeydan and another police officer grabbed his arms and lifted him.

'It must have been a tank shell,' Khamis Zeydan said. 'Are you all right?'

'Tank shell?'

'The Martyrs Brigades were shooting from inside the building. The only way for the Israeli soldiers to penetrate these thick, old walls is with a tank shell. It must have gone in through the living room where the firing was coming from and blown you out of the front of the house. Who else was in there?'

'George's family.'

The dazed gunmen rushed up the steps with the police. In the bedroom, they found Jihad Awdeh. There was blood coming from his head and he was ghostly with the dust of the fallen wall. His men helped him to his feet and took him down the steps. Omar Yussef waited for the Martyrs Brigades chief to look at him, but Jihad could barely keep his eyes open. His gaze was unfocussed and distant, like a troubled man in prayer. He stumbled past amid a crowd of bellowing gunmen, out to the street where the red lights of an ambulance flickered.

The wall between the bedroom and the living room was partially collapsed. Khamis Zeydan and Omar Yussef peered through the gap. George Saba's antique furniture smoldered. The rack of wedding dresses burned, giving off a poisonous smell from the plastic wrappings. The teak dresser was splintered down to its stubby legs. The French statuette that had stood on it was intact, but cast to the flagstones. Omar Yussef remembered that this naked, twisted woman of Rodin's was called *The Martyr*. There were four bodies in the living room, clustered around the three-foot-wide aperture in the outer wall where the shell had entered. Khamis Zeydan peered at one of the bodies.

'Mahmoud Zubeida,' he said.

Omar Yussef looked at the blank face of the dead policeman. The bony face was pale and its lips were drawn back over the brown teeth. It seemed like the skull of a man already years in the ground. The dream of death that he had imagined Mahmoud Zubeida's daughter enduring every night finally had come true. He wondered if he would be able to tell the girl that her father was happy in the firefight before he died, that he was a martyr. He recalled the shame and anger on the man's face when he had recognized the schoolteacher. No, someone else would tell the girl about her father's heroism. He wouldn't be able to talk to her about the way the gunman died. He didn't trust himself not to reveal the ugliness of the corpse and the blood that looked like seeping mud in the dim light.

Or the collapsed wall of the bedroom. What would he tell Khadija Zubeida about that? And the family beneath it.

Omar Yussef began heaving stones from the mound where the bedroom wall had been. Khamis Zeydan and his policemen lifted segments of plaster and stone. When they came to Sofia and the children, the officer closest to the bodies stepped back and puked. The police chief grabbed another of his shocked men and orchestrated the lifting of the last slab from Sofia's legs. George

285

Saba's wife was dead. Her bloodied head lay horribly smashed across her collarbone, her neck broken and shoulders caved in. Under her arms, the children were unconscious, but Khamis Zeydan found a pulse in both. He laid them on the bed. They seemed tiny and battered, though the medic who checked their vital signs gave a brief nod to indicate that they would survive.

Omar Yussef pulled Khamis Zeydan back to the rubble. He was short of breath. 'Habib Saba,' he gasped.

Khamis Zeydan looked at the deep pile of stone. His eyes widened. The policemen began to lift the debris. Sweating, they came to George Saba's father. Habib sat amid the rubble in the same posture Omar Yussef saw him in during the gunfight. His legs were pulled up to his chest and his hands held his ankles. His bald head was gashed along the crown. The deep wound, filled with dust and blood, was a ribbon of black. Omar Yussef thought that Habib Saba had wanted this, so resigned did he seem in death. It was as though he believed there was no reason to save his grandchildren or his daughter-in-law, just as he gave up hope for his son. Perhaps he had been right in his son's case. If Omar Yussef hadn't tried to save him, hadn't gone to Jihad Awdeh and told him what he knew, at least George might have faced a firing squad, not a lynch mob. Yet he couldn't understand the tranquility of Habib Saba. He thought that the old man's body ought to look more crushed than it did. His perfect stillness made him seem immutable, as if the collapsing wall had found his body as unchangeable as stone and failed to break it. Habib Saba's corpse emerged from the rubble neat and self-contained and serene, as though the policemen heaving aside the debris were archeologists unearthing the statue of an ancient monarch.

The policemen lifted Habib Saba. A thick black book dropped from his grasp into the dust and stone. Omar Yussef brushed the powdered cement from the worn leather cover and opened it. On the flyleaf, there was an inscription in an educated, old-fashioned hand: 'To Abu Omar, God willing there always will be such harmony between those of our two faiths as there has been between you and I. Your dear friend, Issa.' These were the words written by the Jerusalem priest to Omar Yussef's father in the days before there was hatred between Christians and Muslims in Palestine. This was the Bible Omar Yussef gave George when he was a student, the solace of his exile and the reminder of his love for his home-town. George's father had clutched it as he died, protecting it with his body as Sofia protected the bodies of her children, as though he could keep intact that better world it represented, even as his bones shattered.

Omar Yussef took his handkerchief from his jacket. He wiped the sweat from his forehead to moisten the edge of the cloth and rubbed the dust from the Bible. The black leather came up as lustrous as the feathers of a raven.

The rain fell more heavily. An ambulance quickly took George Saba's children away, before the shooting started again. Jihad Awdeh climbed unsteadily out of another ambulance. The medics grabbed at him, but he shook them off, angrily. His men, shouting at the police to clear the way, took him to his jeep and sped away.

Khamis Zeydan looked up at George Saba's smoldering home. He issued a few orders to his men to begin the clean-up. Then he put his hand on Omar Yussef's elbow. 'I think I'd better take you to the hospital,' he said.

'I'm fine.'

'Better to be safe. The doctors ought to have a look at you.'

'There's nothing wrong with me.'

'This is the second time in two days you've been knocked off your feet by an explosion. Come on, these things can damage your internal organs, even if you seem fine on the outside. Let's go.'

'No, take me home. I need to change out of these clothes. I'm wet through.'

Shivering, he climbed into the passenger seat of Khamis Zeydan's jeep. They drove slowly out of the street and down the winding hill from Beit Jala. Omar Yussef was silent and angry. Here he was, taking a ride from the police chief, the very man who surely should have prevented all this killing. He had thought Khamis Zeydan was not the one to blame, that it was the corruption all around him that made him ineffectual. But now he believed that his friend was, at best, a passive participant in murder and, at worst, the one who led the killers to their prey.

Khamis Zeydan seemed to sense the meaning of his friend's silence. He looked across at Omar Yussef repeatedly, but the schoolteacher deliberately kept his eyes ahead on the empty road as they passed Aida refugee camp. Eventually the police chief blurted out, 'You blame me for this, don't you. I can tell. You're angry with me. You blame me.'

Omar Yussef was quiet. He wanted to speak, but he still didn't want to hurt his friend and he didn't have the energy for a debate.

'I'm right, aren't I?' Khamis Zeydan yelled. 'You think it's my fault.'

Omar Yussef couldn't restrain himself. 'Of course I do. You're the police chief. Are you telling me it's not the police chief's fault when a man is taken from his jail cell and lynched yards from the police station? It's not the police chief's fault when a bunch of armed thugs draw the Israelis into firing a tank shell at a family's house?'

'You don't know the pressure I'm under.'

'To do what?'

'That's just it. *Not* to do anything. To allow all this to go on.'

'I don't believe you.'

'You think that just because I wear a uniform

I'm more powerful than Hussein Tamari and Jihad Awdeh? Don't believe it. They're the ones with the backing from the top, the very top.' Khamis Zeydan lowered his voice, but it remained bitter, resentful. 'The lynching was too much, even for me. But how could I have known they would do that? I tried to stop them. You saw me, didn't you? I tried to stop them.'

Omar Yussef felt a stirring of sympathy for this man, who had sacrificed his comforts and private life for decades. Now he was betrayed by the men for whom he had fought. If that made him behave like the worthless colleagues around him, it didn't mean he was one of them at his core.

'Why didn't you believe me when I said that Hussein Tamari was the one who led the Israelis to the house in Irtas? The collaborator who helped them kill Louai Abdel Rahman? That he was the one who killed Dima Abdel Rahman to cover his tracks?' Omar Yussef said.

'Don't start on that again.'

'Listen, it makes no difference now. The Israeli helicopter killed Hussein, so the murderer is dead. George Saba is dead, so there's no innocent man awaiting execution anymore. The story is over. My so-called investigation is finished. There's just you and me. Why didn't you believe me? I showed you the MAG cartridge from Hussein's machine gun. I showed you the evidence.'

'The bullets that killed Louai came from an Israeli sniper rifle. But you found a MAG cartridge.

That's not evidence against Hussein, because Louai wasn't killed with a MAG. Dima was killed by having her throat slit, also not by a MAG. Your theory is good, but not necessarily correct.'

'So maybe Hussein didn't shoot Louai, but he guided the Israelis to their target and he left a clue when he accidentally dropped the cartridge casing from his own gun. He must have been the one who identified Louai to the Israeli snipers with the laser sight, the red dot Dima said she saw flicking across his body right before the shots that killed him.'

Khamis Zeydan pulled the jeep over at the side of the road by Omar Yussef's house. 'All right, if it makes you happy, then I'll say that I'm sorry I didn't believe you. But you ought to know that there isn't anything I could have done. You don't have real evidence and, in any case, proof isn't what decides criminal cases here anymore. Belief, influence, and evil – that's what you need on your side.'

Omar Yussef wondered if he should tell Khamis Zeydan just how much more he suspected him than he'd already let on. He felt very weary. He decided to allow the policeman to go. He nodded and, silently, got out of the jeep. He waved goodbye with George's black Bible and watched Khamis Zeydan turn around, slowly jolting over the median strip into the other lane. He felt the rain coming down inside the back of his collar. He put the Bible inside his jacket.

The ditch the Israelis had dug across the street two days before blocked the sidewalk. Omar Yussef climbed over the low wall in front of his house and hurried inside.

CHAPTER 26

When Omar Yussef came through his front door, Maryam was waiting in the salon, wrapped in a blanket. He went toward her. Nadia was asleep against her grandmother's chest. The posture gave Omar Yussef an immediate shudder: it reminded him of the position in which George Saba's wife had died, with her two children huddled against her beneath her arms. The sleepiness of Maryam's face seemed almost as static as death, and he felt an irrational relief when she looked up and spoke.

'I was telling Nadia a story,' she whispered. 'She didn't want to go to bed until you came home.'

Omar Yussef put George's Bible on the coffee table. He lifted Nadia's shoulders, while Maryam took the girl's legs. He moved gingerly, careful not to wake her and not to strain his back, which throbbed again as the rain worked its chill into his bones and his muscles rebelled against the frantic heaving of the stones that had crushed the Saba family. Omar and Maryam took the girl to their bedroom and laid her in their bed.

'You had a call from the UN office in Jerusalem,'

293

Maryam said. 'I wrote down the number for you. It was very late for them to call.'

Omar Yussef nodded. He thought of poor Steadman. The UN people handling that crisis would be working late.

'I'll sleep in the salon, once I've changed out of these wet clothes,' he said.

'I'll make you some tea to warm you up. Do you want soup?'

'No, thanks. Tea, please.'

After she brought the tea, Omar Yussef sat in his silk pajamas and a woolen dressing gown and put his hand out to hold Maryam's fingers.

'What happened, Omar?'

'George is dead.'

Omar Yussef realized that he hadn't said those words before. They seemed so loaded with the grave it felt as though his mouth were full of the dust to which George Saba would now return. It choked him, and he gasped and sobbed.

Maryam reached around his shoulders, stroked his neck, and put her chin against his forehead.

Omar Yussef told her what he had seen, and she cried with him, quietly, deeply. *She knows me*, he thought. *I've hidden things from her over the years and I believed we had grown apart, but she has been with me so long that she simply feels what I feel. Our senses are bonded together, even if we might disagree over politics or things that happen in the town. She didn't want me to investigate George's case, to risk myself to save him, but she knew all along what he meant to me.*

It was a long time before Omar Yussef felt like breaking the tender grip in which Maryam held him. He sat up and looked at the clock on the sideboard. It was 2:30 A.M.

'Why don't you go to bed now, Maryam?'

'I'll bring some blankets for you.'

'I don't think I'll sleep. I'll read a little.'

'Let me sit with you a while. I'll make some more tea.'

Maryam was in the kitchen when Omar heard it. The thudding of the helicopter came through the night and held in place above him. Its rhythm disguised the roaring engines of the tanks and jeeps that came down from the hill above Dehaisha. Omar Yussef went to the window. He wondered if they were coming back to widen the trench in the road, but when they arrived there were no bulldozers. He looked across the street. Two tanks and two APCs took up positions right outside his house. He rushed to turn out the light. The soldiers piled out of the APCs and filed quickly, bent and jogging, up the stairs of the apartment building opposite. Maryam came through the door. In the darkness, her eyes looked haunted.

'They must have come for Jihad Awdeh,' Omar Yussef said. 'Go wake Ramiz and the kids. Just in case they come in here, I don't want anyone waking up with a soldier in their bedroom. But don't panic them.'

Maryam hurried from the room.

The soldiers set sentries on each corner of the sideroad. Omar Yussef opened the window a little. He could hear the radio crackling Hebrew from inside the nearest APC.

Soldiers came down the stairs of the apartment building. Omar Yussef thought perhaps they hadn't found Jihad Awdeh and were leaving. Then he saw that there were only three soldiers, followed by a file of people. The residents of the building were being kicked out while the soldiers searched. The little parade headed across the street toward Omar Yussef's house. He went to meet them at the door.

When he pulled the door back, the first of the soldiers stepped up into the light from the hall. His face was painted in blue and olive camouflage. *What use is that in an apartment building?* Omar Yussef thought. He wondered if the soldier would speak to him in Arabic. The Arabic speakers were always the worst. The more they learned about Arabs, the more they seemed to disdain them.

The soldier said something curt and guttural in Hebrew.

'Do you speak Arabic or English?' Omar Yussef asked in English.

The soldier answered in English. 'You never learned Hebrew?'

'I was always too much of an optimist,' Omar Yussef said.

The soldier smiled a little. His teeth showed

white through the camouflage make-up. He pushed past Omar Yussef and scanned the hall. Maryam and Nadia came out of the bedroom. Omar Yussef heard Ramiz behind the half-open door urging his wife to dress. Maryam's face blanched when she saw the camouflaged soldier. Nadia's was blank.

'Lower your gun, please,' Omar Yussef said.

The soldier let his M-16 barrel fall. 'We're conducting a search in the neighborhood. Some of the people who live in the building opposite have to stay out of the place while we search it. It's raining, so we're going to bring them in here.'

Omar Yussef nodded.

More than a dozen people came through the front door. Omar Yussef greeted them and asked them to come into the salon. Maryam went to make tea, but the soldier stopped her and told her to bring everyone else who was in the house to the salon and to wait with them there. As the people came in, they all bore the same bedraggled, frightened sleepiness. Some of the children whimpered.

The last to enter were Amjad and Leila. Amjad smiled and shook Omar Yussef's hand, thanking him for letting them shelter in his house. Omar Yussef felt bad about his lust for Amjad's wife. Amjad was a good fellow. Even so, Leila was beautiful in the jeans and sweatshirt she must have thrown on as the soldiers turfed them out of their apartment. She had brushed her hair, but it looked slept on, nonetheless, the way it would be on the pillow.

The soldier stood in the doorway, watching the crowd, which now included Ramiz and his family. Omar Yussef knew everyone in the room, except for a woman in the corner with her two children. He assumed they must be the newcomers, Jihad Awdeh's family. He couldn't recall the woman's face from his visit to Jihad's home earlier that night. He stepped carefully through the carpet of children sitting at their parents' feet and greeted the woman.

'You are Jihad's wife?' he whispered.

'Yes.'

The woman was young and quiet. Omar Yussef suddenly recognized the boy standing behind her. He had opened the door of his father's apartment six hours before when Omar Yussef went in to appeal to Jihad to save George Saba.

'Ah, I met you earlier, didn't I?' Omar Yussef said.

The boy nodded.

'What is your name?'

'Walid Jihad Brahim Awdeh.'

It struck Omar Yussef like a lightning bolt. 'You are Jihad's eldest son?'

'Yes.'

Jihad Awdeh's eldest son was named Walid. Jihad was the 'father of Walid,' Abu Walid. Could he have suspected the wrong man all along? Hussein Tamari's eldest son was Walid. Tamari was Abu

Walid. But perhaps Tamari wasn't *the* Abu Walid that Louai Abdel Rahman spoke to just before he died. It could have been Jihad Awdeh. Jihad was Abu Walid, so perhaps he was also the killer, the collaborator.

George had seen Jihad picking something up from the roof of his house and putting it in his vest, when he confronted the Martyrs Brigades gunmen. It could have been cartridges spat out of the breech of Tamari's big MAG. Louai wasn't shot with the MAG, but there was a MAG cartridge at the scene of his murder. Could it have fallen out of Jihad's pocket?

Omar Yussef wanted to lay out this revelation for Khamis Zeydan immediately, but there was no chance of using the phone with the soldier standing guard in the room. He would have to wait until the soldiers completed their search across the street and allowed everyone to leave the salon. He felt a moment of panic. What if the soldiers searched his house, too? They might find the gun, George's Webley in among the socks in his closet. They would surely take him in, and they might keep him for months without trial. By that time, Jihad Awdeh would be far too powerful for him to persuade Khamis Zeydan to arrest him. Even now, he wasn't sure that the police chief would bring him in. He must get to Khamis Zeydan tonight, while the guilt about George's lynching remained heavy upon him.

'The soldiers won't find your father at home, will they?' Omar Yussef said.

Jihad Awdeh's eldest boy stared insolently at Omar Yussef. He lifted his chin, signaling that this was not a question he would ever answer. This boy would never believe that his father was anything but a hero, even if Omar Yussef managed to persuade a court to put the Martyrs Brigades leader on trial.

The soldier kept them in the salon more than an hour. The room grew rank. Some of the small children wet themselves on the carpet as they cried. Several of the women wept and rocked back and forth. All the men seemed to be smoking. The tension was dreadful for Omar Yussef. His back hurt from standing for so long, and he wished he had taken a hot shower when he came home to warm himself after the rain. The smoke in the room made him cough. He wanted to get out of there, to nail the bastard who had set up George Saba. He stared with hatred at the soldier. *Who is this guy to prevent me from getting to the police so that they can do justice? Finish your damned search and get out of my house with your stupid gun and your ridiculous camouflage make-up.* He considered telling the soldier that Jihad Awdeh had fled to the Church of the Nativity, but there was no way to speak privately to him. In any case, knowledge of Jihad's whereabouts would only make him a suspect in the soldier's eyes and he'd be arrested. There was something else Omar Yussef acknowledged: he knew he couldn't bring himself to turn over a Palestinian to the soldiers. He didn't want

Jihad Awdeh killed. He wanted the man arrested, forced to confess. Dead, he would be a hero, a martyr, when he merited only humiliation.

It was almost 4:00 A.M. when the two-way radio clipped to the soldier's shoulder sparked with a deep, incoherent voice. Immediately and without a word, the soldier left the room and went out of the front door. Omar Yussef followed after a moment. He looked out of the door. The soldier jumped into the back of the APC. Two last men got in beside him and pulled the metal doors shut. With a gush of diesel fumes and a grinding bellow, the Israeli vehicles pulled off toward the base on the other side of Dehaisha.

The soldiers were still in sight when Omar Yussef turned back to the people in the salon. They crowded by the window, watching the soldiers leave.

'They're gone,' he said.

'Let me make everyone some tea,' Maryam said.

Omar Yussef desperately wanted to dress and go to Khamis Zeydan. 'Maryam, our guests are tired. Surely they would like to go home and rest.'

'Nonsense, Omar, don't be rude. We have to make some tea for our guests.'

Omar Yussef couldn't argue in front of all those people. He frowned and went to his bedroom. He would dress, so that once the people did leave he would follow them out right away. He put on thick trousers, a shirt and a sweater, because it was the last, coldest part of the night. He dialed Khamis

Zeydan's home and office numbers from the phone on the bedroom nightstand. There was no answer. He dialed both numbers again and let them ring. Eventually someone picked up at the police station.

'I need to talk to Abu Adel.'

'It's very late.' The night sergeant clearly had been asleep.

'You weren't awake? The Israelis are in the town.'

'Do you want me to arrest them?'

Omar Yussef took a breath. 'I need to speak to Abu Adel about a murder.'

A pause. 'Who is this?'

'Abu Ramiz.'

'Abu Ramiz, the schoolteacher?'

'Yes, I'm a friend of Abu Adel.'

'I know. Look, Abu Ramiz, if you're his friend, you'll see him in the morning. He can't talk just now, if you know what I mean.'

Omar Yussef thought of the bottle of whisky in Khamis Zeydan's office. He understood what the sergeant meant. 'Thank you. If you see him, tell him I called.'

As he lifted a pair of shoes from the bottom of his closet, Omar Yussef looked in the sock drawer. He took out the Webley and stuck it into his belt.

Maryam carried a tray of teacups past the bedroom door. 'Omar, why are you dressing?'

He stepped around her and went to the front door. 'I'm going to the church.'

CHAPTER 27

The rain came down cold as Omar Yussef hurried across Manger Square. He halted almost exactly where George Saba had died and looked up at the faint light of the fake gaslamp. The memory of George's humiliated body, swinging from that metal arm, drained so much energy from him that he almost turned and went back down the hill to his house. He felt the jab of the Webley's grip against his stomach, and he knew he must enter the church.

He crossed the slippery flagstones at the side of the Armenian monastery. The rain pattered onto his flat cap with a noise so loud that he almost wondered if Jihad Awdeh, hiding in the church, might hear him coming. A dark figure ducked quickly out of the church through the Gate of Humility. The figure saw Omar Yussef and froze. The two men blinked through the darkness. The wind wafted a wave of cold rain across them. Omar Yussef moved forward. The figure by the gate backed against the wall. It couldn't be Jihad Awdeh. He wouldn't cower that way. Omar Yussef picked up his pace. When he was only a few yards from the man, he recognized him. It was Elias Bishara. His thin black hair clung to his scalp and the rain fogged the thick lenses of his glasses. The water was rapidly soaking his black soutane, but Omar Yussef could see that sweat had already seeped through the robe under the arms. Elias Bishara extended his hands on either side of his body along the wall, as though his terror might propel him up the stones to safety.

'Elias, it's me, Abu Ramiz.'

The young priest appeared not to hear at first, then he wilted as his tension and fear subsided. 'I thought you would kill me out here.'

'He's in there, isn't he.'

'Jihad Awdeh? Yes. I was waiting for him, as I promised you I would be, Abu Ramiz. I was praying for the church and for George Saba. But I was weak. My strength failed and I ran away when Awdeh held his gun on me and told me to leave the church.'

'Is he alone?'

'Just him. Oh, God, I wanted to stay there and guard the church. I'm sorry, Abu Ramiz, I didn't have the strength.'

'You were alone in the church, Elias, You did your best.' Omar Yussef pitied the distraught man before him. 'Where exactly is he hiding?'

'He was in front of the altar, but he could be anywhere now. The soldiers will come here, Abu Ramiz. The soldiers will come and invade the church to arrest him. It'll be a disaster. It was as though I was confronted by the Devil himself.' Elias Bishara wiped his glasses on the loose sleeve of his robe. He looked up. 'But what are you doing here, Abu Ramiz?'

Omar Yussef looked toward the dark gate into the church. Jihad Awdeh was in there, somewhere.

'Abu Ramiz, it's about George, isn't it? That's why you came here.' Elias Bishara held the lapels of Omar Yussef's jacket. 'Don't sacrifice yourself, Abu Ramiz. Jihad will kill you, right here in the church. You can't take him on.'

Omar Yussef laid his hand on Elias Bishara's arm. 'I have to learn my own lessons, Elias,' he said.

The monk gave a barely audible sob. Then, he stepped back and nodded.

Omar Yussef paused at the Gate of Humility. There would be no other monks about. In his pounding heart, he knew there was only one man inside the Church of the Nativity.

Bending, he went through the low Gate. He straightened and rubbed the small of his back. The narthex of the church was pitch black and silent. He remembered what Jihad Awdeh told Leila. As soon as the soldiers came, he would flee to the Church of the Nativity. The Israelis wouldn't dare enter the birthplace of Jesus to arrest him. The world would be outraged, if they did. Omar Yussef thought about that: why should anyone be angry on the part of that man, that murderous bloody man? In Europe they wouldn't know the reality of Jihad Awdeh's life. They might even think of him as a hero, or believe that the people of Bethlehem at least saw him that way. So the Israelis wouldn't come here for him. But Omar Yussef would.

He ran over the layout of the church in his mind. He walked himself through memories of so many visits to the old Byzantine basilica, of the Christian friends who had married or baptized their babies here and invited Omar Yussef to share the occasion. He rarely came to the church now. The Christians had been driven almost underground. They went to Chile, where George Saba ought to have stayed. Or they took Holy Orders, as Elias Bishara had, and hid themselves behind the fortress walls of the church. It seemed appropriate that the church where Christianity was born should be shrouded in 5:00 A.M. darkness, cold and barren, as he found it now.

Omar Yussef moved into the main basilica. He went left to cover himself behind the red limestone pillars of the Franciscan cloister, moving carefully. He hid behind a pillar decorated by the Crusaders with a painting of St Cathal. The Irishman glared down at him, his beard sharp, his oval face terrible and white, lined thickly with black, as though caught in the moment when the Almighty had informed him of the precise tortures that would lead to his martyrdom. Or perhaps it was the severe face of a man who knew the sordid conditions under which *you* would perish, poor sinner, gazing up from the cold stone floor of the church. Omar Yussef shivered and looked away from the harsh portrait. He peered toward the Greek Orthodox altar. The first gray light of a damp dawn glinted through the high windows onto the gold lamps, strung above the aisle on long chains. He had to move fast. He needed the darkness to disguise the antiquity of the Webley.

The sound of a man coughing stuttered from the direction of the altar. The cough was protracted, then the man expectorated. Omar Yussef heard the quick, impatient, repeated rasp of a cigarette lighter that wouldn't catch. The unseen man cursed and tried the lighter again. Then the noise stopped.

Omar Yussef took the Webley from his belt and moved toward the back of the church. He came out into the open aisle, but could see no one at the altar. Then the cough came again, and he knew that Jihad Awdeh was hiding in the Nativity Cave. A dimly flickering glow illuminated the broad, fan-shaped stairs to the cave at the side of the altar. Omar Yussef listened. The cave was silent. He took the first step down, and the next. With each movement, he wondered what the hell he was doing. Jihad Awdeh might not be alone. He might call his bluff with the Webley. Omar Yussef descended further. He remembered that the cave was about six yards wide and ten yards long. The wide staircase funneled down to two entrances, both at the same end of the grotto. Tourists went down one set of stairs and came up the other, after they bent to kiss the ring of bronze beneath which, according to the monks, was the very spot where Jesus's manger had lain. Where would Jihad Awdeh be? Probably as far as possible from the stairs, to give himself time to react in case the soldiers came.

Omar Yussef reached the bottom of the steps. He held the gun in his left hand, so that when he turned into the cave his body would keep its detail obscured from the orange glow. He stepped around the corner.

Jihad Awdeh looked up and smiled at the school-teacher. 'So they sent the special forces.' He laughed and took a pack of Marlboros out of his pocket. He flicked the cigarette lighter a few times before he got a flame. He must have been lighting a candle when Omar Yussef had heard him upstairs, not a cigarette.

Omar Yussef squinted into the dim light. Jihad Awdeh's Kalashnikov lay on the floor in front of him. The gunman had a small rucksack, presumably loaded with food in case of a siege. Omar Yussef wondered if there were explosives in the backpack. He might intend to take the cave, or the church, or anyone who came for him to Paradise at his side. Beneath his Astrakhan hat, Jihad Awdeh's head was bandaged from the blow it took when the tank shell hit the Saba house.

'Get up and come with me,' Omar Yussef said.

'Come where? Are you collaborating with the Israelis still? Are they waiting outside the church for you to bring me in?' Jihad Awdeh laughed, and it echoed like a hundred angry voices around the low cave.

'*You're* the collaborator, Jihad.' He wasn't himself sure if he was bluffing and he didn't care. He spoke with the conviction of a man who had seen so much wrong that he needed now to assert what he knew was right.

Jihad Awdeh's smile disappeared. 'If I'm a collaborator, why am I hiding from the Israelis in the middle of the night?'

'You must have done something to turn them against you,' Omar Yussef said. 'You must have gone too far even for them.'

The bitter grin returned to Jihad Awdeh's face. He pushed the gray Astrakhan hat back on his head and slipped a finger under his bandage to scratch his scalp. 'Fuck your mother, school-teacher. Are you a good shot?'

'How good would I have to be to hit you down here?' Omar Yussef risked pushing the empty gun forward a little, threatening Jihad Awdeh with it. He didn't move toward Awdeh. He wanted to keep him where he was, eight yards away, in case the younger man rushed him.

'So you're going to take me in for what, exactly?'

'You are the collaborator. You guided the Israelis to Louai Abdel Rahman. You used a laser sight to confirm for them that they had the right man and to point out exactly where he was. Your mistake was to leave behind a MAG cartridge at the site of the assassination. At first, when I found those cartridges it led me to suspect Hussein Tamari. Dima Abdel Rahman told me that her husband spoke in the darkness to someone called Abu Walid. Hussein Tamari was Abu Walid. But only tonight did I discover that your eldest boy is Walid, too. George Saba told me he saw you bending to scoop something off the roof of his house before you left that night. But he also said that only Hussein Tamari was firing. You must have picked up the spent MAG cartridges from his gun. You put them in your pocket, because you wanted to cover your tracks in case the Israelis came to Beit Jala to find out who was shooting from the roof of George's house. If they found the cartridges, they'd know it was Hussein, and that made it a little too close to you. You were working for them, and you didn't want them to know that your boss had been shooting across the valley at them, because maybe they'd figure that you were in on it. But when you were lying in the long grass waiting for Louai Abdel Rahman to come to his house, one of the cartridges must have fallen out of your pocket. That's the one I discovered. I kept the shell casing as evidence. I picked up another one that you missed on the roof of George Saba's house. Then you found out that Dima Abdel Rahman had overheard her husband speaking to Abu Walid and you killed her, too.'

Jihad Awdeh waved his cigarette. 'No, I didn't kill that bitch.'

'So the rest is true?'

'Fuck you. You don't know what a mistake you're making. I'm the head of the Martyrs Brigades.'

'So was Hussein, and look what happened to him.'

'Hussein died because he was greedy. The reason the Israelis wanted to kill Louai Abdel Rahman was because his family was operating explosives factories. They were all in on it, including the old man Muhammad. Louai was the family's connection to all the resistance groups. He used to sell bombs to Fatah, but he also supplied Hamas and Islamic Jihad and the Popular Front. He sold to criminals, too. When Louai died, Hussein decided to take over all the Abdel Rahman businesses. I told him he should only take the auto shops. If he took control of the explosives factories, I warned him, the Israelis would come down on him. But he was greedy. The explosives used by the Abdel Rahman boy to blow himself up in Jerusalem yesterday came from one of the labs Hussein took over. So, just as I warned him, the Israelis killed him.'

'Who told the Israelis the bomb was made at one of those labs?'

'Well, of course, I did, Abu Ramiz.'

'You?'

'I planned the mission. I sent the boy off with the bomb. The Israelis weren't sure if they should kill Hussein. But after the bomb exploded in the market, I knew they'd have to get rid of him.'

'And with Hussein gone, you'd be in charge of the Martyrs Brigades in Bethlehem.'

Jihad Awdeh nodded and breathed smoke from his nostrils.

'But why did Yunis Abdel Rahman become a suicide bomber?' Omar Yussef said.

'A martyr, Abu Ramiz. You should refer to him only as a martyr.' Jihad Awdeh smiled sarcastically. 'Self-disgust, I suppose you might say. It's his father's fault really. He's a nasty piece of work, old Muhammad Abdel Rahman. Muhammad told the kid that Dima was fucking Hussein Tamari. He said she had wanted Louai out of the way so she could be with Hussein and that she had persuaded Hussein to help the Israelis kill her husband. Muhammad expected the boy to kill Hussein, so the family could take back their stolen auto business. Maybe the explosives workshops, too.'

'But Yunis killed Dima instead.' The boy had spoiled his father's plan by directing his anger not at Hussein, but at the woman he considered the most unconscionable of his brother's betrayers.

'That's right. He killed her for betraying his brother. It must have seemed easier than killing Hussein – he didn't know the Israelis were going to do the job for him. He killed her and tried to make it look like a random rape. Or maybe he got a kick out of seeing what she looked like in the dirt with her ass up in the air. By the way, you were there too. Did you like her ass? I hear she

312

was a special little pet of yours. How special was she? The police had covered her body by the time I got there, but the guards let me have a look. A lot of the guys got an eyeful.'

Omar Yussef swallowed hard. 'Why were you there?'

'To tell Yunis Abdel Rahman that his dear Dad had made him a killer for nothing. I told him Dima was innocent and that Hussein didn't even know who she was. The boy was quite upset at the news, you can imagine. Disgusted with himself and his father. Guilty. No family business, no future. I told him he could redeem himself by carrying out an operation. He agreed immediately.'

'Why did the Israelis come to your apartment tonight, if you're their collaborator?'

'They wanted to warn me not to keep the explosives factories operating. Or perhaps they just wanted to give me some cover. No one's going to think they'd raid a collaborator's home.'

Omar Yussef pointed at the second staircase out of the cave. 'Let's go. I'm taking you to the police.'

Jihad Awdeh rose and stretched. 'Fine. They will, of course, let me go. And I'll start building another bomb.' He moved along the cave. 'This time it won't be your American boss who gets blown up by it. I'll make sure it takes you out, and your family, too.'

Omar Yussef gestured to Awdeh to keep to the opposite side of the cavern. He followed the gunman up the short flight of stairs, slowly. When his prisoner reached the top, Omar Yussef said: 'Keep going. Not too fast.'

The darkness in the church seemed to have lifted. As Omar Yussef reached the top of the stairs, he pulled the Webley closer to his side, hiding it in the folds of his jacket.

Jihad Awdeh turned. He stared at the old gun.

'Keep going,' Omar Yussef said. His eyes were adjusting. It was too light in the church. He had spent too much time down in the cave. The killer would see the old pistol was useless. 'Come on, move it.'

Jihad Awdeh pointed at the Webley and laughed. 'What are you going to do? Beat me to death with that old thing?'

Omar Yussef felt his mouth dry up. He looked down and saw that the hand holding the pistol shook. 'This gun is an old one. But it works.'

But Jihad Awdeh was already upon him. He punched Omar Yussef in the temple, shoved him backward, and tripped him so that he fell to the floor. From the back of his boot, Jihad slowly drew a six-inch hunting knife. He twirled its jagged blade, smiling. Omar Yussef saw the light glint off the shaft of the knife. How could he have been so stupid as to stay below in the cave until there was this much daylight in the church?

Jihad Awdeh kicked him in the side, just below the ribs. The impact stabbed through his kidneys as surely as if it were a thrust of the knife. He groaned. Then Jihad kicked again and Omar Yussef screamed, a deep bellow.

He grabbed Jihad Awdeh's leg, but the gunman shook free. Omar Yussef looked up. Jihad crouched above him with the knife held to his own throat. He grinned, as though he would bite the schoolteacher and drink his blood. He drew the knife lightly across his throat, sighing with pleasure. It was the same murderous gesture George Saba had described, when Omar Yussef saw him in the jail. Omar Yussef would die now, like George.

The knife was at Omar Yussef's throat. It felt warm from having been stashed inside Jihad Awdeh's boot. He gasped. There was a moment of pressure against the flesh of his neck. Then there was a massive blast, and another. Omar Yussef thought it was the sound of his carotid ripping under the sharp metal, the tearing of the cartilage thundering through his head. But then Jihad Awdeh toppled over onto his victim's chest. He held his head directly before Omar Yussef's face and gave a ghostly moan that was heavy with the stale reek of cigarettes. Then he dropped his head. His brow struck Omar Yussef on the chin. The murderer was dead.

CHAPTER 28

Omar Yussef shoved Jihad Awdeh's corpse away. It rolled heavily onto its back. The dead man's hand released the knife. It tinkled on the stone floor. Blood seeped from two wounds in Jihad Awdeh's side and pooled about Omar Yussef. The schoolteacher felt its warmth melting through his jacket. He pushed himself up to escape the gore and backed a few paces away from the corpse, as though unsure that the murderer wouldn't rise and try to take his life once more.

There was a silhouette in the doorway to the church. It moved toward Omar Yussef. This was the man who had saved him, firing from the other end of the church with enough accuracy to strike Jihad Awdeh, rather than the victim pressed to the stone beneath him. As the shooter came on, his footfalls echoed about the ancient walls. Omar Yussef stared at the dark figure. When Awdeh had held the knife to his throat, he had been sure he was about to die. So sure that the relief of his reprieve was still somehow unreal.

The figure passed through the first dusty shaft

of light from the high windows. The police beret on the man's head was askew. Omar Yussef saw a hand gloved tightly in black leather straighten it. The footsteps came closer. It was Khamis Zeydan. Now was the time when Omar Yussef would learn if his suspicions were misplaced, if the police chief were as befouled by murdered blood as he thought. Khamis Zeydan had saved him by killing Jihad Awdeh, the man who had beaten and humiliated the police chief only two hours before. But would he finish off Omar Yussef too?

Three other policemen rushed through the Gate of Humility and ran down the aisle behind their commander. The police chief turned to look at them and then quickened his pace toward Omar Yussef. He reached the schoolteacher and stared at him hard, tapping the barrel of his pistol against his false hand. His face had the fierce callousness of one who has killed, one who will kill. Omar Yussef lifted his eyes toward the sunlight where it cut the blackness high inside the church. He filled his lungs, and in that moment he pictured Khamis Zeydan, young and suave and filling their favorite student café in Damascus with laughter, and he knew that whatever his old friend had become, he would remember that youthful warmth on his face and it would draw him far from this gloomy church in time and space. Omar Yussef held that breath.

Khamis Zeydan holstered his gun. He looked down at Jihad Awdeh. 'This bastard's dead,' he said. He turned to his men. 'Get this son of a whore out of the church. I don't want anyone to know that I shot him, and certainly not that it happened inside this holy place. You two, carry him over to the station. You, get a bucket and a mop. Clean up the blood.'

'His rifle is down in the cave,' Omar Yussef said.

'Let's go and get it. We'll see what else he left down there.'

Omar Yussef hesitated.

Khamis Zeydan cocked his head and wrinkled his moustache. 'I just saved your life. Do you think I'll murder you, now?'

'I'm sorry, Abu Adel,' Omar Yussef said. 'I'm not thinking straight.'

'Well, that has been to your credit lately. You had reason to suspect people. Even me. But now you can start taking things at face value once more.'

'I don't know if I will, ever again.'

Khamis Zeydan went down the steps to the Cave of the Nativity. Omar Yussef followed. His legs felt weak. In two days, he had been near to his own death three times, and he had seen even more dead bodies, of people he loved and of those he feared. It was too much. He sat on the bottom step and put his hands on his head.

'He was about to kill me,' Omar Yussef said.

Khamis Zeydan slung Jihad Awdeh's Kalashnikov over his shoulder and looked inside the rucksack. 'What's in here? Food.' He looked over at Omar

318

Yussef. 'You're right about that. You'd be dead now for sure, if Maryam hadn't told me you were coming to the church.'

'Maryam?'

'You left a message with my desk sergeant. I'm sorry to say that I was drinking after I dropped you at your home. I kept thinking about George Saba's wife, the way we found her with her children under her arms. I've seen so many people dead, Abu Ramiz, but I hated myself for letting that happen to Sofia Saba. So I locked myself in my office and started back on that bottle of whisky. I came out to take a piss, and the sergeant told me you had called. I drove down to your house. Maryam was in a terrible state. She told me you'd gone to the church. It seems I got here just in time.' He came toward Omar Yussef. He pulled Jihad Awdeh's black vest from the rucksack, stuck his hand in one of the pockets, and pulled out a fistful of shiny copper tubes, a dozen spent MAG cartridges. 'Well, look at this.' He let them drop back into the rucksack. 'I guess we'll call this Exhibit A.'

'No, that's Exhibit C,' said Omar Yussef. From his jacket, he took the old MAG cartridge he had found outside Louai Abdel Rahman's home and the one from George Saba's roof. 'These are Exhibits A and B.'

The long, thin devotional candle Jihad Awdeh had lit in the cave sputtered to its end. Omar Yussef and Khamis Zeydan went up the stairs.

A policeman jogged down the aisle to the dark pool of Jihad Awdeh's blood.

Khamis Zeydan looked at his watch. 'See to it that the blood is gone before the priests come in here. Be quick. They'll be arriving any moment now. They probably will have heard the shots.'

The policeman saluted and slapped a soapy mop onto the flagstones.

'I found your friend Father Elias outside the church. He was in a bit of a panic, but when he calms down he can make sure none of the priests get too curious about what went on here. Later I'll dump Jihad's body and make it look like the Israelis got him.'

Omar Yussef nodded. 'It seems miraculous that you saved me just at the very moment he was about to slit my throat. Did you really shoot him, or was he killed by bolts of lightning from heaven?' he joked.

'It might have been divine intervention,' Khamis Zeydan said, as they came out of the Church of the Nativity into the crisp air of dawn. The rain had stopped. The sun was bright on the wet flagstones. The bell rang in the Armenian monastery. 'In that church, you were as close to death as it's possible to be.'

Omar Yussef laughed with deep relief. 'Evidently God didn't want another martyr.'

CHAPTER 29

Khamis Zeydan dropped Omar Yussef at his house when the dawn was still new. The police chief leaned across and gripped his hand through the open window. Omar Yussef expected the police chief to caution him to give up the amateur detective game. But Khamis Zeydan said nothing. His handshake and his expression were firm, and he nodded approvingly at his old college friend. Then he drove his jeep away, back toward the church.

Omar Yussef entered his house. Immediately he calmed Maryam with a finger on her lips. He held her tightly and wondered how long it was since he'd grasped his wife so strongly. He lay on his bed until it was time for the UN office in Jerusalem to open. Then he found the telephone message Maryam had written on a scrap of paper the night before and he returned the call to the UN regional director, a Swede named Magnus Wallender.

'Mister Yussef, I'm pleased to hear from you. Sorry to have disturbed your family with my call so late last night. It's a very worrying time, isn't it?' Wallender said.

Omar Yussef felt so relieved and elated after his rescue at the church that he paused a moment before he remembered why Wallender should be anxious.

'We are all very sad about Christopher's death,' Omar Yussef said. The severed hand. The face and chest flayed like a cut of meat in an abattoir. It seemed a long time ago.

'This is why I wanted to talk to you, Mister Yussef. We consulted with New York and Geneva overnight. We think it's simply too dangerous right now for an American, or any other Westerner, to run the Dehaisha school. Christopher Steadman's death was a shock that rippled all the way though the organization, right up to the Secretary-General.'

It was hard to imagine the Secretary-General of the United Nations in his office high above Manhattan hearing the news of an assassination in Dehaisha. Omar Yussef thought that if the killers had struck their true target – namely, him – it would, of course, not have reached the attention of the Secretary-General.

Magnus Wallender continued. 'We feel it would be preferable and safer in the current environment to fill the vacancy as head of the Dehaisha school with a local. You're by far the most experienced of the teachers and a figure respected throughout Bethlehem. So we'd like to offer the position to you.'

'As director of the UNRWA Girls School in

Dehaisha?' It was a matter of days since Omar Yussef had thought his time at the school was over. Now he was to take charge? 'Well, that's very kind of you. Do you mind if I think it over for a day?'

'Not at all. We shall send someone down today to pick up your personnel file, just to be sure that there's nothing to block the appointment. But that's really just a formality.'

Omar Yussef thought of the sheets of blue paper, the negative reports his former boss, the Spanish lady, had written about him. They were at the bottom of a muddy pool across the street from the school. There was nothing else in the file that would be out of the ordinary. The collection of whining letters from parents would be easily dismissed. He thanked Magnus Wallender and hung up.

Here was Omar Yussef's opportunity to stand up to the government schools inspector and anyone else who wished to feed hatred to the children of Dehaisha refugee camp. He would take this chance. He had focused on George Saba as the evidence he would leave behind him of his goodness, his morals. Now he wondered if his legacy might not be constantly unfolding, one for which he must fight with each new intake of students at the school.

The thought of retirement from teaching seemed attractive to him. He acknowledged that he had enjoyed the chase that led him to Jihad Awdeh.

But what was he going to do? Set up a detective agency in Bethlehem?

Nadia entered the salon carrying a cup of coffee. She wore the sky-blue shirt and long, navy skirt of the Frères School. She came to Omar Yussef, gave him his coffee, and kissed him on the cheek.

'Did you find him?' she said.

'Who? Who was I looking for?' Omar Yussef pretended to search beneath the cushions on the sofa.

'The man who killed George Saba.'

Omar Yussef smiled. He hadn't known she was aware of the aim of his investigation. 'Yes, Nadia, I found him.'

'Good, I knew you'd get him,' she said. 'Are George's children going to come and live with us?'

That's not a bad idea, Omar Yussef thought. *I should do that for George*. He decided to ask Maryam.

Nadia looked at the black Bible on the coffee table, where Omar Yussef had left it when he returned from the destruction of George Saba's home. 'What's this?'

'That belonged to my father. It was a gift to him from a friend of his who was a Christian priest. I gave it to George Saba many years ago. I rescued it from the ruins of his house.'

Nadia flipped the cover open and read the inscription to Omar Yussef's father from his friend the Catholic priest. She smiled. 'It's a beautiful book,' she said. 'I have to go to school now.' She kissed her grandfather again and left the house.

324

Omar Yussef watched Nadia pass outside the window, leaning forward under her pink backpack. There was a legacy, he thought, that might be found in detective work, just as much as in teaching. It was a mistake to believe that detection was a matter of figuring out what had happened in the past and then taking revenge for it. He understood now that it was about protecting the future from the people who committed evil and who would do so again.

Omar Yussef picked up the slip of paper with the U.N. phone number scrawled across it. His accountant had told him he had the money to retire from teaching if he wished. He looked at the message and dropped it on the coffee table next to George Saba's Bible.